"Nice to meet you, Lily. I'm DeShawn."

"Are you friends with my momma?"

He looked at Tiana, who was trying to scowl, but the effort of keeping a six-year-old balanced on her hip in the jostling crowd required too much effort. "DeShawn and I are acquaintances, Lily. That means we know each other but aren't friends."

"Can we still go watch the dogs with him?"

"It's a great spot," DeShawn said with a smile.

Tiana huffed out a breath. "Fine. For Lily."

"Absolutely. Completely for Lily's sake," he replied. He held his hands out and Tiana let him take Lily. Swinging her easily up to his shoulders, he laughed at Lily's excited squeal. "Hold on tight," he said. "And, Momma, follow close. We're going in."

"Do not drop her," she snapped.

Tiana grabbed a handful of his jacket and the feeling of her fingers brushing against the muscles of his back, even through the layers of fabric, sent a rush of heat down his spine.

Dear Reader,

This is a story I hadn't planned to tell. DeShawn was such a popular character from *Spying on the Boss* and *Boss on Notice*. Then Tiana showed up, as some characters do. I needed a friend for Mickie in *Boss on Notice*, and there she was. No planning. No notice. She was a character who pushed me aside and said, "I've got something to say here."

The chemistry between Tiana and DeShawn was unplanned, just one of those happy writer moments when your characters come alive and surprise you. So of course they needed a happily-ever-after.

Many, many thanks to my prereaders: Vera H., Gabriella Brown, RN, Yashica Green, RN, and Djuanna B. Thank you for your input! I appreciate your time and support!

As a white woman, I hope I have done justice to my characters and their experiences. Any errors are mine and mine alone.

I hope you enjoy this conclusion to The Cleaning Crew miniseries.

Janet Lee Nye

JANET LEE NYE

—

The Littlest Boss

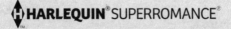

HARLEQUIN® SUPERROMANCE®

Recycling programs
for this product may
not exist in your area.

ISBN-13: 978-0-373-64044-7

The Littlest Boss

Copyright © 2017 by Janet Lee Nye

Printed in U.S.A.

www.Harlequin.com

Janet Lee Nye is a writer by day and a neonatal nurse by night. She lives in Charleston, South Carolina, with her fella and her felines. She spends too much time on Twitter and too little time on housework and has no plans to remedy this.

Books by Janet Lee Nye

HARLEQUIN SUPERROMANCE

The Cleaning Crew

Spying on the Boss
Boss on Notice
Boss Meets Her Match

Visit the Author Profile page at Harlequin.com.

This is for all the nurses and caregivers out there. And to my WIC crew, who have cheered me on through every disappointment and every success. Thank you. Club 1035 rocks!

CHAPTER ONE

THE GUY IN the produce section of Publix was about to make an amateur mistake with the avocados. He had two of them in his hands, ripe and ready to eat by the look of them. The way to do it, Tiana Nelson knew, was to buy one for now and one for later. *Swap one of those for one a bit more green*, she thought. *You'll be glad you did a few days from now.* What to do? Approach and tell him? She was tempted. That arm. He wasn't even flexing it, just had it angled enough so he could give the lush fruit a little squeeze, and *Wow. Okay. That's a well-built fella.* The jacket he was wearing didn't conceal his muscles at all, did it? Hard curves moved beneath the fabric.

She maneuvered her shopping cart, trying to get closer without being conspicuous, dodging a flustered mom who was trying to snag a singing child in an *Adventure Time* sweatshirt pirouetting between the apples and the bananas. There was something about the guy with the avocados—besides the fact that he was exceptionally easy on the eyes—but it wasn't until he glanced over at her and she caught a spark of recognition in his expression that she understood.

I know him. He knows me.

She was running all the possibilities through her mind—work, school, gym, here—when he grinned at her and it clicked. That grin. She knew that smug, snarky grin. *Sugar sticks! That smart-alecky maid. What was his name?*

"Nurse Ratched!" he said, setting the avocados in his basket and looking entirely too pleased with himself. "I'd recognize that scowl anywhere."

And then she did actually scowl, and frowned at the realization that she'd done so, and immediately tried to cool her expression into a kind of bemused grin. *Oh, that guy. One of Josh's guys from the Cleaning Crew.* She waved a hand toward the juice aisle and said, "Did they call for a cleanup in aisle two, Man Maid?" She felt a flush of heat in her neck and cheeks as she said it.

He laughed and strolled closer to her with a purely casual confidence that irked her. All at once she was acutely aware of how she must look, straight off the end of a long, crazy shift in the ER, in wrinkled blue scrubs and beat-up Asics that probably should have been swapped out six months ago. *Wait, there isn't vomit on my pants or anything, is there?* Random bodily fluid stains were always a possibility on her shift. Tiana pulled her coat closed and tried to keep her expression casual, amused but disinterested. But darn if he wasn't a fine-looking man.

"They actually let you take care of people now?" he said. His grin had reappeared—big, wide and goofy, making everything feel like it was all in fun.

"Take care," she said, reverting to Stern Nurse Mode. "More like save lives, Mr. Maid. Why are you here? I thought you were joining the army or something."

"Or something," he repeated, putting a hand over his heart. The grin faded a bit—just a bit—as if those words had hit him a little too hard.

Uh-oh. There's a story there, she thought.

But he bounced back right away. "You do remember me," he said. "I'm touched."

"Tetched maybe," Tiana said with a laugh.

The grin may have faded but the mischievous gleam in his eyes had not. "Life. You know. You have a plan and sometimes it falls through." He paused, just for a beat or two, then added, "I went with Army National Guard instead of active duty. Got a great job as a civilian here at the Corps of Engineers."

"Oh. Okay," she said. "Well. That's good." She put her hands back on the shopping cart handle and felt something brush by her at hip level. The whirling child had reappeared, the pirouettes now alternating with mini jetés, and his flustered mom gave Tiana a glance of apology as she scooped her budding ballet dancer up into her arms. She needed to get home. Wednesday night was some prime Netflix watching.

"Sorry," the boy's mother said as he thrust a sticky handful of Gummi Bears toward Tiana. "Caleb, I swear..."

Tiana laughed. "Not a problem," she said. She smiled in solidarity as she watched the mom plop her squirming child into the shopping cart and buckle him in. *The struggle is real—don't I know it.* That reminded her. She needed to get herself moving so she could be back home before Lily went to bed. She winced as she watched Caleb rub the handful of candy against the cart handle and then stuff the entire wad into his mouth. *Ah, well, it'll give his immune system something to do.*

As Caleb and his mom disappeared around the corner, Tiana remembered Mr. Hottie Maid's name. *DeShawn Adams!* He was still watching her, his mouth twisted up into that grin, suggesting he was barely holding back on a snarky comment. Mmm-hmm. He may have lost the little goatee he'd had when she last saw him, but he was still the perfect picture of tall, dark and handsome. His hair was short and once again she considered how not even the light jacket he was wearing against Charleston's February chill could hide that body. Tall and strong and muscled and probably even a really good guy once you got past his Mr. Smarty Pants facade. *Ugh. Stop.*

"Yeah," she said, tapping her fingers on her cart. "Well, hey, DeShawn, nice to see you, but I do need to get going." She gave him a little wave, then remembered. "Oh, wait. The avocados." She gestured toward his basket. "I was going to say. Get one that's ripe now and one that's going to be ripe soon. That's how my mom always told me to do it."

He nodded, that twisted-up smirk still concealing a zinger, and then he reached into the pile, plucked out not one but two green avocados and placed them in his basket beside the pair of ripe ones.

One of Tiana's eyebrows went up.

"Hey," DeShawn said, "I *really* like guacamole. Now and later."

Tiana groaned. "Later, Man Maid."

His laugh was rich and warm. It was a good kind of laugh, a hey-we-just-connected laugh, and it followed her as she tried to make her exit and slip on down an aisle. "Hey, Tiana?" DeShawn called out. "Speaking of later…"

She turned just long enough to give him a decidedly chilly look. "Later," she repeated. "Good to see you." She regretted the aisle she'd turned into as soon as she chose it, but there was no way to turn around now without looking flustered. She so wanted to appear casual but she felt like she was going to trip over her own feet. Was she overtired? It had been a long shift at the hospital. Was he still watching her? He was still as infuriating as ever and she had enough on her plate right now. New job. New city. Settling in with Lily. Her mother had moved to Charleston with them to help her, so that was another adjustment. Living with her mother again made her feel like she was still fifteen years old rather than a grown woman, a working professional. The last thing she needed was a smart-ass man on top of that tangled knot. She looked around, one hand up as if trying to decide on an item. When she finally looked back, trying to make it appear nonchalant, he was gone. Good. She looked at the shelf in front of her. Nothing but applesauce, fruit cups and dates. She picked up a box, inspected it. What? No. No way. She definitely did not need any dates, ha-ha. Even though Man Maid was super yummy.

What was wrong with her?

LILY, HER ARMS wide and a huge dimply-cheeked smile on her face, was running toward her as soon as she opened the front door. "Momma! You're home!"

Tiana dipped down to eye level with her child, smiling but serious, and put a hand up in the universal sign of stop right there. "Hold up, Lily," she said. "What's the rule?"

Lily skidded to a halt and her little face became serious. "No hugging in nurse clothes," she recited. Tiana's heart skipped a beat, she loved this girl so much. Lily standing there in her lavender pajamas trying to play at wearing a stern face. Was it possible for anyone to be so adorable?

As much as Tiana wanted to scoop her daughter up and squeeze her tight, the reality was there could be *anything* lurking on her scrubs after twelve hours in the emergency department. And this shift had been all kinds of hot messiness, the kind of stuff usually reserved for the night shift when the moon was full. Old guy coughing like he was going to heave a wet lung across the back of the hand that he held halfheartedly in front of his face. A gunshot wound rolled in by ambulance; just a kid, really, late teens, lying there stunned, groaning, as the paramedic—Rachel, one of the best—called out the particulars to Dr. Dean. The kid had made it. Dr. Dean could go stone-cold in the worst of traumas and direct every person in the room with a flat precision that was almost eerie to behold. What else? The toddler with the telltale inspiratory whoop. The dude who walked in wanting a sperm count, of all things. She was still shaking her head over that one.

A whirlwind, that's what the last twelve-plus hours of her life had been. She sighed. And that wasn't even counting the awkwardness that was the ill-advised stop at the grocery store on her way home.

But…that was then. *You leave that there, if you can, and you can because you have to.* That was the first thing she'd learned after nursing school. It was required, for your own sanity. Nurse Tiana needed to take a breath, let go and ease back into being Mommy. She smiled and blew air kisses to Lily as she put the bags down on the counter.

"I could have picked up groceries, Tee," her mother said as she entered the kitchen. "Go get changed. I'll put these away." Vivian took the bags from her and placed them near the sink. She could have at least tried not to shake her head side to side as she inspected each purchase. "Lot of salt in these," she said as she shook a pack of corn chips en route to the pantry. She pursed her lips as she reached back in the bag, rummaging around. "Sugar, sugar, salt. Oh, well, now, here's a vegetable. Not bad!"

"I know," Tiana said, bristling. "I just wanted to grab a couple of things." She sensed Lily reaching to pat her waist and she caught herself just in time.

"Germy-wormy," Lily said, wearing a pout. "I remember."

"Oh, sweetie, I'm sorry. I'll get cleaned up right now, okay? Then we can cuddle."

Lily nodded, then asked if she would read her a bedtime story. Tiana smiled and told her that was all she wanted in the whole world. And it was the truth.

The shower ran long and hot, easing the knots bunched up in her back and shoulders, and she stood there, indulging herself in the luxury of it. Say what you wanted about this place, the water heater alone was worth it—it just kept churning out a steady, soothing rush of heat. When she finally stepped out of the shower, she felt 99 percent human again.

After slipping into her favorite Hello Kitty sleep pants—shut up, she could if she wanted—and an old, comfy T-shirt, Tiana let herself relax. She curled up with her little girl and opened up one of her favorites. She remembered her own mother reading it to her when she herself was little.

As she read the story to Lily—the poor girl was exhausted; her eyes struggled to stay open even as she nodded along with the rhythm of the words—Tiana reflected on how the peace and comfort of home was so *necessary*. A refuge. A need right up there with food and water. You had to have a place where you felt safe and loved, where you could just be you.

"Are you going to be here all night?" Lily asked in a low mumble. Her cheek was already pressed to her pillow and her eyes were shut.

"Sure, honey," Tiana said. "I will." She brushed her fingertips along Lily's shoulder.

Lily nodded. By the look of it, she'd be out soon, sleeping soundly.

Sound sleep, now there's an idea, Tiana thought. She'd have to get some of that for herself.

"Do you have to go to work tomorrow, Mommy?" Lily asked as Tiana placed the book on the bedside table and pulled the comforter up to her daughter's chin.

"Not tomorrow, honey. I get to take you to school and pick you up after. Maybe we can go on a special date, just the two of us. What do you think about that?"

Lily snuggled down deep in the blankets. "Fun. Mommy?"

"Yes, love?"

"I was thinking. I don't want a fish pet. I want a kitten pet."

Tiana kissed Lily's forehead. "We'll talk about that later." Lily murmured as she turned toward her pillow. Tiana and slipped out of the room, pulling the door almost, but not quite shut.

Standing there in the hallway, she considered how much had changed since she'd first stepped foot into nursing school. Talk about whirlwinds! And then there was the day she'd sat in her car in utter despair after taking her boards, sure that she'd tanked it and that it had been all for nothing. But it turned out she'd done okay. Better than okay, really. Now her workdays were filled with helping other people deal with the worst day of their lives. She was still in her orientation phase, working under the guidance of an experienced nurse. The skills were easy to learn. Charting. Which doctor to call. All of those things were simple. What was hard was finding that line within herself: the line that allowed you to be a caring and compassionate nurse yet still keep your heart safe.

You can't bleed for your patients or you'll burn out in a year.

Those words, the first thing her preceptor had taught her, were the most difficult part of the job to master. Because she was a problem fixer. She wanted to fix every aspect of a patient's life. But she couldn't. She knew that. But it didn't stop her from wanting to.

"I HAVE YOUR supper warmed up," Vivian called from the kitchen.

Walking toward her, Tiana felt the fatigue of the day beginning to weigh her down. She put an arm around her mother, pulled her close. "Thanks, Mom."

"Rough day?"

Tiana shrugged. "No more than usual."

At the small dining room table, Tiana looked around at the apartment. She'd just moved her little family in a week ago, and it still seemed surreal. After years of cheap college apartments and two months in an extended-stay hotel while she began her orientation, it was certainly the nicest place she'd ever lived, even though the monthly payment about gave her heart failure. A small smile crossed her lips as she looked around. She could afford it though. Finally. Financial freedom was the ultimate freedom. Three bedrooms, hardwood floors, walk-in closets, granite-topped counters, sleek black brand-new appliances. She'd done this. Yeah, it was expensive, but she'd made it. Lily was in a great elementary school, living in a great town with endless opportunity. Everything she'd worked for when she left Lily with her mother and went away to school. Sometimes, she would stop and look around, still surprised she'd made it out the other side.

Her mother's hand closed over hers as if she'd read her thoughts. "You've done well, Tee. I'm so proud of you."

Squeezing her mother's hand, she nodded.

"We did it. Together. I couldn't have done it without you. We did this, Mom."

"The Three Musketeers. Now eat your food and go to bed."

That made her laugh. "Okay, *Mom*."

She took a few bites. Her mother could cook, that was a truth. Even when she followed the recipe perfectly, her food didn't taste like her mother's. Tiana suspected secret ingredients.

"Lily wants a kitten now instead of a fish."

"Ha! She'd rather go for furry and snuggly than for scaly and slimy? Imagine that!" Vivian mimed locking her lips and throwing away a key. "Not even going to touch that battle. Good luck."

Letting out a tired sigh, Tiana finished the rest of her food. As much as she hated to admit it, Lily had inherited her determined streak. When Lily put her foot down, crossed her arms, and held her chin high, she looked like a mini CEO getting ready for a meeting with the Board of Directors. In pajamas! Tiana shook her head, smiled, and sighed again. As hard as she had to be, tried to be, that girl had her heart wrapped around her little finger. The littlest boss.

But a kitten, gah.

Maybe a few more trips to the aquarium?

Find some super enthusiastic intern who could spin tales of clever clownfish, sunlight sparkling across rainbow-colored scales just below the surface, mermaids, sails and all the wonders of the deep blue sea?

Hey, it was worth a try.

CHAPTER TWO

"DESHAWN!"

He'd barely stepped inside the restaurant when—wham—there was the tackle hug. Sadie Martin nearly knocked him over. He returned the exuberant hug, lifting her off her feet for a moment. Aw, Sadie. Seeing her was good medicine. He'd been feeling low, falling into that woulda, coulda, shoulda trap, but all that fell away as soon she'd crushed his ribs with her trademark Sadie Squeeze. He was glad to be home. Happy to return to Charleston. Where he had friends he considered family. "Boss-Lady Sadie," he said with a smile.

She gave him an appraising look, a single worry line between her eyebrows. "You look skinny," she said, after a moment's pause. Then: "Are you eating?"

"Sure, I'm eating. Just don't have to maintain the muscle mass required for my previous employment." He rolled his shoulders and puffed his chest out, flexing just enough to make her laugh, keeping it light.

"That's all right, that's all right," she said. "Blame me for you being too lazy to work out. I see how you are."

"God, I missed you, Sadie."

"Glad to be home?"

"You don't even know."

"How's that ankle?"

The ankle. The stupid accident had held up his entry into the army but had opened a new path for him. It had been a momentary lapse in concentration, one slight misstep on a ladder followed by five months of casts and surgery and rehab. If he hadn't been careless, yeah, well...woulda coulda shoulda, right?

"It's fine," he said. "I'm back up to full speed. Thinking about doing the Cooper River Bridge Run this year. But the ankle, yeah... it does predict rain very accurately. There is that."

He looked around the bustling restaurant. Busy Friday night. It was new. The West Ashley area of Charleston was booming. Booming could be a good thing. Lots of work. But the traffic—the traffic was definitely not an upside. New houses and apartments going up everywhere he looked, from out past Summerville all the way up to Mount Pleasant. Used to be scenic drives out to those places, nothing but green trees and Carolina sun. Now it was a slow roll through bumper-to-bumper traffic. Still, the scent of barbecue was making it hard to dwell on all that. He was here now and his stomach growled. The hostess led them to a booth in the back.

"The potato salad is to die for," Sadie said. "It's made with horseradish."

"Is it hot?" he said.

"Surprisingly cool and creamy. Just enough of a zing to let you know it's the good stuff."

"Huh."

After the waitress brought them each a glass of ice water, jotted their orders down with a few quick swipes of her pen and walked off toward the kitchen, Sadie turned serious.

"How's the job?" She leveled her eyes at De-Shawn. It was her business look. It was a kind professionalism, to be sure. Sadie was good people. But business was business.

"Good. I like it. It feels a little odd. I'm actually doing the things I studied in school. Who would have expected that? But I'm excited."

"You're part of the navy base transition?"

"Yep. Working on the new I-26 and Cosgrove interchange."

"What does that entail?"

"Right now, a lot of walking around in the cold and measuring things."

"Sounds divine. I'm glad you're happy. I was worried about you."

"You always worry about everyone."

"True. But I was extra worried about you."

He took her hands and looked her in the eyes. "I'm fine. You know, not gonna lie. I was disappointed that I couldn't go into the army. That hit hard. But it's okay. I love my job. I still get the opportunity to travel. And I'm in the Army National Guard. It's still everything I wanted. Just…scaled down a bit."

She nodded. "So, it's going well?"

Her tone was casual but her gaze was locked on him. She could win her a staring contest. That was a fact. That was how she climbed to the top of her business. Made it with sheer determination, absolute focus. Resisting the urge to squirm when the silence stretched too long, DeShawn shrugged. "Yeah, okay," he said. "So there's a learning curve. But that's normal right?"

"Yes." She drew the word out into at least four syllables. "Spit it out, DeShawn. What's wrong?"

That made him laugh. Momma Bear. That

was what he and the other guys in the Cleaning Crew would call her. She could smell a problem from three miles away.

"It feels weird," he said. "I feel weird. I look around at my coworkers and they know everything. They're just going around doing their jobs and I feel like I'm acting in a play."

Her expression softened and she bobbed her head. "I know that feeling well. When I have to go to those professional women's meetings, I feel the same way. What in the hell am *I* doing here?"

He nodded, tapped his fingers on the table. "Well, okay, so that's what it is. But how do I fix it?"

"Keep showing up," she said. Her right eye got a little twitchy. She looked down and to the left for a heartbeat, then met his gaze directly. "That's how. Eventually it wears off. Well, it gets better. Just a twinge now and then."

He nodded along with her and smiled. It did make him feel a little better, being on the same page with Momma Bear. Sadie was his biggest role model. She'd gone from being essentially homeless—she hadn't even had a high school degree—and from that place and time in her life, she'd went on to build an award-winning cleaning company. She'd even made herself rich along the way. It wasn't the typical out-come one would expect. Sadie was definitely an outlier, definitely two or three standard de-viations from the mean at least. But she was also right here in front of him—real, honest, relatable—and it gave him hope. He thought about that a lot these days. Hope, and what it meant to people. The difference it made in their lives, having it. Thought about the crazy idea he'd been bouncing around in his mind. About how he could maybe start spreading some of that hope around.

"I never really thanked you," he said to her. "For all you did. For me. For a lot of people."

She frowned, her brow wrinkling slightly. "What do you mean?" she said. She picked at a corner of her napkin.

"For hiring me," he said. "That was crucial. That was more than just a cameo role in the story of my success."

"I gave you a job, DeShawn. That doesn't make me a hero." She cleared her throat and took a sip of water, watching him over the top of the glass.

"No, you did more than that. The only job I'd had before that—before you took a chance on me—was washing dishes in a diner. You showed me how to take pride in a job well done, how to behave like a professional adult."

Her cheeks flushed and she looked down at the table to fiddle with the silverware. "Ugh," she muttered before taking a deep breath and looking up at him. "Thank you, DeShawn. You're very kind."

That surprised a laugh out of him. "What was that?"

"Lena is trying to teach me how to gracefully accept a compliment."

"Keep practicing," he said. "It'll get better. Someday it'll just be a twinge."

"Smart-ass."

DeShawn sat back, grinning, as the waitress returned with their plates, piled high with pulled pork and all sorts of deliciousness. He looked at the bottles of sauce on the table and reached for the mustard-based one.

"Try a dab of the white sauce," Sadie said as she poured a generous dollop of it on her plate before handing him the bottle. "It's lured me away from mustard sauce."

DeShawn made a concerned face and leaned closer. "Is it legal to not use mustard-based sauce in Charleston now?"

Sadie snort laughed and that made him

laugh. Add another point to why coming home was the best decision. He and the guys used to keep score of how many times they could make Sadie snort laugh. Highest score got Friday night drinks free.

"Charleston has become very progressive in its acceptance of diverse barbecue sauces."

He tried the white sauce—"Meh."—and went back to his favorite one.

While they ate, he gathered the courage to speak his idea out loud. Maybe it was too soon. Maybe he needed some time. Stop feeling like a fake. How could he help others when he didn't fully believe in himself yet?

"Hey, Sadie?"

"Yeah?"

"Do you know where Henry is teaching?"

Sadie wiped her mouth with her napkin and swallowed a mouthful of pork. "Henry? My Henry?"

"Yes, your Henry," he said with a smile.

Once a Cleaning Crew member, you were family for life. Henry had oriented DeShawn when he first joined the Crew. He'd graduated and gone off to teach a few months later.

"I don't remember the actual school, but it's

down near Hilton Head, Beaufort, that area, but inland."

DeShawn nodded. That sounded like Henry. Inland. Rural. "Do you have his number?"

"Yes. Why?"

He shrugged and felt a bit of heat on his cheeks. Saying it out loud was scarier than he'd expected. But this was Sadie. She wasn't going to let him wiggle out of an answer. Maybe that was why he'd come to her. He fiddled with his silverware and, keeping his eyes on the table, he blurted it out. "I was thinking that maybe I could talk to kids who come from backgrounds like mine and, I don't know, help them somehow." He looked up at her. She had sat back in her chair and was looking at him appraisingly. He looked back down. "Never mind. It's a stupid idea."

"No!" she said. She looked at him directly. "I think it's an amazing idea. What would you talk to them about?"

"Well, I haven't gotten that far with it yet. I think I need to talk to Henry first. Find out if there's a need. What that need is."

Sadie was nodding. "I'm sure there is. There's always a need."

Sighing with relief, he sat back in the chair.

Wasn't that the truth? Always someone who needed a hand up.

Sadie pulled her phone out of her purse. "Do you remember Lena? My accountant?"

DeShawn laughed. "Remember? How could anyone forget her? She's remarkably unforgettable."

Sadie narrowed her eyes in a mock show of suspicion. "What are you saying about my best friend?"

Lifting his hands, palms up, DeShawn smiled. "Not saying anything. She's a delight. Sunshine on spring flowers."

Sadie snorted out a laugh. "Let me give you Henry and Lena's contact information. Lena did something very similar for the kids out at the Toribio Mission. I'm sure she'd be happy to help you develop this."

He loaded the numbers into his phone with a growing sense of excitement. He hadn't been able to pinpoint the flat feeling he'd had the last few months. Not until this idea had begun to form. All his life, he'd been striving for a goal. Get through high school. Get through college. Get into the army. Even when he'd broken his ankle and his plans changed, it was also a goal. Get the ankle healed, rehab done, qualify for Army National Guard, and get a job. Once all that was accomplished, he'd thought he was done. But instead, he felt like everything had gone too slow, too quiet.

He needed a new goal. And he thought he might have found it. The quiver of excitement of a new project brought a grin to his lips. "So, what's this I hear about Lena? She found a man who isn't afraid of her? Is that actually possible?"

Sadie laughed. "Matt. Yeah. She's goofy in love."

"Speaking of goofy in love—when's the wedding? Soon, right?"

"April." She rolled her eyes. "It's gotten out of hand."

"That's just you. Only thing you'd be comfortable with would be going to a UPS store and having the notary marry you on your lunch break or something."

"See!" Sadie exclaimed, spreading her arms. "That's exactly what I wanted. And they all act like I'm the crazy one."

DeShawn laughed. He'd missed this. Missed the Crew. Missed Sadie. For the first time since he'd slipped off that ladder and sent his careful plans flying in the wind, he felt everything was going to be okay.

AFTER WRESTLING OVER the check and winning, DeShawn gave Sadie another hug and headed to his car. As he slid behind the wheel, his phone vibrated in his shirt pocket. He fished it out while cranking the engine to get the heat going. Charleston winters were usually mild, but a cold snap was in progress and the temperatures were dipping down into the twenties at night. He swiped left to reject an unknown call and then dropped the phone back in his pocket.

As he pulled out of the parking lot onto Savannah Highway, the phone meep-meeped, signaling a new voice message. Ignoring it, he drove to the little apartment he called home for now. He didn't need much. A bedroom. A kitchen. Charleston real estate was crazy expensive right now, so his plan was to live as cheaply as possible, pay off his student loans and start building his meager savings. He hoped to buy a condominium after the loans were paid off. If his car held up that long. Start to put down some roots. Build a life here.

Once home, he changed out of his work clothes into a pair of Deadpool sweat pants and an Iron Man T-shirt. Hey, he liked Marvel Comics. *Time to kick back and relax. See what's new on Hulu*. But first he had to make sure that unknown call wasn't work related. He was sure he had everyone properly identified in his phone, but didn't want to take a chance.

He hit the voice mail number and put the phone on speaker. He had one new message. There was a brief pause. He was just about to delete it, thinking it was a robocall, when a hesitant female voice began to speak.

"DeShawn? This is your mother. Denise? I know we've had our troubles but I've been clean and sober for three months now. I'd like to talk to you. If you want. Okay? Just…uh… call me back? If you want."

He stared at the phone as it went through its beeps and prompts. Save this message? Delete? He hit Delete with a shock-numbed finger and let the phone slip from his hand. His mother. *Damn*. The stunned feeling began to wear off and he slowly became aware of a simmering anger building in his chest. Not now. Not when he was finally settled. Not when he'd finally crawled out of that whole situation. He'd washed his hands of his family after his grandmother, Momma G, had passed away. She had raised him, had done as right as she could by him.

But the memories he still had of the times

when he had been with his parents, the memories of his parents showing up at all hours of the night after she'd taken him under her wing, made him feel as if he were right back there, in those powerless childhood days and nights of knowing. Of knowing about the drinking, the drugs, the emotional blackmail they'd leverage against Momma G. And it was always money, needing money, when they'd show up and try to make her—Momma G, the only one who'd shown him love and compassion, the one who believed in him—feel like she was the problem, she was the one in the wrong.

He'd never forget the way his gut would twist when he heard that first hissing sound of a beer can being cracked open, knowing that it was just the start of a night or a weekend-long roller-coaster ride through hell. He remembered feeling his body tense as he heard one or both of them shouting at Momma G. Alone in his room, he'd be too far from the argument to pick out the details, the specific words being thrown out in the air, but the intent, the tone—that was unmistakable.

He remembered how strong Momma G had been. The weight she'd carried, all those years, on her shoulders. What must it have been like for her, looking at her child, trying to speak reason, and seeing only the empty eyes of a blackout drunk who wouldn't even remember what she'd said or done when she woke up in the morning? Eyes are supposed to be the windows to the soul, right? So what does it say when you look into someone's eyes and see nothing, not a hint of compassion, nothing that can be appealed to, only that addict's need for more?

And that someone is your child?

Momma G must have been a lion inside, to be that strong. Because in those harrowing days, she'd had to make a choice: her daughter or her grandson. What do they call it on the battlefield, when the medics wander from screaming body to screaming body, figuring out who might survive? *Triage.* That was the word.

Momma G, his beloved grandmother, had to triage her own family. And when she looked at her grandson, she saw something in him that made her say: *Him. I choose him. He has a chance and I'm going to make sure he keeps that chance.*

He caught himself spinning on the edge of all those memories. He closed his eyes, took a deep breath. Held it, way down deep in his gut. He slowly released his breath.

Okay. Let go of it. It's not now. It's not happening now. Let go.

Standing, he paced around the small living room area. *Sober for three months? Come back when you got three years on you. Then maybe I'll believe you. Trust? Huh. Don't push it. A few months is a hiccup, not a change.* He couldn't deal with this right now. It did all the wrong things to him, getting these memories stirred up.

Pulling on his running shoes and finding his hoodie, he grabbed the keys, intending to go for a run. Stepping out into the cold, dark evening, he paused. Maybe he should go to the gym, use the treadmill. Save the running in a hoodie for daylight. He shook his head in exasperation. *This world just doesn't stop, does it?*

At the gym, he set a grueling pace. Running. Running from the ghosts. Trying to sweat the poison out of his body. His anger twisted and turned. Finally, he hit the stop button and lifted his feet off the belt and onto the sides. Head down, heart pounding, his ragged breathing loud in his ears, he realized he was angry at himself. He'd thought he'd put it all behind him. That phone call should have had no more emotional impact than a mosquito buzzing around his head. Instead, it had enraged him.

Kindled all the pain and fury he thought he'd exorcised from his life. *Just like a damned addict. Knows exactly the right time to pop up and mess everything up. Not this time.*

CHAPTER THREE

"IT'S THE BABY! It's the baby!"

Lily was jumping up and down, waving her hands in the air. Tiana grabbed her to keep her from rushing into the parking lot as the SUV pulled into a parking spot. "Ian's not a baby, honey. He's two years old."

"But he's not a big boy," Lily said. "I'm six and I'm a big girl and he's littler than me." Her eyes were wide and sparkling. Tiana felt her own mouth spread into a smile. She gave her daughter a quick hug and booped her nose.

"True," she said. "But he's really a toddler."

"Baby."

Tiana grinned and waved as Mickie climbed out of the car. "Mickie!"

"Tee!"

They met at the sidewalk and embraced. "It is so good to see you," Tiana said as she stepped back to look Mickie up and down. "Pale skin. Bags under the eyes. Permanent worried look on the face. Yep. You are a full-fledged nursing student!"

Mickie made a sound. Half laughter, half frustrated growl. "You are one hundred percent correct. Let me get little man out."

They laughed and chattered all the way back to the apartment. Lily took Ian off to her room so she could read to him. She was very proud of her reading skills. Tiana settled down on the couch next to Mickie. She hadn't yet made many female friends here, so it was good to have a friendly face, even if only for a few hours.

"How's it going?" They both asked at the same time. Then laughed.

"How's school going?"

"Good. It's stressful, like you said. But I'm running fast as I can to stay ahead of it. And I was able to land a patient care tech job on the mother-baby unit. Not where I want to be, but I've got a job reference now and I'm in the hospital system. How are you?"

"Feels like the first few months of nursing school all over again. But with patients and blood. I'm just now starting to feel like I've got a handle on it."

"But do you love it? Is the emergency department still where you want to be?"

"Yeah. The chaos of it all can make me wonder if I've lost my mind, but it's exciting. I'm never bored. It's always a challenge."

"Good. I'm trying to really make myself take a good look at each of the specialties as we rotate through. I don't want to be so focused on being a labor nurse that I miss an interest somewhere else."

Tiana nodded, remembering how it had been, being there, doing that, and not all that long ago. She looked up at Mickie and smiled. "That's my girl," she said.

They both started speaking at once—eager to share their stories, compare notes, when the front door opened and Vivian walked in carrying what seemed like her own weight in grocery bags.

"Mom!" Tiana scolded, getting up. "You should have called. I would have helped you carry those up."

Viv laughed. "No, girl. I'm the gold medal winner of carrying all the groceries inside in one trip." She set the bags down and motioned at Mickie. "Come here, sweet girl, how are you doing?"

"Perfect, thanks to your daughter. She got me completely ready for nursing school."

"Where's that little boy of yours?"

"In the bedroom with Lily," Tiana said. She side-eyed Mickie. "Here's where she completely forgets we're in the house because she has babies to play with."

"Well, that leads me to my rude question," Mickie said. "Would it be okay if Ian hangs out here for a while?"

"Of course," Vivian said automatically. "Long as you need."

"Thank you. I know it's short notice, but this thing with my boyfriend, Josh, this afternoon. I didn't know he'd be like this. Now that the time is near, he's devastated. He needs my full support for this."

"What's going on?" Tiana asked.

Mickie glanced down the hallway, listening to Lily's lilting voice as she read aloud to Ian. "He's moving his mother's body to another cemetery," she said in a lowered voice.

Vivian put a hand over her heart and turned a worried look at Mickie. "What's up with this?"

Mickie sighed. "His father abused his mother. When she tried to leave, he killed her and himself. Josh found out they were buried side by side and he wanted his mother moved away."

"Oh, honey," Viv said, pulling Mickie into her arms. "I'll be praying for you through this."

Tiana wrapped her arms around Mickie also. "We're here for you. All of you."

"Thank you," Mickie said, stepping back and wiping her face. "But there's more."

"More than that?" Tiana asked.

"A good more. Josh got a call from DeShawn. He's working on putting together a project for a teacher he knows. He's looking for people from disadvantaged backgrounds who've gone on to college and successful careers. He wants to put together a program for his students. I thought it sounded like something you'd be interested in doing."

Tiana narrowed her eyes. "DeShawn?"

"Yeah, you remember him, right? From last summer?"

Tiana got up off the couch and went to the kitchen. Dumping fresh ice into her water bottle, she shook her head and let out a breath. "Did he tell Josh that he saw me at the grocery store the other day?"

Mickie stood. She walked over, closer to Tiana, and leaned against the kitchen countertop. "No," she said. "Not that I'm aware of."

"Hmph," Tiana snorted. The damn man would say anything. "Tell him I'm not interested."

"Really?" Mickie said. Her eyebrows went

up and she pursed her lips, just slightly. Then her face relaxed. "I thought you would have liked that. You're such a natural teacher."

"It's not the project. It's the man. Is he really doing this or is it a scam to get my phone number?"

"I doubt it. DeShawn's a good guy."

Tiana nodded and her eyes narrowed.

"I'm sure he is, but I don't have time for games."

Mickie frowned and pushed away from the counter. "What should I tell him then?"

Tiana sighed, sucking in one corner of her lips and dropping her chin. She shook her head side to side once, then again. She picked a piece of lint off of her sleeve, examined it and then walked over to drop it in the trash can. "Give me his number," she said. "And tell him I'll think about it."

Mickie slipped her phone out, then swiped and scrolled a few times. Her brow knit and she bit her bottom lip. "Come on, come on, where are you?" She swept her finger across the screen. "Ah, okay. Here we go." She grabbed the closest pencil and scribbled a number on the top of the calendar hanging on the wall. "Ugh," she said, obviously noticing all Lily's school projects, tests and meet-the-teacher nights listed. First graders had so much to do. "I don't know if I'll be able to manage this when Ian gets to school." She tapped the calendar with the pencil eraser and turned to look at Tiana.

"It doesn't stop," Tiana said. She was smiling now. "I'm not going to kid you."

"Yikes," Mickie said, glancing at the time. "I need to get going. Let me say goodbye to Ian." She pulled Tiana in for a hug. "Thank you again for helping me out."

"You just be there for your man."

FEBRUARY GAVE THEM the gift of one of those rare cold days with sunshine and blue skies. The occasional icy breeze was the only reminder it was deep winter. DeShawn sat on one of the black folding chairs set out around a bright green awning over an open grave. Josh sat unmoving like a stone. Mickie leaned against Josh, holding his hand tight in hers. Kim, Josh's sister, was on his other side, holding his hand also. Beside her were her adoptive parents.

He'd been to funerals. Many. Too many. But this was…a reinterment. What an odd word. What an odd thing for a beautiful Saturday afternoon. A word for repeating what should only ever have to be done once for someone. He glanced to his left at Sadie. Wyatt, her fiancé, had her left hand clasped in both of his. Her lips were pressed tightly together, moving her gaze from Josh, she reached out and took his hand. He squeezed her fingers and leaned in close to her.

"Is he okay?" he whispered.

Sadie didn't answer, but gave a shrug while shaking her head, just barely. DeShawn turned his attention back to the chaplain, who was giving the standard funeral oratory. At the end, Josh stood and approached the coffin. He set a bouquet of red roses on the gleaming wood.

"Be at peace, Momma," he said, his voice wavering. He patted the coffin. "You're safe now." He stepped back.

Mickie and Sadie simultaneously began crying. DeShawn felt his own throat close up tight. He wanted to put his arm around Sadie, but Wyatt already had her. He clasped his hands together on his lap and looked down at the ground.

"It's okay."

He looked back up at the sound of Josh's words. Josh sat back in his chair and pulled Mickie into his arms. "It's okay," Josh repeated.

DeShawn reached out and put a hand on

Josh's shoulder. As did Sadie. For a moment, he felt the strength and fierce love that joined them. Sadie. Josh. They'd been his family for so long. And now look at them. Starting their own families. He looked back down. Thought about the phone call from his mother. He shook his head. *There's nothing to salvage from my family.*

Josh and Kim had requested to be alone as the coffin was lowered into the ground. De-Shawn leaned against his car, watching from a distance. Most the guests had left. Mickie, Sadie, Wyatt, Lena and Kim's parents remained. They didn't speak. He went to Mickie and pulled her into a hug.

"You're looking mighty cold, my Mickie."

She wrapped her arms around him and pressed a cheek to his chest. "I'm from Minnesota. This is shorts and flip-flop weather. I'm glad you were able to be here."

"It's crazy. Is Josh okay? I can't wrap my mind around this."

"I think so. She was buried next to her murderer. You know? I can't even… The anger. He was using it, I guess. It kept the grief down. It caught up with him, though. This morning." She stepped back and glanced over her shoulder at the grave site. When she turned back, the troubled look on her face deepened just a bit.

"What?" he said.

"I asked Tiana about the project."

"Great! What'd she say?"

"No."

DeShawn was taken aback for a moment. Despite all the teasing between them, he thought she'd definitely be interested in his idea. Then he noted the look in Mickie's eyes. That I'm-waiting-for-an-explanation look. "What?"

"Are you scamming for her phone number?"

"What? No! Is that what she thought?"

Mickie glanced over her shoulder again. "What happened at the grocery store?"

Shaking his head, he lifted his hands, palms up. "Nothing. Never mind. Don't need her."

Mickie pushed his hands aside. "Actually, it wasn't a hard *no.* She said she'd think about it."

He tilted his head, scrunched up his chin then looked off to the right.

"Here they come," he said.

Josh and Kim walked back to the small group. Kim went straight into her parents' arms. Josh held his hand out to DeShawn for a high-five, but DeShawn pulled him in close and held him there instead.

"You okay, brother?" DeShawn asked.

"Yeah," Josh said. "I am. Feels good to have it done. I feel as if I've… I don't know how to say it."

DeShawn put his hands on Josh's shoulders and looked him in the eyes. "You freed her, Josh. She died because she was trying to save you and Kim. She's free of him now."

Josh nodded and looked away as he swallowed hard. "You coming to Sadie's?"

"Yeah, man. I'll be there."

"Okay. We're going to pick up Ian. See you there."

CHAPTER FOUR

DeSHAWN LOUNGED BACK in a chair around the table in the conference room of the Cleaning Crew offices. He'd spent four years of his life working here. He closed his eyes and tried to put himself back in the head of the young man he'd been when he first walked in here, all those years ago. He couldn't do it. He didn't fit there anymore.

What those years had been, for him, was work, hard work. He'd caught a little side-eye, at first, from those who couldn't see a man in that role. Cleaning houses? But he figured out was that there was a world of difference between just doing the job and doing the job right. You did the job if it was a good day or a bad one. If you were sore or under the weather, you pushed that to the other side of your head and kept going. You learned to see more, to notice, to take pride in that wow in the client's eyes. Yeah. And the friends he'd made here. The family he'd made.

He felt at home. There was no other way to say it, was there? He smiled. He liked that, a lot. At home.

Sadie came in and sat beside him. He smiled at the sight of her huge cup of coffee, steam still rising. Getting between Sadie and her coffee could drop a guy into seriously dire straits.

"I miss seeing you sitting here," she said.

"It feels strange to be here. Like seeing your bedroom from when you were a kid. It's perfectly the same, but somehow looks and feels completely different."

"How are you doing, DeShawn? I know you're going to say fine, but losing out on your Army commission was a huge blow. Are you really okay?"

"I am," he said. He slouched back in his chair, looked up and then back at her. "I know I had a vision of myself traveling the world, building things, experiencing life. It was a hard decision to make, but I'm okay. On a different path is all."

"You can still travel."

"I know. Stop. Recalibrate. Make a new plan. I'm good. Actually beginning to feel a Divine hand in it. I feel like I've come home. Like this is where I belong."

"Good. We're your family. You should be with us."

"My mother called me."

And, hell. He hadn't meant to say that. The words just fell out of his mouth without permission. The small part of him that wasn't stunned into silence by the unexpected announcement was amused by Sadie's transformation. She went from relaxed and happy to momma grizzly standing over a cub.

"And?" Just one word, but a word crackling and sparking with little pops of not-so-slight hint of am-I-going-to-have-to-kill-someone around the edges.

"And I don't know. It was completely unexpected. I don't even know how she got my number."

"What did she want?"

Tipping the chair back against the wall, he laced his fingers behind his head. "To tell me she'd been clean and sober for three months. Wanted to talk to me." He shook his head, still not wanting to believe it ever happened.

Sadie put her foot on the cross rung of the chair and sent the chair back to the floor with a jarring thud. "Told you not to do that to my chairs. Clean and sober? Three months. She's

probably doing that AA step where you're supposed to make amends to those you've hurt."

He stood and pushed the chair slowly back
under the table, his fingers gripping the back.
"I don't know how I feel about that."

Sadie stood and took his hand. "Come on.
Let's go upstairs and talk."

It was easier here. Sitting on opposite ends
of the couch in the apartment Sadie had built
above the office. More like he was talking to
his sister than his former boss. "If she is trying to stay sober, then I'm glad for her. That's
no way to live," he said.

"But?"

"But do I have to go back down that road
with her? What's this amends stuff? She reminds me of all the horrible things she did and
said? All the times she made Momma G cry?
Dragged me out the house to hide me away
with her wherever she was living until...until
Momma G gave her money. Money for drugs.
That's what Momma G had to give her to get
me back."

He stood and paced around the living room.
It was still right there, always just below the
surface. That cool exterior was thin, and all
it took was the right trigger—a word, a picture in his head, the whiff of something—to

snap it and release all that poison. He'd only been hiding it from himself, pretending he was over it when really, he was just ignoring it. He rubbed at his face with shaky hands and tried to slow the pounding of his heart by taking a few deep breaths.

"Then what?" he asked quietly with his back to Sadie. "I say I forgive her? And she walks away feeling happy and free? I don't want to go back there. Mentally. Emotionally. I walked away from all that."

He heard Sadie's footsteps and looked down at his feet. He felt selfish. Petulant. He should be a better person than this. Sadie put her hands on his shoulders.

"No." The word was spoken firmly. "You do not owe her that. You don't have to put yourself through that, DeShawn. That is your right. This mess is hers. You don't have to help her clean it up. Okay?"

He felt the anger drain away. His shoulders relaxed under her hands. "Okay," he said, turning to face her.

"But," she said as she looked him in the eyes.

"Of course there's a but with you." He tried to make it a joke. Tried to grin. Because he knew what it was and didn't want to hear it.

"Think about it, DeShawn. Don't dismiss it automatically. You are obviously still angry and hurt, with good reason, but that means it is still affecting you. I had to forgive my mother so I could let go of all those feelings. I'm not saying that is your answer, but think about it, okay? I love you too much to know you are hurting like this."

That got a real smile from him. "I'll think about it, Boss."

"Promise?"

A clatter arose from the kitchen downstairs. Josh and Mickie were back from picking up Ian. Relief flooded him. He shouldn't have said anything. Sadie was going to hound him until this issue was resolved. "I promise," he said. "Let's go see that kiddo. You have to see Josh if there is any snot on Ian's face. It's priceless."

Sadie scowled. "Ew. Snot? There better not be snot."

PEEKING DOWN THE HALL, Tiana felt a sense of walking on eggshells. People were either sitting quietly or doing busywork. No one was acknowledging the truth: there were only two patients in the entire ER. A laceration that needed stitches and a migraine. Even for a Sunday night, this was unprecedented. No one dared to utter a word lest the magical spell be broken and an avalanche of critical patients buried them.

Stepping into Bay Six, Tiana pushed the cart she'd loaded with supplies to the cabinets. Shaking her head impatiently, she began restocking supply drawers. Yeah, it was nice to have a break, but dang! Without the constant flow of adrenaline, her body began to remind her it was two in the morning. Eyelids were heavy. Head all muffled. Thoughts of how much she loved her pillow. It was a great pillow. She missed it right now.

Kasey Rattigan twirled around in the room's chair, her ponytail swinging from side to side. "Tell me something," she said.

Kasey was her preceptor in the emergency department. Smart, tough, fearless and in possession of a sense of a wicked and black humor, she and Tiana had bonded over a particularly heinous code brown.

"What?"

"I don't know. Something interesting."

Tiana snorted out a laugh. "There is nothing remotely interesting in my life," she said, stacking packages of sterile gauze. "I work, I sleep, I eat."

"Let's take the girls to the Children's Museum this week."

Moving on to the cabinets, Tiana checked the supply list. *Needs more pulse oximeters. EKG leads. What about this DeShawn thing?*

"Earth to Tiana!"

"Hmm?"

Kasey brought the chair to a sudden halt and stood up. "Whoa!" she said, grabbing at the counter. "Dizzy. What's going on with you?"

"Nothing. I'm trying to memorize what's in the cabinets."

"You aren't memorizing anything at two a.m. Save that for day brain. You keep zoning out. What's on your mind? I'm your preceptor—you have to tell me."

Tiana closed the cabinet drawers. Kasey was right. Her brain was passing the information through with zero storage. "It's not a work thing."

"Then as your newest best friend, you have to tell me."

"It's nothing really. I got this offer to do this…thing."

Kasey's eyebrows disappeared into her bangs. "Oh," she said, each word dripping the sarcasm. "An offer. For a thing. Wow."

Tiana leaned against the counter and looked

around the bay. The more she'd thought about DeShawn's project, the more she wanted to do it. But it came with DeShawn. And she couldn't deny that their playful bickering was cover for some real attraction. At least on her part.

Kasey returned to the chair, this time flopping back in it with her arms hanging over the sides and her head lolling on the back. "Tell me," she whined. "Before I say the *b* word!"

Tiana laughed but a flash of superstitious fear that jolted through her overruled the laughter. The *b* word was *bored*. It was worse than uttering the *q* word: *quiet*. To speak either of those words aloud would bring disaster raining down upon any nurse foolish enough to say them. She hooked the rolling stool with a foot, pulled it toward her and sat.

"I got asked to be part of a group to speak at a school. It's a rural school with disadvantaged students. They are looking for speakers from similar backgrounds who've graduated college."

Kasey sat up straight in the chair. "I didn't know that was your background."

"Small town. Crappy school system. Yep. That's me."

"So, you'd be perfect for this group. Why the hesitation?"

Making a face, Tiana began to swivel the stool from side to side. "The guy who's putting it together…"

"Wait." Kasey pushed off with her feet, sending her chair rolling toward Tiana's stool. Their knees crashed together. "A guy? Tell me about this guy."

"Nothing to tell," Tiana said, even as the heat of her blush stung her cheeks. "I met him last year."

"If there's nothing to tell, why are you blushing?"

"It's really nothing. There's just this…like… chemistry there."

"Chemistry? How horrible!" Kasey said, putting her hands to her cheeks.

"It's not horrible. It's just not what I need in my life right now."

"Bullsheeeet." Kasey sang out. "You could use a man in your life. Break up that work, sleep, eat routine you've got going on. Tell me about Mr. Chemistry."

Tiana stood and walked to the bay door. Glancing down the hall, she saw everyone was still milling around or sitting at the nurses' station. She pulled sliding glass door of the room almost shut and turned to look at Kasey. "I have to be careful," she said as she went back to her stool.

"Of what?"

"Lily. I was seventeen when I got pregnant with her. Her dad and I tried to make it work, but we were so young. We wanted different things. He tried at first. But as Lily got older, he came around less and less until he finally just disappeared from our lives. Lily was old enough to know that her daddy left her."

Kasey's hands closed around Tiana's with a gentle squeeze. "So you can't have men coming and going from her life."

Feeling her shoulders relax, Tiana nodded. She'd known Kasey would understand. "Exactly. I don't know how to navigate that minefield."

"And an explosion could hurt Lily. As your friend, I understand. As your preceptor, I'm going to tell you to seriously think about it though. Management eats that stuff up with a spoon. It would look amazing on your post-orientation evaluation that you participated in a project like that. Mr. Chemistry or not."

"Thanks," Tiana said, her eyes glazing. "That makes the decision so much more easy."

"Just do it." Kasey glanced up at the clock

and made a celebratory pumping motion with her first. "Woot! It's two thirty! Only thirty minutes left on our shift!"

Tiana closed her eyes and silently counted backward. Did Kasey really just jinx it? Every nurse knows that you never, ever...

She was cut off by the sounding of an alarm, the incoming trauma alarm. Jumping to her feet, Tiana headed for the door with Kasey close behind her.

"This is all your fault, you know," Tiana said as they joined the others in preparing for the ambulance's arrival.

Kasey said nothing, but from the expression on her face, she didn't have to.

"Lena? Sadie's accountant Lena?" Malik took a step back but his eyes shone with interest. A mixed of fear and admiration ran through those four short words.

DeShawn laughed as they leaned against the side of his car in the parking lot of a strip mall along Savannah Highway, not far from 526. He'd talked to both Henry and Lena about his idea. They'd both been on board. Malik, a former Cleaning Crew member, was now in medical school, was his best friend and first recruit. He could feel a not-so-small sting of disappointment. He hadn't heard anything from Tiana. "Yeah. She's driving. Refused to pick us up at the apartment."

"So this is why I'm standing in the cold on the side of the road, waiting? Instead of being in my warm bed?" Malik asked.

"She's got a BMW. Unless you want to risk a hundred miles in my death rattle mobile? When it gives out, we could kick our feet through the floorboards and drive it Fred Flintstone style."

Malik rubbed his hands together. "No, hard pass on that. I'll take the BMW. Huh. Get a little comparison shopping in for when I'm a rich doctor."

He closed his eyes, spread his arms wide and tilted his head up toward the sky. "What's that you say, Mr. Car Dealer Man? Do I want this full custom package in Smoked Topaz or Silverstone? How about one of each, two sets of 444 horses side by side…"

"Uh-huh," DeShawn said. "Didn't you say you wanted to be a family practice doctor in an underserved area?"

Malik shook his head, still in his daydream. "You know, at this exact moment in time, I do not recall making that statement."

"Ha!" DeShawn said. "You'll see."

A white BMW pulled into the parking lot and came to a quick stop beside them. The window powered down and Lena Reyes looked at them over the rims of her sunglasses. "Get in. Don't track dirt."

"Hi, Lena. Nice to see you again," DeShawn said with a laugh.

"Get in, it's cold."

The window powered back up. DeShawn climbed into the front passenger seat, grinning. Lena liked to play tough but she was a softy when it came to kids. Mention poor kids and she opened her wallet and her heart.

She glanced at Malik as he got in the back seat. "Hi, Malik. Good to see you. How's school going?"

"Great. Thanks."

"So, DeShawn," Lena said as she turned the car back onto Savannah Highway, heading south. "What is your goal, your vision for this project?"

The question startled him. "Uh," he stammered. When he started thinking about it, he realized that he hadn't really thought it all the way through. "I thought we could talk to the kids about our experiences. Show them that it can be done. Help them find resources."

She nodded. "That's a good start, but I think

you've got something here that you can turn into a long-term project."

"How?"

She grinned at him. "That's for you to figure out. This is your idea, DeShawn. You want to help these kids? They need more than a parade of people lecturing them."

That's when the first wave of doubt soaked him. He tried to keep it off of his face, but inside, his mind was checking off all the boxes he hadn't even noticed were on the list. Lena was right. She had that way of laying truth out flat in front of you. This was going to have to be more. Much more. The idea seemed so good when he was talking with Sadie. Inspire the kids. Point them in the right direction. But Momma G hadn't just pointed off toward some picturesque horizon and made a nice speech. She'd been there, day after day, doing the hard work. Being a consistent model of goodness in his early, troubled life.

These kids were real people with real problems and real day to day needs. And having hope in the first place was to start hoping and then have it snatched away. To believe that *this* time, someone was going to actually keep a promise. He'd been there, done that too many times with his own parents. He began to consider the true depth of the waters he was diving into.

This wasn't a weekend project. This was a commitment.

Malik reached over the seat to clap his hand against DeShawn's shoulder. "It'll be fine," Malik said. "He's an engineer. Solving problems is what he does." He looked at DeShawn. "You got this."

The doubt dialed down a few clicks. It wasn't that he didn't have a plan at all. He simply had insufficient data to make a comprehensive one. "We'll talk to Henry," he said. "Find out what the needs are and go from there."

"That's good," Lena agreed. "Build the program around the kids. That's how it should be."

Charleston stretched out a while longer as they motored down 17 South. There was a long patch of green space, especially around the USDA lab, but really it kept that west of the Ashley vibe all the way up to the intersection of 17 and Main Road, where you could take a left and go high up in the sky on the new bridge over the Stono and get a breathtaking view of Johns Island. That's usually how DeShawn saw it in the ever shifting map of the greater Charleston area he kept in his head. But they weren't going to Johns Island today.

No Stono Market or Tomato Shed Cafe, sad to say. Nope. Today was all a steady straight drive past the tractor supply places and you-pick berry farms that meant you were easing through Ravenel.

Lena put the pedal down as the road opened up and there was nothing but trees whizzing by on both sides, the car riding as smooth as silk. It was peaceful. He even let himself close his eyes for a while, just breathe the clean air and feel…good.

Don't overthink it, he thought. *Just go with it. Like she said. Build the program. Let it go the way it wants to go. What the kids need.*

After some time of just watching the trees, he heard Malik muttering, "Gonna change to surgery. Get me one of these."

DeShawn laughed, then cautioned Lena as they crossed the Edisto River that it was wise to tap the brakes a few times before entering historic Jacksonboro. That was a stretch of road where the constabulary liked to keep an eye and Radar out for southbound motorists in a little too much of a hurry to get to Beaufort or Savannah.

"Hm," she said, slowing down. She looked around. "We're good on gas. Do either of you need to stop for anything? Last civilization for a few miles at least." She nodded toward the gas station at the fork where you could either cut north up into Walterboro or keep south along the ACE Basin Parkway.

"I'm good," DeShawn said.

"Good," Malik said.

They kept south.

"Do you know where this place is?" DeShawn asked. Once you were in the ACE Basin, the world just opened up, bursting with blue skies above, lush green all around, vast tea-brown waters snaking beneath the bridges. It was beautiful. An almost pristine estuary, one of the largest on the Eastern seaboard, pretty much undeveloped save for the highway they were traveling down.

"Nope," Lena said with a wave of her hand. "Following GPS."

About a dozen miles from I-95, DeShawn pointed up ahead to a dark, dragonesque shape in the marsh grass. "Is that a gator?" he asked.

"In February?" Lena said. "I don't think so."

"South Carolina Lizard Man, more likely," Malik said.

"What?" DeShawn and Lena asked in unison.

It turned out to be a long curl of thrown-off truck tire, twisted up like a burnt cruller.

"You two hush up with your horror movie stuff," Lena said. "I'm driving here."

DeShawn looked back. "That's a really big tire, though. That can't have been good, when that thing blew."

"Lizard Man's a real thing," Malik said. Lena's eyes caught him in the rearview mirror. He shrugged. "Seriously. He lurks around in the swamps and tidal creeks, occasionally stumbles upon family picnics and hilarity ensues. What? You guys never saw that TV ad?"

Lena smirked. "Lurks," she said, tasting the word. "Sounds like one of the charmers my family tried to hook me up with last year."

DeShawn looked out the window and whistled. Lena laughed. "Relax," she said. "It's not far now."

And she was right. They kept motoring down the big roads for a while longer, then took an exit to a smaller road, then turned off again. Farm houses with single grain silos, sun-faded barns. Another turn, this time onto a bumpy winding road where they drove past small houses ringed by clusters of mobile homes. Finally, they found themselves on a small-town main street. It was almost as if it was secreted away in the green, one of those Southern towns that had once been part of something—farming, textiles, trade—but were left behind and forgotten about in the wake of the great global industrial machine. Lena pulled into a small lot next to a neat red brick building, with only the words *County School* above the door.

"This is where Henry arranged for the meeting," Lena said as they got out of the car. The lawn was brown and patchy beneath their feet in the relative cold of the South Carolina winter. DeShawn noticed that the paint was peeling and cracked. As they made their way inside, he had a strange feeling of déjà vu. The floor was clean but old. The ceiling tiles were sagging in places. The desks in the classrooms they passed looked like they were left over from the sixties.

He shook his head. "Damn."

"I know, right?" Malik said. "You'd think they'd have fixed this by now."

"Reminds me of my elementary school," Lena said.

"Me too," DeShawn echoed.

Lena stopped in the doorway to the library. She looked in and he saw her shoulders slump. "When I got to high school," she said slowly, "we were in a better school district. It was such a shock. They had computers and books in the library. I mean, you know that schools aren't going to be exactly equal, but…until you see it, until you *really* see it, you don't understand. You don't get how wide that gap really is."

When she stepped back, he leaned in through the door. The library was no bigger than a classroom. Many of the shelves were empty. It was dim, sad, smelling faintly of mildew and old paper.

"Yeah," DeShawn said. "I was in the top in my high school class but still barely scored well enough on my SATs to get into college. Had to do the first two years at a community college to get caught up."

The look on her face made him take a step back. He knew her well enough to know she was a powerfully determined woman. What Lena wanted, Lena got. She looked at them. "This is bullshit," she said in a voice much quieter than the anger in her eyes. "Let's try to fix something here."

"Damn straight," he said.

"Hey!" a voice called out. "I'm down here."

A man stood in the hall outside a classroom. "Henry Gardner," he introduced himself as he shook Lena's hand.

"I remember you, Henry," Lena said with a smile.

"And I you. Your visits to the Cleaning Crew office were a source of awe and fear."

Her mouth fell open and the three men laughed. "What? Why?"

"Ahem. Well, you do have a certain sense of…determination about you," Malik said diplomatically.

"Come on," Henry said with a motion toward the door. "Let's sit down."

As they pulled chairs into a small circle, Henry looked at Lena. "I'm surprised to see you here, Lena. Are you funding this?"

She shot him a look. Quizzical with a touch of do-you-want-to-die. "I grew up in a trailer park. I *am* one of your students."

"Perfect," Henry said smoothly. "We have a good percentage of Hispanic students so your input would be more than welcome." He looked at DeShawn. "What's the plan?"

"The plan is to try to provide what you need," DeShawn replied. "What do the kids need? Besides role models?"

Henry's laugh echoed around the small empty classroom. "Need? Books. Computers. Internet access."

"Wait," Lena said. "The school doesn't have internet?"

Henry shook his head. "The public library

does, usually. It's slow, but it's there. Most of my kids don't have it at home at all."

DeShawn looked at Malik and shook his head. Same old story. Different generation. "I'd guess that the best way to start would be getting the kids' trust," he said. "I'm trying to recruit more people. We could start with a series of class visits for people to tell their stories."

"Definitely," Henry said. "I can tell them they can do it all day long, but in the end, I'm just a white guy from suburbia. They like me, but they don't identify with me. They need to hear it from people who've lived it."

"We can help you with that," Malik said with a grin.

They spent the next hour learning about the kids. As they spoke, DeShawn began to get a better idea of just how large the need was out here in the rural, almost forgotten places. The kids needed more than role models. They needed mentors. They needed to see the world outside this crossroads town.

CHAPTER FIVE

SOMETIME DURING THE NIGHT, Lily had crept into bed with her. Tiana rolled over and pulled Lily close to her, snuggling down into the warm blankets. This was heaven, right here. A lazy, easy Sunday morning. Nowhere to be, no work, no school, no lunches to be packed. Maybe she would make bacon and French toast later. She was drifting into a light doze when there was a single sharp rap on the door. Groaning, Tiana opened her eyes. She knew that knock. It was her mother's patented get-your-ass-out-of-bed knock.

"Is Lily with you?"

"Yes, Mom," Tiana replied. She pulled an arm out from beneath the covers to grab her phone. *Eight in the morning? Woman's gone crazy.*

"Well, get up. I'll get breakfast going. Don't want to be late."

Lily stirred beside her. Tiana sat up, shivering in the cool air, her skin missing the heat of the blankets. "Late for what?"

"Church."

Church? What church? Tiana hadn't even started looking for a home church yet. Flopping back on the pillows, she sighed. *No use to argue.* She'd not won an argument with her mother ever in her entire life.

"What's wrong, Momma?" Lily asked.

"Nothing. We need to get up. Granny wants to go to church."

"She doesn't like to be called Granny."

"I know."

"You don't like church?"

"I like church just fine. I don't like to get out of bed when it's cold."

"Me either. Maybe we can have church under the covers."

Lily squirmed down under the blanket. Laughing, Tiana pulled the covers over her head and scooted down. "Now what?" she asked.

Lily put her hands together in prayer and Tiana copied her. "Dear Jesus," Lily said in her clear, sweet voice. "Thank you for saving us. We really appreciate it. But it's cold so Mommy and I are going to stay in bed if that's okay. Amen."

"Amen," Tiana echoed. She smiled at her daughter. How'd she gotten such an amazing child, she didn't know. Funny, smart, sassy.

Lily grinned back, a gap-toothed grin. She was so innocent it made Tiana's heart hurt a little to know it wouldn't last. The door to the room opened. Lily put a finger against her lips.

"What are you two up to under there?" Vivian asked.

"We went to church under the covers," Lily said.

There was a moment of silence. Then a huff of irritation. "Both of you get up. I need someone to stir those grits while I tend to the bacon."

"Bacon!" Lily cried and scrambled out of the bed.

"Fine. Leave me all alone," Tiana called after her.

"But, Momma! Bacon!"

"That's all right, Lily," Vivian said. "She'll get up once she starts smelling it. No one can stay in bed when there's bacon sizzling."

They left the room but didn't close the door. Tiana pulled the covers away from her face. She had to get her mother to go back home. Somehow. She loved her mother and was grateful for all she'd done to help with Lily over the years. But it was time for her and Lily to have a little breathing room. And for her to sleep in when she wanted to.

Grabbing her thick robe, Tiana shrugged into it while crossing the room. In the kitchen, Lily was standing on a step stool, studiously stirring a pot of grits. A large pot of grits in the morning meant shrimp and grits later on. That was Mom's way. She knew how to plan out her meals and to use all that she cooked. As she poured coffee, Tiana laughed.

"What's so funny over there?" Vivian asked, moving bacon around with a fork.

"Nothing," she replied as she stirred sugar and creamer into the coffee cup. "I remembered how shocked I was the first time I saw bacon in the college cafeteria. They cooked the whole strip."

Her mother had her own style. She'd chop the rasher of bacon into three sections, dump the entire pile into her frying pan and just keep stirring until it was done. "Huh," Vivian said with a slight snort. "That's fine. If you got all day."

Tiana went to the stove to check the heat under the grits. The burner was off and the pot was barely bubbling. They looked done to her, so she guessed Lily's stirring was just to give her something to do. "Be careful with those grits, Lily. They are very hot."

"I'm being careful, Mommy."

"What church are we going to today?"

Vivian had been visiting churches every Sunday to find a good fit. This was the first Sunday Tiana either had off or hadn't worked a late shift since before they'd moved in. It was on her list of things to do, just not quite as close to the top as her mother's list.

"Emanuel."

"The one downtown?"

"Yes." Viv turned to look at her. "Why?"

Tiana looked at Lily, then back at her mother, eyebrows raised. The look she got back was pure steel. "No one's going to say things in front of the children."

"Say what?" Lily asked.

"Nothing, sweet girl," Vivian cooed. "Keep stirring those grits. Your momma needs to drink her coffee and get in the shower."

AFTER CHURCH, THEY walked the few blocks along Calhoun Street to have brunch at Saffron Restaurant Bakery. A nice cup of coffee and a trip through their divine brunch buffet was worth the early wake-up time.

"Can we go to the aquarium too?" Lily asked.

As they walked to the South Carolina Aquarium, Tiana wished once again that she could live downtown. It was such a walkable town, so utterly charming in its own way, but the real estate market was unreal. Once, while dining at Jestine's Kitchen, she'd overheard someone quip that prices in the Historic District were on par with Manhattan. She didn't doubt it. All those magazines talking Charleston up as the best travel destination in the country, as the best wedding destination, the most polite city... Well, maybe Charleston was polite when an elderly gentleman walking the family poodle tipped his hat to you on Chalmers Street, but it was considerably less polite on 526 during rush hour bumper to bumper traffic.

She smiled, shook her head. This place. What a beautiful mess of contradiction.

The day was perfect. Cool but sunny. The wind coming off of Charleston Harbor was redolent with the unique scent the locals called pluff mud. Thickly pungent, strong enough to tickle the insides of your nose. To a Charlestonian, it was a sweet perfume. But then, Charlestonians also thought that the tip of the peninsula was where the Ashley and Cooper Rivers merged to form the Atlantic Ocean, so there's that. To Tiana it smelled like… Hmm. Funky oysters?

They made their way to the South Carolina Aquarium, which was one of Lily's favorite things about her new hometown. From the giant shark tank to the smaller exhibits, Lily loved it all, everything in an around there. After her first visit to the aquarium, she'd decided she wanted to be a fish doctor when she grew up. As Lily skipped ahead of them, Tiana linked her arm with her mother's.

"Any thoughts on going back home?"

Vivian swiveled her head and raised her eyebrows. "Are you trying to get rid of me?"

Yes. "No. I'm just starting to feel selfish, keeping you here so long."

"You aren't ready for me to leave yet."

"We'll be fine, Mom."

"Who's going to watch Lily when you work late? How are you going to get her to school when you have to be at work before her school even opens?"

Tiana watched as Lily leaned in to get almost nose to nose with one of the smaller sharks in the big tank. That was a problem. Her work schedule wasn't compatible with school hours. "I'm working on that. A few of the other nurses have kids in the same school.

They take turns getting the kids to school and watching them after."

"So you're going to let total strangers watch after your baby?"

"They aren't total strangers, Mom. I work with them. And speaking of total strangers, what about all the kids you normally watch? Who's taking care of them now?"

"They're all in school now. I haven't had little ones since Lily."

Tiana's heart sunk. There went her main leverage to get her mother moving. Her only hope was if one of her sisters got pregnant. That would be perfect. She considered just flat out lying and saying one of them was trying. But the retribution she'd get for that would make trying to get her mother to go home look like a day at the beach.

Vivian pulled her arm away and stopped walking. She turned to look Tiana in the eye. "Do you want me to leave?"

"I don't want you to feel like you have to stay."

"That's not what I asked."

Glancing at the shark tank, Tiana noted Lily was in deep conversation with a little boy about her age. They were pointing at various fish and nodding with great seriousness. She must have found another future fish doctor. "Let's sit down," she said, gesturing at the row of benches.

"I don't want you to leave," she said, feeling her way slowly along the words. "It's just that Lily is so used to being with you, which isn't your fault, it was my choice…"

"And she sees me more as a mother figure than you," Viv finished.

Blinking against the sudden sting of tears, Tiana nodded. "I feel selfish about it, but yeah. She calls me Mom, but she still goes to you for everything. She bumps her knee, she goes to you. She wants a snack, she goes to you."

"When she wanted a cuddle this morning, she went to you."

Tiana dropped her head and stared at the floor. "Yeah. I guess. But that was for fun times. If she's scared or hurt, she goes to you."

"Don't feel selfish. It's normal. We both know it's going to take some time. She knows you are her mother. She's just used to coming to me."

"Because I wasn't there."

She couldn't look at her mother as she spoke the words. Instead she watched Lily, who was slowly pacing along the edge of the tank.

"I'm not fighting this same old battle with

you, Tiana. If you want to beat yourself up about it, go ahead. You had a hard choice to make. It was a huge risk. You took it. Yes, you lost some of Lily's childhood while you were gone. But you gave her a future."

Vivian walked to Lily as Tiana leaned forward, staring at the floor and feeling pretty much like a six-year-old herself. Pouty and petulant. She hated it. Hated feeling at odds with her mother. But there it was. She was jealous. Of her own mother. She looked up as Lily scampered back with Vivian trailing behind.

"Did you have fun looking at the pretty fish?" Tiana asked.

"Yes. There's a pink one today," Lily answered.

"Pretty. I wonder if we could find you a pink fish for your pet."

Lily's eyebrows came together in an all too familiar frown. "I want a kitten."

Tiana sighed. *Mission not accomplished.*

"Ready to go, darling?"

"Yes." Lily looked up at her grandmother. "Can we get ice cream on the way home?"

Vivian lifted a hand to point at Tiana. "Ask your mother."

Tiana tilted her head up to catch her mother's gaze. Dipping her head in a quick nod, she stood.

"We can go get some *sorbetto*, that's better than ice cream," she said, taking Lily's hand in hers. As they made their way out of the building, Tiana hooked an arm around her mother's waist for a quick squeeze.

"It'll be all right," Vivian said.

That made her smile. That was her mother's answer to everything. A broken nail. A bad grade. A dead car battery. A flat tire at midnight in the middle of nowhere. Tornado. Hurricane. Exploding septic tanks. *It'll be all right.* And it usually was. Except the exploding septic tank. That hadn't been all right at all.

DeSHAWN HAD SPENT most of Monday morning out at the former Charleston Naval Base, which was now being repurposed into private and industrial usage. The building of a railway extension to serve a shipping container facility included moving two major highway intersections. And moving two intersections meant a lot of data gathering. Even the best coat and hat couldn't protect against the winter cold seeping in after several hours outside.

He was more than happy to return to his desk at the headquarters and, once he thawed out his fingers, upload all the information into the computer, where he could prepare it for presentation.

"What's the grin for?" his office mate asked as he returned from lunch.

DeShawn shook his head. He hadn't realized he was smiling. "Just happy to be out of the cold," he said.

That was only part of the truth. He couldn't believe he'd done it. Sometimes, he'd stop and look around, completely stunned that this was his life now. He had his degree. He had an awesome job. He loved the orderliness of it. Data. You gathered it. You put it together, you applied it to your project. Adjust as necessary. Simple. Factual. Same with the rest of his life. Simple. Orderly. No crazy family creating drama. Tiana's face flashed in his mind's eye and he felt a little tug of disappointment. He really wanted her involved in his project. He'd have to figure out a way to change her mind. How, he had no clue.

"I wouldn't complain. Wait until July and August."

"Not complaining. Not at all."

He returned to the task at hand. He wouldn't complain about surveying in the heat of the summer either. Well, not too much. His cell phone buzzed from inside the top desk drawer where he'd stashed it. Pulling it out, he saw an unknown number. The happy feeling he'd been riding fell away. He swiped left on the screen to reject the call. That was the past. Momma G had made him swear to finish his degree and he had. He'd busted his ass to get out of there and now that she was gone, he had no reason to ever go back. They could call a billion times and he wasn't going to answer. Drawing in and letting out a long, slow breath, he refocused on the job in front of him.

Later though, as he sat in traffic on the commute home, a thought exploded in his mind. *What if it had been Tiana?* Mickie had said she was thinking about the school project. Curiosity piqued, he reached for his phone at the next red light. Thumbed through to listen to the voice mail. It was a woman, but it wasn't Tiana.

"Hi, DeShawn. My name is Gretchen and I am your mother's sponsor in Narcotics Anonymous…"

He hit Delete before he could hear any more. *Damn it. Now she's giving out my name and number to other druggies?* Slamming his hand against the steering wheel only fueled the frustration and anger. *Why can't they leave me alone?* As traffic started moving, he merged into the right lane with a halfhearted wave in apology to the person he'd sort of cut off. Pulling into a parking spot in a strip mall, he put the car into Park and wiped at his face with both hands.

Maybe if he just talked to them. If he told them to go away, would they? He could be the bad guy. In fact, he'd willingly be the bad guy if it meant he was finally done with them. Staring without seeing out into the passing traffic, he became acutely aware of the anger that was coursing through his body. All the happiness and satisfaction with himself and his life were gone. Wiped away by a single phone call. He had to deal with this.

He needed to talk to Sadie. Now. Before this got out of hand. Looking around, he got his bearings. He'd driven all over the Charleston area in his four years as a member of the Cleaning Crew. Drop him anywhere and he could be back at the Crew office in less than fifteen minutes. Well, in this traffic, maybe thirty.

It was twenty. He glanced at his watch. As he pulled around to the parking lot on the side of the house, his stomach dropped. Sadie's car wasn't there. *Now what? Go to the gym and run until you're too tired to think about this anymore?* A movement at the back door caught his attention. Molly. She locked the door behind her and turned to peer at his car over the tops of her glasses. He rolled down the window.

"DeShawn!" she called out in delight as she crossed the small lot to greet him.

He climbed out of the car to give her a hug. Just seeing her face made him feel better. If Sadie was a big sister figure to him, then Molly was certainly his substitute grandmother. Short, round, white hair, constantly reading romance novels at her desk, but she missed nothing. She could go from sweet grandmotherly love to drill sergeant tough in a heartbeat.

"I was looking for Sadie," he said as he stepped back.

"Oh, it's PTA night," Molly said with a self-satisfied grin.

"PTA?" Parent-teacher thing?

"Exactly," Molly said with a knowing smile, "Parent-Teacher Association. She's at the elementary school with Wyatt and his daughter."

He stared openmouthed at her. *Sadie? At an elementary school meeting?* "I… I," he stuttered. He shook his head. "I can't even process that information."

Molly laughed. "It's mind-boggling. What did you need, honey?"

It came back to him, cutting short the humor. "Nothing really. To talk."

He felt her gaze on him but couldn't quite meet it. She had a way of knowing things. "Well," she said. "I was going to hop on the bus, but if you aren't hurrying off anywhere, would you give an old lady a ride home?"

"Of course," he said. Why hadn't he known Molly rode the bus to work? He felt a little ashamed of himself. He and the guys should have been giving her rides home every day.

"Thank you. And I put a nice pot roast in the slow cooker this morning. If you'd like, there's plenty for two."

He followed her directions into the cozy Byrnes Down neighborhood. "I wouldn't want to impose."

"Same pot roast I made for First Friday dinners."

That made him smile. On the first Friday of the month, Sadie and Molly would cook up a huge dinner for all the Crew members. It was family time.

"I'm also a fairly good listener," Molly added.

"Okay. I can't pass up your pot roast."

"Good, you're looking a bit skinny."

At the front door, Molly turned to him. "Mind your step. Wee furry ones everywhere."

"What?"

As he followed her into the tidy cottage-sized house, he was surrounded by tiny mewling kittens. One, two, three, four... "Molly? Are you a crazy cat lady?"

Ten. There were ten of them. And one grown-up cat slinking along a wall.

"Heavens, no! I'm a foster home for pregnant mommy cats. They stay with me until they have their babies and then go out for adoption when the kittens are old enough. I usually only do one litter at a time, but there was an emergency placement and I ended up with two momma cats and all their kittens."

A tugging on his pant legs made him look down. Three of the tiny beasts were climbing him like a tree. As he bent to pick them off, two more started up his other leg. "I'm under attack!"

Molly's laugh rang out and with a tug at his heart he realized how much he'd missed her. She was basically a white version of Momma G. "Let me get some cat food. They'll leave you alone then."

He followed her into the kitchen and sat at

the small dining table while she attended to the cats. He'd never seen so many kittens in one place before. The mewling rose in pitch as the food was being prepared then complete chaos as they fought for a spot on the platters.

Molly sat beside him once she was finished. "Want one?"

"No. Absolutely not."

"They'll be ready for adoption in a month or so."

"I'm not a cat person."

"Everyone is a cat person. You just have to meet the right cat."

Nope. If he was going to get a pet, it'd be a big dog. "I'm concentrating on taking care of myself right now. Not sure I'm ready to be responsible for another life."

Molly patted his hand and stood. "Let's get that roast served up. I'm starving."

Over dinner, she asked about his new job, his apartment, his love life, his health. Basically every exact same thing his grandmother would interrogate him about. He found himself relaxing into the comfort of it. After leaving the Crew, he felt he'd lost his family. But they were still family at heart.

"I'll get these," he said as Molly reached for his empty plate. As he cleared the table, Molly began to fill the sink with water. He paused. "Do you not use the dishwasher?"

"It's broken. Makes a horrible racket when I turn it on. I just haven't called anyone to come look at it yet."

"Sounds like something stuck in the drain. Want me to take a look?"

"Would you?"

"Of course."

Ten minutes later, he was disassembling the drain trap with two kittens inside the dishwasher with him, several more sitting on the open door and one perched on his shoulder. "Dude," he said to the gray kitten sitting on his shoulder. "You really aren't helping."

"Cats are natural supervisors," Molly said.

He looked at the kitten and it looked back at him with mint-green eyes. "Is that what you're doing?"

He got a tiny little mew and it made him laugh.

"You were looking for Sadie," Molly said. "Is something wrong? Could you talk to me?"

For a moment, he felt off-balance. He'd forgotten all about his mother and her mess. He turned his attention back to the dishwasher. "You know about my parents, right?"

"I know your grandmother raised you."

He nodded, carefully placing the screws out of kitten reach on the counter above him. "Yeah, my parents were addicts. Back and forth with sobriety for years, but when I was about six months old, it got really bad and my grandmother took me away from them."

"One of them come back?"

It was said with such a knowing, yet compassionate, tone that he looked up at her. "Yeah. My mother."

Molly nodded. "Time for amends?"

He shrugged and pulled loose the drain trap. "Here's your problem," he said as he held out a small chunk of plastic. He put it on the counter above him and scooped up the screws. "I guess that's what she wants. She gave my name and phone number to some lady who says she's her sponsor. I'm guessing she called to say I should let my mother to talk to me. I just don't know."

There was a long silence as he put the drain trap back together. As he was removing kittens from the inside, Molly stood from where she'd been sitting at the dining room table. "Come sit in the living room with me."

After disposing of the bit of plastic and washing his hands, he settled down on the opposite end of the sofa from Molly. She turned toward him with her hands clasped. "My former husband was an alcoholic."

He blinked. He'd thought she was a widow. "Oh," he said slowly.

"He would get sober for a year, slip up, drink for a year or two. It was a never-ending cycle. After about twenty years, we separated. I couldn't do it anymore. It's a horrible disease but you can't help someone who doesn't want help."

He felt something, some sort of release. She understood. "That's why when my grandmother died I just walked away from the entire family. Even though my aunts and uncles are great people, being with them exposes me to my parents and I just can't do that anymore. I feel bad about it and I try to keep up with them on Facebook and stuff, but I can't be there."

Molly was nodding. "You have to take care of yourself first, DeShawn. You deserve a happy life. It's not selfish, it's self-preservation."

"So, what is this amends stuff about?"

"Just that. The person acknowledges the harm they did to you, takes responsibility, apologizes."

Thumping his head back against the couch, DeShawn stared up at the ceiling. "I don't know if I can listen to that," he said quietly.

He felt the cushions of the couch shift and Molly's warm hand clasped his. "You don't have to, DeShawn. Self-care first. This is why I had to separate from my husband. It became too much to hear him apologizing for the same acts over and over and over again without results. It became harmful to me to have to relive all the bad times. I said *No more*."

"I get that," he said. But there was still some squirmy, wrong feeling twisting in his gut. "But I still feel… I don't know."

"Guilty? Like you aren't helping her recover or stay sober? Wondering if you say no and she goes back to using, it will be your fault?"

He stared at her. "That's exactly it. I feel like I should give her a chance, but I just plain don't want to. I've got my life on track—I'm in a really good place now. Do I want to go back and wallow in all that pain again?"

"Only you can answer that, DeShawn. Remember, it will also be a time for you to tell her exactly what impact her drug addiction had on you. Some people find that cathartic."

Great. Back at square one. He shook his head. "I don't know what to do."

"Then don't do anything until you do know. If you want, I will call the sponsor lady and tell her you are deciding what you want to do and to please not contact you again."

He looked back to the ceiling. Was that a solution or would he be pushing responsibility off on someone else? "No," he said, shaking his head. "I'll call her. I'll tell her."

A tugging on his pants leg made him look down. The little gray cat climbed up and sat on his lap. Mewed. Molly laughed.

"I think you've been claimed."

He reached out and rubbed its tiny head and felt a low rumble. The kitten walked straight up his chest and sat on his shoulder, purring loudly in his ear. "I am not taking this kitten."

Molly nodded. "Okay. Anything you say. I'll hold him back for you. They'll be ready to adopt in three or four weeks depending on their weight gain."

He lifted the kitten off his shoulder and handed it to Molly. "Nope. Thank you for dinner. And the talk. But I'm not going to let you turn me into a crazy cat man."

"Anything you say. Thank you for fixing my dishwasher. I do miss you. You should come to the Friday dinners."

At the door, he hugged her and kissed her cheek. "Thank you," he said again. "I mean it.

Talking to you really helped. I don't feel quite as crazy."

"Anytime. I'm right here, okay? Me and your cat."

CHAPTER SIX

HER CHEEKS WERE starting to hurt. The fake, polite smile she had plastered on her face was faltering. This was too much to ask for on a Monday night. The concentration she needed to keep from rolling her eyes was distracting her from keeping that smile in place. Discreetly checking the time on her phone, Tiana resisted the urge to sigh. Lily sat beside her, happily swinging her feet and drawing in a sketch pad. She checked the image. Another cat. Lily's bedroom walls were covered in the evidence of her never-ending campaign to get a cat. *When she's old enough to scoop up cat poop, she can have one.*

Reinforcing the smile, Tiana turned her attention back to the meeting. She'd never been to a PTA meeting before and if this was how they were, she'd never go back. These two damn women had been passive-aggressively discussing what the theme of the spring carnival should be for at least ten minutes. Felt like ten years. She wanted to jump up and scream, "How about springtime?"

Glancing around, she met eyes with another parent. The woman mimed putting a gun to her head and made a face. Tiana nodded. *I put on a bra for this?* Unfortunately, the price she was paying for getting Lily into the creative arts magnet school was parental involvement. She was required to attend so many meetings and do volunteer work in the classroom. She liked the volunteering. She loved that she could come have lunch with Lily when she wanted. She hated these meetings.

Lily looked up. "Are those women still talking?"

And not in her library voice. Heat flooded her face as others nearby turned to look. "Shh. Yes, honey. They are."

"I think the theme should be cats."

Oh Lord. Parental politics on one side. Cat demands on the other. I need a drink. A movement to her left caught her attention. Kasey plopped down beside her.

"Sorry I'm late," Kasey whispered. "Had a fatal gunshot come in ten minutes before my shift ended."

"Lucky. I had an impacted bowel end of my last shift," Tiana whispered back. "Did you pick up an extra shift?" She already felt more relaxed. It was Kasey who pulled some strings to get Lily admitted to the charter school mid-year.

"Just a couple of hours. Jordan wanted to leave early. She's taking Shay to Disney for her birthday. So I covered for her."

"Where's Claire?" Lily asked, leaning forward to look over.

"She's at home with her daddy," Kasey explained.

Another bonus. Kasey and Jordan both had daughters about the same age as Lily and the three were already best friends. Great school. Great friends. Everything Tiana had been working so hard to get for her daughter.

Kasey slid down the chair, stretching her legs forward and slipping her feet free of her clogs. "Ahhh," she whispered, wiggling her toes. "Feels so good to sit down." She looked up at the front of the room where the two mothers were still standing off. May Day vs. Baby Animals. "For the love of hearing your own voice. Those two. We'll be here all night."

Tiana slouched down so they were touching shoulders and leaned in. "It's been at least fifteen minutes. Isn't that against the Geneva convention or something?"

"Yeah. Pro tip, when you are asked to be on any sort of committee, ask who is in charge. If it is either of these two, run. I'll give you a list of names. Who to avoid. Who is easy to work with."

"Seriously. It's a spring festival. The theme should be spring."

They listened for a few more minutes. Kasey stood up and raised a hand. "I motion we table this discussion until the next meeting. I'm curious about the findings of the gender-neutral bathroom committee."

About ten *second the motions* hit the air before Kasey even finished speaking. When she sat down, Tiana deployed her most epic side-eye. "Gender-neutral bathroom issue? Do you *want* to be here all night?"

An hour later, it was finally over. "Come on, girly girl. Let's get you home," Tiana said, taking Lily by the hand. As they crossed the parking lot, Tiana pointed up at the full moon. "Ugh."

"I was ignoring that," Kasey said. She shook a fist at the sky.

"Three to three. On a full moon night. Double ugh."

"See you at three. Wear your roller skates. Oh, yeah! We're taking Claire to see the Wildlife Expo exhibits this weekend. Y'all want to come with us?"

Tiana made a face. "Sure, but I got this thing on Saturday. We can go on Sunday."

"What's with the face? And define *thing*."

"It's just there's this…nothing. It's fine."

Kasey caught her by the elbow. "Oh. No, ma'am. There's this what? What are you hiding?"

"Nothing." She glanced down at Lily and lowered her voice. "It's the school project I told you about."

The slightly puzzled look on Kasey's face quickly changed to sly deviousness. "Oh. The *project*. With the…"

"Yes," Tiana interrupted. She gave a slight head tilt in Lily's direction. "The project."

"I thought you were finished with school, Mommy," Lily piped up. "Why do you have homework?"

"It's a different kind of project, Lils," Tiana said.

"Very different," Kasey added with a grin.

Tiana made a face at her. "Gee. Thanks." She hit the unlock button on her key fob. "Miss Kasey is being a silly pants, Lil. Climb on up."

"Bye, Lily! See you on Sunday," Kasey called out as she moved to her own car. "I'll call you to arrange details. Have fun on Saturday with *c-h-e-m-i-s-t-r-y* man."

Tiana waved a certain finger in the air. "Bye, Kay-Kay."

"What project?" Lily asked as Tiana buckled her into the booster seat.

"Nothing, baby. Ms. Kasey was just being funny."

She climbed behind the wheel with a grin on her face. It felt good. The crushing fear of failure that had dogged her all through college was gone. She still felt nervous on the job, but that was normal and she was learning and feeling more comfortable every day. What felt good was getting back to being normal. Having friends. Doing things. Living a life that included more than studying and attending classes. She'd even begun reading for pleasure again.

She shouldn't have let the DeShawn thing slip out though. Kasey was too quick. And she never forgot a thing. "Ugh," she said, slipping the car into gear and slowly backing out.

"What's ugh, Mommy?"

"Nothing, love. Was just thinking of something I have to do later."

"Okay. I was at the library at school the other day and the librarian helped me look up stuff about taking care of kittens. Did you know you can train a kitten to use the bathroom on a toilet? So you don't have to have those boxes you said you didn't want?"

"No, I did not know that," she replied in a neutral voice. Oh, she was going to have a talk with this librarian.

DeShawn waited outside on the sidewalk, watching the busy Saturday afternoon shoppers scurry through the parking lot. With a grin, he remembered Tiana's terse voice mail agreeing to meet him to talk about the school project. She still had those iron walls up high. Which only made him more curious as to what was beyond those walls. Was she like that with all guys? Or just him? He bounced on his toes to keep warm. *She has a kid. Maybe that's why. Ever think of that?* And Mickie had a kid and Josh still went hook, line and sinker for that. "Aw, man," he said out loud in a low voice. "You are getting way ahead of yourself."

With a glance at his watch, he frowned. She'd said quarter to eleven and it was almost eleven now. Scanning the parking lot, he spotted her. *Finally.* A smile spread across his lips. Then faded as... *She brought the kid?* He watched as Tiana helped the little girl out of the back seat. Then she paused as… *Oh hell, she brought her mother too?*

He lifted a hand as they walked closer. She looked at him and shook her head, making the curls bounce.

Letting go of her daughter's hand as they reached the sidewalk, Tiana turned to her mother. "Go ahead and take Lily in for story hour. It's starting now."

Once they were inside, she turned to him. "I'm sorry."

"What for?"

"Being late. Once Lily found out I was coming to the bookstore, she wanted to come too. Then I had to get my mother to come to watch her so I could meet with you. And it turned into a drama."

"No problem. Come on, I'll buy you a coffee."

Once they settled at a table inside, DeShawn with a bottle of water and Tiana with a cup of tea, he bobbed his head toward the bookstore. "I'm not allowed to meet them?"

Her eyes were cool as she looked at him over the rim of her teacup. "*Allowed* isn't the right word. I'm very careful with my daughter."

"Understood. She's cute though. Looks just like you."

"Thank you. Now tell me about this project."

Okay. All business. He quickly outlined the idea of the project and the needs of the kids at the school for her. "I'm now looking for people of similar backgrounds to come talk to the kids and to be mentors."

"Where is this school again?" Tiana asked. When he told her, she nodded. "Corridor of Shame."

He leaned forward, not sure he'd heard her right. "The what?"

"Corridor of Shame. It's the area in South Carolina along Interstate 95. Predominantly black, very poor. The entire infrastructure is crumbling along with the schools."

"That's…" He couldn't find the right word. "It's known enough to have a name but no one has done anything about it?"

Tiana leaned forward. "Poor. Black. Rural."

"Now I'm mad. First I was shocked by the school conditions. But to know it's a statewide problem? That just makes it worse."

"So whatcha going to do about it, Mr. Maid?"

The words were a teasing challenge that came with a bonus of one of her smiles. "I guess I'm going to have to keep my promise to the kids at that school while I educate myself on what's being done to solve the problem. Are you on board?"

She put down the teacup and held her hand out. "I'm in."

He put his hand to hers, ignoring the heat the feel of her palm against his generated, and shook. "Great. Thank you."

"So, what's next?"

"Tuesday evening after work, we're having a planning meeting to discuss the next steps. Can you make it?"

Pulling out her phone, she tapped through to the calendar. "Yep. What time and where?"

FINISHING HER NOW cool tea, Tiana watched as DeShawn left the coffee shop. He'd thrown her for a loop by waiting outside. Her plan had been to get Lily settled in the children's section and meet him in the coffee shop. But he'd handled it well. Her mother realized also and had smoothly taken over Lily and hustled her inside. Tiana didn't think Lily had noticed.

She shook her head, trying to get rid of the thoughts. *Think about this project. The kids.* It was a great idea. She'd come out of Corridor of Shame schools herself and knew first-hand what those kids were facing. Gathering her things, she made her way to the children's section. The story reading was still in progress. Lily was sitting on the floor with her knees up and her arms wrapped around them. Her chin rested on her knees as she listened to the story. A warm feeling of love and pride flowed through her.

"Your meeting all done?"

She turned to her mother. "Yes. It's an interesting project."

"Interesting man. What do you have to tell me about him?"

"Nothing. He used to work for Josh… Wait. What do you mean by interesting? You've never even met him."

"Tee. I've got eyes, don't I? Good-looking. Single. Wants to get involved to help kids? That's interesting, don't you think?"

"I need a man like a fish needs a bicycle."

"That doesn't even make sense. Of course you don't *need* a man. But they are good to have around sometimes."

Tiana felt her cheeks burn. "I'm not even having this discussion with you, Mother. Besides, story time is over, and here comes Lily."

"You don't have to shield her from everything."

Tiana turned away and waved at her daughter. Her mother just didn't understand.

"Momma? Can I buy the book too?" Lily asked as she joined them.

"Yes. And then we can go over to that place that makes your pizza just the way you want it for lunch. Hungry?"

Lily wrapped her arms around her waist and flung her head back dramatically. "Starving!"

While waiting in line to pay, Tiana's thoughts drifted back to DeShawn. Her mother was right, although she'd never let her know that. DeShawn was drop-dead gorgeous. Educated. Good job. Army National Guard. And creating a project to help poor kids? If he was a church-goer, her mom would have them engaged in a month. *Yeah, that's all great, but remember he annoys you by just breathing.* She couldn't forget all his snarky flirting from last summer. *You liked it. That's why you get so annoyed.* She let out a huff of air, unsure who exactly she was angry with. Him or herself.

"Why so mad?" her mother asked when she met them at the front door.

"I'm not mad. I'm thinking."

"I'm thinking too. I'm thinking it's about time for you to take time for yourself. Have some fun."

She got a light nudge from her mother's

elbow. "I'm having fun. We're going to the bird show thing tomorrow."

"Grown-up fun."

Tiana pushed open the door and held it open for Lily and her mother. "Stop it, Mom. You're kind of grossing me out."

"What's grown-up fun?" Lily asked.

Tiana shrugged. She wasn't stepping in that. "Ask your granny."

"Her nana."

"What's grown-up fun, Nana?"

"I'll tell you when you're a grown-up."

Shaking her head, Tiana strode across the parking lot. Her mother needed to go home. Soon.

TIANA JOSTLED HER WAY through the crowd in Marion Square, trying not to drop the four plastic containers of shrimp and grits she was carrying. The Southeastern Wildlife Expo was in its final day and the Birds of Prey flight demonstration was one of the most popular events. Mother Nature had been kind enough to bless them with a mild midfifty-degree afternoon with lots of sunshine and no wind.

She made it back to where Kasey was waiting with Lily and Claire. They'd come early so they'd have a front-row seat to the demonstration. The grassy center was roped off for the show. Around the perimeter of the park were booths where local chefs were cooking up samples of their menus.

"Lord," Kasey said as Tiana approached the blanket they'd spread on the ground. She jumped up to help with the containers Tiana had tucked into the crooks of her elbows. "They didn't have a bag for those?"

"No," Tiana said as she sat down and began pulling spoons and napkins from her coat pockets. She checked her sleeves. This was her good coat. No spillage, thank God.

The savory dish tasted extra good in the crisp air. Tiana practically gobbled hers down, she was so hungry. In the chaos of getting Lily up and out of the house, she'd forgotten to eat breakfast.

"When do the birds start flying?" Lily asked.

"Not too long now." She checked the time on her phone. "Less than thirty minutes. I know it's been hard waiting—you've both been very good."

They'd had the idea that the girls could play while they waited. A plan dashed once they saw the size of the crowd. Luckily for Tiana, Kasey was one of those über-organized mothers who traveled with a magical purse that held something for every emergency. Books, sketch pads and crayons. Juice boxes. Snacks. Wet wipes. She wouldn't be surprised if there was a full change of clothes in there.

After they'd eaten and gotten the girls cleaned up, Kasey volunteered to brave the crowd to dispose of their trash. As she left, there began to be some activity in the area roped off for the demonstration. People were moving in and setting things up. The crowd pushed closer.

"Up, girls," Tiana said. She gathered up the blanket and put the girls in front of her. "Spread apart a bit. We need to save room for your mom, Claire."

"That's a hawk! That's a hawk, Mommy! I recognize it from my bird book," Lily said in her most outdoor of voices. Several adults nearby smiled.

"Oh! Look! It's an owl!" Claire said, pointing.

"I see them. This is going to be fun, huh?"

Kasey returned and took her place beside Tiana. She leaned over to whisper in Tiana's ear. "Don't look but there is one super-hot man back there checking you out. Like seriously checking you out."

"Where?" Tiana whispered back.

"To your right, few feet back from the rope. Black leather jacket, red knit hat."

Tiana turned, trying to appear as if she were casually glancing around at the crowd but her gaze froze. *DeShawn. Of course. That damn man showed up everywhere.*

"Ugh," she said.

"What? He's hot."

"He's annoying."

"Is he the project guy? *C-h-e-m-i-s-t-r-y* man?"

Claire looked up. "We know how to spell, Mom. We're six, not stupid."

Kasey stuck her tongue out at her daughter. "What did I spell then?"

The two girls whispered back and forth. *"Chimney,"* Lily announced.

"Close enough," Tiana said. "Look! The birds are starting to fly." She elbowed Kasey. "Stop looking at him."

"I'm not looking at him. I'm looking at that guy he's with. The ginger. Yum."

"Oh, I'm telling your husband."

Kasey laughed. "I'm allowed to *look*. He's coming this way."

Alarm rang through her body as Tiana looked over. Sure enough, DeShawn was weaving his way through the crowd toward them. She shook her head. *No.* He smiled and kept coming. She put on her fiercest nurse no-nonsense expression and shook her head again, adding in a quick head dip in Lily's direction. That stopped him. The smile faltered as he glanced down and saw Lily. He nodded and retreated back to his friends.

"What was that about?" Kasey asked.

Tiana leaned in close. "Not in front of Lily," she whispered.

"SHOT DOWN?" ERIC asked with a laugh as De-Shawn returned.

"Naw. She's got her kid with her."

Malik shook his head. "Run, man, run. Women with kids? That's way too complicated."

DeShawn ignored them and pretended to watch the graceful flight of the owls. They really were beautiful creatures. His gaze kept straying to Tiana. He should have known she'd have her kid with her. He felt a twinge of some unidentifiable emotion. Not quite pain, not quite sadness, something balanced between the two. He couldn't stop watching. Tiana had her hands on her daughter's shoulders, laughing and nodding at the girl's excited gestures and exclamations. She looked like a mini Tiana except her hair was caught up in two puff balls at the sides of her head. *Loneliness.* The word rose in his mind, but that wasn't quite right either. He wasn't lonely. He had friends. They did stuff. It was more a lack of connection. He'd watched one of his best friends fall in love last summer. He wasn't jealous, but it did show him a part of life he was missing.

"Dude, stop staring at her," Malik said.

Turning his attention back to the show where hawks were now demonstrating their skills, he repressed a sigh. The fun was gone. A family. She had a family. Her mother. Her kid. She *was* a mother. What could he offer her? *Nothing. You've got nothing. Let it go. Whatever you think this might be, just forget it.*

A nudge brought his attention back. Eric tilted his head toward Calhoun Street. "Let's head over to Brittlebank Park and watch the Dock Dogs dive. We should still be able to get a good spot."

DeShawn nodded. *Yeah, great idea. Get out of here.* He glanced over one more time. And caught Tiana's direct gaze. She was smiling at him. A real smile. A flare of warmth lit him up inside before it faded away. He lifted a hand and gave a little salute and turned to shoulder his way out of the crowd. *What were you thinking anyway? That she'd want the likes of you? She's going to want better than some crackhead's kid.*

Eric stopped and waited for him to catch up. "You okay, man?"

"Yeah, I'm good."

"So, who was she? You lit up like it was Christmas when you saw her."

DeShawn felt his face go hot. He shook his head. "We've met a few times. I don't really know her."

"Sounds like you want to move that forward."

"I thought so. Not so sure anymore."

"Move on then. Come on by my place next weekend. We're going to watch the All-Star Game. There will be lots of women there."

Forcing a grin, DeShawn slapped the palm Eric held out. "Sounds great, man," he said. The words rang hollow in his ears though. The realization that he didn't want to get with just any woman hit him. He wanted Tiana. He wanted to search for a chink in that armor of hers and find who she was behind those walls. Following Eric and Malik to the parking garage, he shook his head. *Never going to happen.*

His mood lifted once they arrived at Brittlebank Park. The crowds were just beginning to form and they were able to grab a prime viewing spot. The Dock Dogs competition was one of the expo's most popular. Dogs of all types competed in spectacular leaps off the end of the dock into the Ashley River. The air was humming with excitement and the yips and barks of the dogs as they waited.

"When does it start?" he asked as they settled down on the grass.

"Not for another hour. Good thing we got here so early."

DeShawn leaned back on his hands as he looked around at the crowd. It was growing larger by the minute. The remainder of his dark mood left him. It was impossible to be gloomy when the day was so perfect. Warm, sunny, the sky as blue as it could be without a cloud in sight. Good friends. Dogs jumping into the water. What more could he ask for?

"So what's going on with Josh?" Eric asked.

"Huh? Nothing."

"That's not what I hear. I hear he's shopping for rings."

DeShawn shrugged. "Wouldn't surprise me. Mickie's an awesome woman."

"Man," Malik said with a laugh. "You leave

the Crew, I leave and look what happens. Everyone starts falling in love and getting married."

"That's what happens. It's called life."

"The circle of life," Eric said. Malik and De-Shawn simultaneously began singing the song from *The Lion King.* "Aw, shut it, you two. You sound like cats fighting in a bag."

Lying back in the grass with his hands behind his head, DeShawn smiled up at the sky. "Dang, I've missed you guys."

"Sadie's always hiring."

"Naw. She said I was too skinny. I'll be at the next first Friday dinner though."

A while later, Eric gave him a not-so-gentle nudge. "Get up, man, it's close to starting time."

Getting to his feet, he saw the crowd had grown even more and people were pressing in to get close to the water. "Wow. Did I fall asleep?"

"Yes. And you snore, dude. Probably why you can't keep a girl."

"Kiss my ass, man."

The good-natured ribbing was forgotten as the dogs began their show. It was impressive. The dogs reached amazing heights and lengths before splashing down in the muddy water of the Ashley River. The air was filled with excited barks and the oohs and ahhs and cheers of the crowd.

Over the noise, DeShawn heard a very loud voice that caught his attention.

"I can't see, Mommy!"

He glanced up at the rear of the crowd. The park was a slope from the parking lot to the edge of the river and he could Tiana struggling to lift her daughter high enough to see over the crowd. He hesitated a moment. She obviously didn't want to interact with him while she had her kid with her. But come on. He lifted his hands above his head.

"Tiana!" he yelled, projecting his voice over the crowd and waving until she saw him. He gestured for her to come forward.

Even from a distance, he could see the struggle on her face. She wanted to say no to him, just to say no. But she wanted her kid to see the dogs. He hit Malik in the ribs with an elbow. "Be right back, dude, hold this ground."

He waded through the crowd to Tiana. "Come on, we've got a prime spot right up front."

Tiana's daughter looked at him from where she was riding on her mother's hip. Barely. "Hi. I'm Lily."

"Nice to meet you, Lily. I'm DeShawn."

"Are you friends with my momma?"

He looked at Tiana, who was trying to scowl, but the effort of keeping a six-year-old balanced on her hip in the jostling crowd required too much effort. "DeShawn and I are acquaintances, Lily. That means we know each other but aren't friends."

"Can we still go watch the dogs with him?"

"It's a great spot," DeShawn said with a smile.

Tiana huffed out a breath. "Fine. For Lily."

"Absolutely. Completely for Lily's sake," he replied. He held his hands out and Tiana let him take Lily. Swinging her easily up to his shoulders, he laughed at Lily's excited squeal. "Hold on tight," he said. "And Momma, follow close. We're going in."

"Do not drop her," she snapped.

Tiana grabbed a handful of his jacket and the feeling of her fingers brushing against the muscles of his back, even through the layers of fabric, sent a rush of heat down his spine. Ignoring that, he focused on weaving his way through the tightly packed crowd back to his friends on the bank.

Malik and Eric looked up as he returned and swung Lily down to her feet. "Tiana, this is Eric and Malik. We all used to work together at the Cleaning Crew." Tiana put her hand on Lily's shoulder. "Hello. This is Lily."

"Malik, Tiana is going to be joining us on the project with Henry."

"Awesome. Welcome to the team."

DeShawn pulled off his jacket and spread it on the ground. "Y'all sit down. Enjoy the show."

"Thank you," Tiana said, giving him a real smile. "This is very nice of you."

"I'm a nice guy."

"No, he isn't," Malik broke in. "He's a bum. Now, me? I'm a nice guy."

"You're in med school. By law, they've removed your soul and replaced it with ego," Eric said. "Now, *me. I'm* a nice guy."

"You're also twelve years old. Both y'all stop your yapping," DeShawn said. Tiana's curls bounced as she shook her head in amusement and a flush of satisfied happiness went through him. It had felt nice, doing a good deed. Helping her out.

Everyone returned to watching the dogs but DeShawn couldn't keep his gaze from straying to Tiana as she sat on the grass, her arm around her daughter, holding her close, pointing at the dogs and sharing in the cheering. The warm feeling faded a bit. She was a good mother.

Which brought back the low-level simmering anger at his mother. He still hadn't called the sponsor woman to tell her to back off.

He clapped at a spectacular leap from a black Lab but there was no joy in it. He was going to have to take care of that problem eventually.

As the show ended, Tiana stood and brushed off his jacket before returning it to him. "Thank you, DeShawn. That was very kind of you to share your spot with Lily."

"Not a problem," he said, feeling suddenly awkward. He turned his attention to Lily. "Did you like the dogs?"

"Yes. It was amazing. Momma, maybe instead of a fish doctor, I'll be a dog doctor. Or an owl doctor."

"You can be all of them," Tiana said. "Veterinarians are doctors who treat all animals."

DeShawn grinned at the look of gleeful realization that washed over the little girl's face. She looked so much like Tiana, it was a little strange to see such a huge smile. "Y'all need a walk back to your car?"

"No. We'll be fine," Tiana said. "My friend had to leave early so we're just going to get an Uber home."

"You sure? We can give you a ride, no problem," Malik offered.

"Thank you, but we're going to get some dinner first." She turned to DeShawn. "I'll see you on Tuesday for the meeting. Nice to meet you guys. Thanks for letting us share your spot."

And, just like that, she was gone.

CHAPTER SEVEN

TOAST! RESTAURANT IN downtown Charleston had been a great success. Rather difficult in a town of local foodies and tourists from all over the world seeking modern Southern cuisine. Recent expansions were proof of the success. One thing DeShawn knew about the West Ashley area was they were starving for good restaurants. The new mayor's promise to revitalize West Ashley should help with that, he hoped.

The parking lot wasn't crowded. But six in the evening on a weekday night wasn't prime restaurant time.

DeShawn pulled into a parking space. He didn't see Lena's car. Glancing at his watch, he saw he was early. The weather had turned cold with a dampness that was more than mist but less than a drizzle, making it seem colder and darker. He hurried across the parking lot and pulled open the door. Warmth and all sorts of wonderful food smells hit him as he entered.

Looking around the small space, he spotted Tiana at a table near the back. She lifted a hand.

"Hey. Looks like we're both early," he said, slipping into the seat across from her. She was in her nursing uniform and looked tired. A glass of wine was half finished on the table in front of her. "You worked a whole shift today?"

"No, they were busy so I went in for a couple of hours to help out. That big accident on 526."

"I heard about that. What was it? Five or six cars?"

"Yeah. Three people dead. Two of the seven who came to the ER probably won't make it."

The waitress approached and asked if they were ready to order. He grabbed the menu. "We've got two more coming," Tiana said.

"Anything to drink?" the waitress asked.

"Just water for me," he said.

"Another wine, ma'am?"

Tiana shook her head. They sat for a moment in silence after the waitress left. Tiana swirled her wine, but didn't drink, keeping her eyes on the glass. It was more than worrisome to see her like this, all animation gone. Not even a hint of her usual snarky annoyance at him.

He reached over to still the spinning glass. "Are you okay?"

She brought her hands up and rubbed her face. "Yeah. It was my first mass casualty event."

"That sounds terrible. I can't imagine how you do it on a normal day, but something like that?"

Her shoulders rolled in a slow shrug and she met his eyes. "Honestly. I don't know. Most the time I can sort of lock it away. Sometimes it really bothers me."

"Today it bothered you?"

Her dark eyes met his. "One of the patients was a little girl. She had the same shoes that Lily wears all the time. Little Hello Kitty sneakers. I came around a corner and all I saw was this one little shoe and for a moment, I didn't think I'd be able to function. I had never felt terror like that before." She turned her head away and wiped beneath her eye with a knuckle. Took in a shaky breath.

"Hey," he said, reaching out to take her hands. "But you did."

"Yeah. I did. She's going to be okay. Mostly scrapes and bruising."

"You okay?"

She nodded and took a swig of wine. "Yeah. I will be. I'm actually glad we had this sched- uled. Gives me time to clear my head before I go home. I need to get right or I'll break down and cry on Lily."

DeShawn squeezed her hands. "But I'm betting she's going to get a couple extra hugs and kisses tonight."

Tiana looked down to where his fingers covered hers and he almost pulled away. But she didn't so he didn't.

After a long moment, she casually broke the contact to reach for her silverware rolled in a napkin. "Here comes Malik."

He turned to look over his shoulder. Malik and Lena were making their way to the table. He stood as Lena approached, earning him an eyebrow raise from Tiana. He grinned at her just to get—yep, there it was. Her irritated eye roll. Then he held Lena's chair for her. Might have been poor, but Momma G always said manners were free.

After introductions were made, Tiana sat back in the chair. DeShawn transformed before her eyes from smart aleck to seriously organized man. The change was very impressive.

"We've got another planning meeting with Henry on Saturday," DeShawn said as he pulled a notebook from his briefcase. His eyes met hers. "I hope you can make it, but it's okay if you can't." He turned to the others. "Tiana is a nurse in the ER and works odd hours."

"That's where I've seen you before!" Malik said, pointing at her.

"Are you in your residency?"

"No. Still in med school. But I notice beautiful women."

Her expression didn't change as she slowly blinked. Her eyes came open as her head tilted a bit. Malik withered under her stare.

"Just saying..." he stuttered.

"Sheesh, Malik," DeShawn said. "You got zero game."

"Knock it off, both of you," Lena barked. "This is a professional meeting. And I have to be back downtown in less than an hour." She turned to smile at Tiana. "I'm going to steal that look."

Tiana raised her wineglass in a toast. "Feel free."

"All right," DeShawn said. "Lena. You were looking into getting Wi-Fi for the school?"

"Yes. We can get it installed no problem. It's going to take a while to get computers in the numbers we need. Teachers will be able to bring personal laptops in to run lessons. My Saint Toribio group is working on funding."

"Good. Malik?"

"My med school class has agreed that for our community outreach program this year, we will restock the school's library. We've been contacting libraries and literacy programs for book donations. And we'll be holding fundraisers throughout the year to buy books."

"Perfect. I've got three more people to agree to come talk to the kids. I've touched on this before, but I think the next step is to start arranging for the kids to visit workplaces. Either in groups or as individuals."

Tiana nodded along. "I can ask about the learning lab at the hospital. Both the med and nursing students use it. They can simulate anything from a heart attack to the birth of a baby."

DeShawn nodded and gave her a smile that sent a jolt of heat through her gut. "Perfect. Thanks, Tiana."

"Another thing to consider, something I ran up against when setting up the college assistance programs at Saint Toribio, is that some of these kids have no interest in college," Lena said. "We are adding in vocational training jobs. Electricians. Plumbers. HVAC technicians. Jobs with livable incomes that don't come with college debt."

"Never thought of that," DeShawn said.

"That's a great tip. We have to reach as many kids as we can."

Lena nodded. "We found that kids with borderline grades were feeling left out and slightly insulted by the college-only focus."

DeShawn looked around the table. "Anyone know anyone who can help us with this aspect?"

No one did. "It's okay," Lena said. "I can get you the information we gathered for the Toribio Mission. Also all the forms and handouts we used."

"Thank you. That'll certainly jump-start the process," Tiana said.

"The head of the diversity office at Charleston College said she'd be happy to give a talk also," Lena said. "I know I had a lot of fears about going to college. She can dispel any of those concerns for them."

"Me too."

Tiana looked at DeShawn. They'd both spoken the same words with the same intonation. He smiled at her. A real smile. She fought against the feeling of inclusion and understanding in that smile but lost.

She felt a growing respect. There really was a lot more to him than met the eye. Her body reminded her of the searing heat that had almost overwhelmed her when his fingers had touched hers. This was moving beyond chemistry. Putting the wineglass down, she pressed her lips together. *You need to stop thinking these thoughts.* But her brain didn't listen. They wrapped up the meeting and Tiana realized Malik and Lena were leaving without ordering dinner. They were going to leave her alone with DeShawn. And all her shiny new feelings about him.

AFTER LENA AND Malik left, Tiana reached for DeShawn's notebook, spinning it around with her fingers. Despite how mentally and emotionally exhausted she was from the horror of the afternoon, she felt something in his presence. More than the physical thrill of his touch, more than how his easy smile lifted her own spirits, she had a new understanding of him. The kind of man he was. *There's a saying for that. Something about the soul.* She'd felt it at his answer about being ready for college. How they instantly understood each other. *Kindred! Kindred souls. That's it.*

The waitress approached to ask if they were ready to order. "I'll have the shrimp and grits," Tiana said without looking at the menu.

"Same," DeShawn replied. He spoke without

breaking the thoughtful gaze he had aimed at her. "What were your fears about college?" he asked as the waitress moved away.

"Mostly that I wasn't smart enough. I remember exactly when I knew I wasn't ready. My first go-round at the SATs. I was on track to be class valedictorian. Four-point GPA. And I sat there, staring at the math part of the test in absolute horror."

"Yes," DeShawn said, nodding. "I couldn't afford tutors or the special classes, so I just read everything my school library had about taking the tests. Hours on the school computer looking up stuff. And I still sat there, feeling like I was a complete failure."

"So, how do we help those kids? Just telling them our stories isn't enough. I know how I felt. I felt alone and ashamed. I'd been the smart one, the one who was going to make it out of that small town. I sat in that classroom feeling like it had all been for nothing. I wasn't going anywhere."

DeShawn was nodding. He pulled the notebook back to him and clicked the pen. "Support systems once in school," he said as he wrote.

"Funding or supplies for multiple practice SAT testing," Tiana added.

"Yes," he said as he wrote it down.

"That's good. Also, an idea for down the road a bit, but when I was in nursing school, one of the things we did was create a private Facebook group. We used it for asking for help or advice. For venting. To coordinate projects. It was a great way to connect."

"That would be good. If enough of us committed, we could follow the kids all the way through high school."

"And they could help each other, encourage each other so they don't feel alone."

They each sat back and smiled at each other.

"Damn," DeShawn said. "We're good."

The waitress returned with two steaming plates of shrimp and grits. Tiana picked up her fork. "Don't sound so surprised. I'm always good."

As they finished eating, they talked about the presentations they'd do. They eventually decided to give their talk first and together, cut the personal story down to a few minutes and then spend the rest of the time talking to the kids about the plan and then getting their feedback.

After a minor skirmish over the check—he wanted to pay for both and she insisted on paying for her own—she pulled on her coat.

He held the door open for her. And put his hand on the small of her back as they walked to their cars. She tried to be annoyed with it, but couldn't ignore how nice it felt. Not to be a nurse or a daughter or a mother, but to just be herself. And herself was really liking the feel of a strong, warm, male body near hers. She may have leaned into that warmth a bit.

At the cars, he turned and his hand moved from her back to cup her shoulder. "You going to be okay, Nurse Ratched? Is your head better?"

She smiled and nodded but tears rose in her eyes. Pressing her lips together, she turned her head away. It wasn't that he'd reminded her of that horrifying moment when she rounded the curtain in the bay and saw that Hello Kitty shoe, it was that his words were tender and caring.

"Hey? What's this?"

His hand touched her cheek and she looked back at him. A blink sent twin tears down her cheeks. "It's not what you think," she blurted out, embarrassed by her loss of control.

"What is it then?"

She wiped at her face. "I'm tired. It wasn't a good day. And thank you for being so nice."

His hand moved to cup her chin and he tilted

her face up to look her directly in her eyes. "You're welcome."

His eyes were amazing. Light brown, almost amber, and those flecks of hazel and she had to stop staring into them but she couldn't. *Hypnotizing. That's the word.*

His hand moved. Their breath clouded in the frigid air but she didn't feel cold. *He's going to kiss me.* Before the thought fully formed in her brain, his lips pressed lightly against hers. Then all rationality ceased as her body reacted to that barest of kisses. A sound left her throat and she clenched his jacket in her hands.

Then he was there. All there. Arms around her. Pressing her back against her car. His mouth on hers. Open. Their tongues colliding. The contrast of the icy-cold metal of her car on her back and his fiery heat pressing against her front was deliciously torturous. And then he stepped back, his breath pluming quickly, one hand to his mouth.

She stepped away from the car, dizzy with the sudden absence of his touch and the intensity of feelings the kiss had stirred. It'd been a long time since a man had made her feel this way.

"I've been wanting to do that for a very long time," he said.

She nodded. "I know. We've got this thing." Making a vague back and forth motion between them, she scrambled to find a working brain cell.

"I'm sorry. I don't want to make things weird, Tiana. I should have asked first."

"Don't be sorry. It was a great kiss. I just… I'm not in, uh, a place right now."

"I get it."

She looked him in the eye. He shrugged and grinned.

"It's just…"

He caught her hand. "Tiana. It's okay. I understand. You've got a lot going on in your life."

"It's not that I don't want…"

Damn. What is coming out of your mouth, woman? She felt her cheeks go hot as his eyebrows raised. Because her hormones were screaming, *Yes, please. Let's have hot sweaty sex with this gorgeous chunk of man.* And he looked like he was reading her mind. She clapped her mouth shut.

"Be safe driving home," he said. "I'll see you Sunday."

"Okay," she breathed out in relief and scrambled into the safety of her car. Buckling up, she cranked the engine and banged her head off the steering wheel a couple of times. *Stupid stupid stupid. What is wrong with you? One kiss and you turn into a blithering idiot. Get yourself home right now.*

SHE GOT HOME just in time to hop in the shower and have story time with Lily before bedtime. DeShawn had been right. Lily had gotten some extra hugs and kisses. Tiana felt the horror of the day slip away as she curled up beside Lily on her small bed.

"Why don't you read one to Momma?" she asked.

Lily's eyes widened. "Two stories? That's against the rules."

"Just this once," Tiana replied. "Momma needs more snuggle time."

Later that night, she lay in her own bed staring at the ceiling. Every time she closed her eyes, she'd see that shoe. That impossibly tiny shoe. And feel the gasp tear at her throat again. Weeks ago, she had been in the hallway when a patient pulled out a gun and threatened to kill everyone if he didn't get his oxycontin. That had been less frightening.

"Come on, Tee. Get it together," she whispered aloud in the dark, twisting and turning on the pillows, jerking the covers up to her ears. *Fine. Fine. That little girl is fine. Her family is fine. It wasn't Lily. Calm your nerves. Think about something else.* Her brain helpfully loaded up an instant replay of that kiss. *Not that!* "I give up," she muttered and flung the covers off. It was wine time.

"Can't sleep?" Vivian asked from the living room.

Tiana poured some merlot in a glass and went to sit on the couch with her mother. "No. I had a bad scare at work."

Vivian made a mmm-hmming sound as her knitting needles clinked. "You can talk to me about it if you think it'll help."

Tiana scrunched up into a tight ball at the end of the plush couch and took a sip. Haltingly, she tried to put into words the horror she'd felt. Vivian nodded and knitted. When her words ended, Vivian glanced over.

"You remember when Jayla Fraiser passed?"

Tiana frowned. "That was, what? Fifteen years ago?"

"About that. Remember what happened?"

"She went out on the lake with too many kids in a rowboat. It tipped over and she drowned."

"And where were you supposed to be?"

"Helping Daddy at the vegetable stand."

"And where were you actually at?"

Tiana sipped more wine. Strange how her mother could make her feel ten years old again. "At the library."

"We heard a girl had drowned in the lake. Didn't know who. I went to tell your daddy and you weren't there. Your daddy thought you were home. I thought you were with him. I felt like my soul had been ripped straight out of my body and sent to hell. Went flying down to the lake. That's when Trey told me you weren't with them."

Tiana nodded. *Soul ripped out. Sent to hell.* "That sounds just about how I felt. How long did it take you to get over it?"

Vivian shook her head and returned to her knitting. "A mother doesn't ever get over that. A child is her heart walking around loose in the world. Nope, Momma's going to be worrying over you forever. Just like you with Lily. Go back to bed, Tee. Say some prayers. Do your best."

CHAPTER EIGHT

DeShawn waited on the steps of his apartment building. Looking up into the blue sky, he realized it was getting warmer. February was over. In less than a month, the temperatures could be up into the eighties. Spring was on the way. He felt oddly nervous as he waited. *That kiss. My God. That kiss.* Tiana had a million excuses but none of them had stopped her. She'd kissed him back. Those had been her hands twisting the fabric of his jacket. Propping his elbows on the step behind him, he smiled. It had been an amazing kiss.

More than those curls, those hips, those lips. The little he knew of her, she was smart and determined. He'd looked up the whole Corridor of Shame thing. Tiana graduating from college after a lifetime spent in the schools in that area was like winning the lottery. The woman had grit and strength. He liked that.

A quick beep of a horn brought him back to the here and now. The window of Tiana's car powered down. "You getting in, Mister Maid, or are you sitting there collecting frost?"

He approached the car and leaned in the window. "Depends. Where's it frostier? Out here or in there?"

Her smile felt like a victory.

"Get in, DeShawn—stop letting all my heat out." The window powered back up as he climbed in. He lifted a stack of papers from the seat before settling in. Tiana held a hand out. "You can give me that."

"'One thousand and one reasons I should have a kitten,'" he read from the top page.

She snatched the papers from his hand and put them in the back seat. "My daughter. She's waging war upon me."

"If you need a kitten, I know where you can get one."

"I don't need a kitten. I don't want a kitten. I don't have time for a kitten."

"I'm just saying. When you lose that war, let me know. A woman I know has ten foster kittens almost ready to be adopted."

"It's not the kitten. It's the litter box."

"You can train them to…"

His words were cut short by a frustrated growl. Tiana shot him a murderous look. "This kitten woman you know? She's not a librarian, is she?"

"No. She's the office manager at the Cleaning Crew."

Putting the car in Reverse, Tiana backed out of the parking space "I don't want to talk about kittens. I'm so sick of hearing, reading, seeing crap about kittens."

"Sounds like your daughter inherited your stubborn streak."

"I'm not stubborn. I just know what I want and I don't stop until I get it."

"Stubborn."

"Want to walk, Man Maid?"

"Want to talk about that kiss, Nurse Ratched?"

She cut her eyes at him. "No."

He held on to the car door and kept his mouth shut. After they'd made their way out of the city and into the countryside, he turned his head to look at her. "Why do you always seem mad at me?"

"No more questions."

"Why not?"

"Because you annoy me."

"Name one way I annoy you."

Her dark eyes cut in his direction, brows arched high enough to disappear into the curls across her forehead. "Breathing."

"Breathing? I annoy you by breathing?"

"Yes."

"Huh," he said, settling back in his seat. "You're just going to have to deal with that because I'm not planning to quit breathing anytime soon."

Silence played out for a few more miles.

"You've got a smart-ass attitude."

"And you're Miss Suzi Sunshine?"

She didn't respond and he peeked over. Her lips were pressed tightly together. "You're right," he said. "I do have a smart-ass reputation. But I only smart-ass with people I like. Like that woman who had her tongue down my throat the other night."

Her hands tightened on the steering wheel. "That was a moment of weakness. And I don't want to talk about it. You said I was mean."

"No I didn't. I asked why you always seem mad at me." More silence. He shook his head. *Why bother?* "Forget I asked."

He leaned forward to pull off his coat. It was getting hot in there. Tiana reached out and turned the heat down. "I'm not mad," she said. "I just don't need any…distractions."

Turning the word over in his mind a few times, DeShawn bit down on about twenty snarky comments. "Okay," he said, drawing the word out.

She threw a quick glance in his direction, sending those curls bouncing. "Okay."

As if they'd settled anything.

FINALLY, HE SHUT UP. Tiana focused on the winding country road before her. It wasn't his smart-assedness, it was his voice. The low, sweet baritone like Reverend Al Green was sitting next to her. Made her feel things. Want things. Like more of those kisses. But this wasn't college anymore. She had Lily back now. She took in and let out a breath. Nothing could be about what she wanted.

She knew it was a mistake to offer him a ride. Trapped in the car alone with him, there was no hiding from her feelings. *Ignore it. Focus on the project.* She made a left onto the last stretch of road. About four more miles, then he'd be out of her car. And she could breathe without the scent of his leather coat and soap or aftershave or whatever it was that made her want to take a bite out his neck. A small figure was walking along the highway and she slowed and moved to the center line as she passed.

"Wait," DeShawn said, twisting in the seat to look out the back window. "That's just a kid."

She slowed further and studied the rearview mirror. He was right. It was a little girl, clutching a hoodie tight around herself. Glancing at the dashboard, she saw it was forty degrees outside. "I hope she's not walking to town," she said, braking and doing a three-point turn.

She stopped in the middle of the road and powered down the window. "Honey? Are you okay? Do you need a ride?"

The girl stopped. She looked like she might have been around twelve. "I'm not allowed to get in cars with strangers."

Tiana nodded. "That's a very good rule. Are you going to town? We are going to the school to meet with Mr. Gardner. Do you know him?"

The girl pulled the hoodie closer. "Yes. He's my social studies teacher."

Tiana pulled the car off the road and put it in Park. Grabbing her phone, she climbed out. "What if I called him and he said it was okay to ride to town with us, would that be okay?"

Before the girl could answer, she dialed Henry's number. She explained the situation and handed the phone to the girl.

"Mr. Gardner? It's Patrice. This lady okay? She has a man with her."

"Tell him it's DeShawn."

"No, sir. My momma had to get another shift so she rode the bus out this morning. Yes, sir. Okay."

Patrice handed the phone back to Tiana. "He said I can ride with you."

"That was a smart idea," DeShawn said once they had her settled in the back seat and had turned around.

"I've been known to have one from time to time," Tiana said. She glanced at the girl in the rearview mirror. "Patrice, tell DeShawn what you meant by your mother having to ride the bus out. He's not from around here."

"You don't know about the buses?"

DeShawn turned to look back. "No."

"Ain't no jobs out here," Patrice said. "Best place for work is at the hotels on Hilton Head. The hotels run a bus out here, pick up all the maids, then bring them back at night."

"What time does your mother get on the bus?" Tiana asked and shot DeShawn a knowing look.

"To be at work by seven, she gets on the bus about five in the morning, I'd suppose."

"And she gets home, when? About six at night?"

"Yes'm."

Tiana looked at DeShawn. "That's what it's like out here. To get work, these kids' parents are gone for thirteen, fourteen hours. And those are the good jobs."

They rode the last mile in silence. Patrice jumped from the car with her thanks and scurried down the street toward the library. DeShawn caught Tiana's hand as she was gathering her things. The feel of his fingers on her palm sent a lightning-fast and hot sizzle up her arm. She looked into his eyes.

"Is that what your parents did?" he asked. "Ride the bus?"

She pulled away. "No. My daddy was a farmer. Mostly soybeans. Just a couple acres. My mother, she ran what was supposed to be a day care but it was really a one-stop community center and after-school care. Some days, there'd be ten of us sitting in a circle on the floor, doing homework."

"That sounds nice."

She smiled. Yeah, it sounded nice. Made her mother sound like a saint. And she had been for many of the kids she reached out to. Truth was, she was desperately trying to keep them out of the street, off drugs and in school. She didn't succeed in that with all the kids. Unrelenting poverty has a way of grinding people down.

She popped open the door. "Come on, they'll be waiting on us."

He followed her up the sidewalk, walking quickly in the brisk air. At the entryway, he touched her elbow. "Does it ever freak you out?" he asked in a low voice.

"Does what freak me out?"

He shook his head and reached for the door. "Nothing. Doesn't matter."

She stepped into the warm building but caught his wrist as he walked past her. "Yes. It freaks me out," she whispered. "I sit at the nurses' station and listen to the nurses my age talking about their sororities or ski vacations or going to Europe like it's no big thing. And I sit there, feeling like I've wandered into a place I may not quite belong. Is that what you meant?"

He stepped closer to her and she resisted the urge to step back. Up close, those eyes were too direct, too bold, too entrancing. "Yes. Coming here, to talk to these kids, I feel like a fraud."

"Imposter syndrome. I looked it up."

Some of the intensity left his eyes and the beginnings of one of his snarky grins played at the corner of his lips. "Of course, you would have."

She smacked playfully at his arm. "It's a real

thing. Especially in first-generation college graduates who are the first in their families to move into white-collar professions."

"Now you sound like Mickie reading off her index cards while she's studying."

Tiana shook her head. "Where do you think she got the idea?" She began walking down the hall, toward the classroom and he followed.

"But what do you do about it?"

"Fake it. Fake it 'til you make it, baby. Come on, Lena is waiting on us and she doesn't seem the type you want to keep waiting."

That made him laugh. "Now, there's an understatement."

THE PLANNING MEETING only took a few minutes. Everything was in place to have speakers come once a week for the next month. They would add in other things as they discovered needs. After that, DeShawn, Malik and Henry were dispatched to Lena's car to haul in the first boxes of donated books.

Tiana looked around the small room that was the library. "Dang, this is tiny. Is it supposed to be the library or was it a classroom?"

Lena shrugged. "I have no idea. I'm just glad someone cleaned it out already. I'd be sneezing and wheezing for a month from the dust and mildew that was here."

A wave of frustrated anger rolled through Tiana and her fists clenched. Taking a deep breath, she let it out slowly. Getting mad never solved anything. "It's still a gloomy place. I think a nice bright coat of paint might cheer it up, hmm?"

Lena looked at her. "That's a great idea. When we fixed the room at the mission, we had the kids put their handprints along the wall. Gave them a sense of ownership."

Feeling her frustration slip away, Tiana nodded. "A class project, perhaps?"

"Definitely. We'll put it on the list."

The men came back with boxes. Putting her hands on her hips, Tiana looked at Henry. "We've had an idea."

Malik laughed as he set down a box. "Why does that sound so ominous?"

"Paint. Who would want to come in here? Looks like a room in a haunted house," Tiana said.

Henry looked around, nodding. "You're right. I'm so used to looking at it that I don't really see it anymore."

"Can we get the kids involved with it?" Lena asked.

"Absolutely. I'll work it out and get back to you."

"Great," Tiana said. "Now. Anyone have any idea how we should sort the books? I know fiction and nonfiction."

Henry pushed a box against the wall with his foot. "Just leave them. I'll catalog and store them until after we get the painting done. No need to shelve them twice." He reached out and grabbed DeShawn's hand. "Thank you for coming up with this idea. I think we're really going to do some good here."

DeShawn ducked his head and his cheeks darkened. Tiana raised her eyebrows. *What's this? Humility? Shocking.*

"Naw," DeShawn said. "Having an idea is easy. It was all of us who made it real."

Dammit! Stop being perfect! She tried scowling at him, hoping that would remind her heart that she was not going to fall for this man. But her heart didn't seem to want to listen.

Henry turned to her. "So, we'll be seeing you two Tuesday to kick off the program?"

She quickly rearranged her face into a smile. "Sounds good."

"WHAT ARE YOU going to talk about?" she asked as they got on the road home.

"Well. I was going to talk about how I lived with my grandmother. That she encouraged me to excel in school and made me promise I would graduate from college. But neither she nor I had any clue about applying for college or getting scholarships or grants. I was lucky to have had a good guidance counselor at school who helped me with all that."

Tiana nodded. "And were you ready for college?"

He laughed. "Hell no. I wasn't top of my class but I was in the top ten percent. Even then, when I got to college I realized I was behind in math. Had to take remedial courses to catch up. That's why it took me five years to graduate instead of four."

"That's exactly what happened to me. I had to go to a community college for a year just to get caught up, then transferred to the nursing program at the University of South Carolina."

DeShawn pulled a pen from his shirt pocket. "Got paper?"

She did that thing. That parent thing where she managed to reach into the back seat without taking her eyes off the road and produced a picture of several brightly colored fish. "From the fish doctor phase," she said as she handed it to him.

"You sure you don't want to keep it? Put it on the fridge? Isn't that what you're supposed to do?"

"Man, my fridge isn't big enough for her fish pictures. Point number one—good grades do not equal college readiness. Be prepared to catch up."

She tapped the paper and he began to write, using the dashboard as a desk.

"Point two," he said. "Use your school's guidance counselor. Don't take no for an answer."

"Why'd you live with your grandmother? Where were your parents?"

The question took him by surprise. She usually tried to distance herself from him.

"My parents had substance abuse issues. Momma G just sort of took over caring for me."

"You were lucky."

He didn't feel very lucky but he merely nodded. "I was. What's point three?"

"Feeling like you don't deserve to be there."

"God, yes. That's a big one." He shook his head. "Tell me more about the Corridor of Shame. You mentioned it before."

Tiana gathered her thoughts. He smelled amazing, as usual. She cleared her throat.

"It refers to the swath of South Carolina along Interstate 95. Like I told you, it includes the poorest, blackest, most economically isolated counties in the state. The schools are literally falling apart. No supplies. No technology. Barely any books."

"Worse than this school?" he asked, sounding surprised.

"This school is in pretty good shape. My fifth-grade classroom didn't have glass in the windows. Boarded up in winter and screens nailed over them in the warm months."

"I… I can't wrap my brain around that. I grew up outside of Charlotte. We were poor but our schools weren't falling apart."

"Welcome to South Carolina," she said.

"Why do you stay though? You have a kid. Wouldn't you want to get out?"

She shrugged. It was a question she'd asked herself many times. "It's home. My family is here. I got my daughter out of that small town. She's in a good school. She has more opportunity in Charleston than I ever had. It'll do for now."

They each fell silent for several miles. De-Shawn shifted in the seat and faced her. She cut her eyes at him. "What?"

"Why do you always go defensive? I was

going to ask if you had any ideas about how to get the kids out to see us doing our jobs in the real world, like we talked about. I might be able to get permission to have one of them follow me on the job."

The comment stung a bit and Tiana held her tongue. She didn't always go on the defensive. Just with him. Because she wanted to get to know him. In all sorts of ways. Her curls bounced as she shook her head. *Job. Lily. Get your mother to go back home.* That was enough for one person. She did not need anything—or anyone—else in her life right now.

"I know I can't have a kid come into the emergency department," she said as she fiddled with the heat setting. "I talked to the simulation lab manager. I can setup a tour for the kids interested in the medical field. All I need is a date, time and headcount."

"Do you do most of your work in the ER?"

She side-eyed him again. *Why does he have to be so interested? It's really unfair.* "Yes."

"Do you like it?"

"Barring nights like the horrible one I told you about, yes, I do."

He shifted again to face forward in the seat. "All right. I'll shut up. I don't know why making ordinary conversation is a problem with you."

Pressing down hard on the impulse to apologize, Tiana focused on the road ahead. Thirty more minutes and this would be over. As the miles ticked by, the silence began to feel decidedly uncomfortable. "It isn't a problem," she said firmly.

"Okay," he replied and the neutrality in his tone irritated her.

"Look, DeShawn, you seem like a really nice guy. But I just started this job—I'm working crazy twelve-hour shifts. I've got a six-year-old in a new school. I've got a mother who has moved in and won't take any hints about going home. Now I've got this project with you all, and while I'm excited about it, it is another thing I have to do."

"And what does any of that have to do with having a conversation with me while we are in this car right now?"

She pursed her lips and felt her cheeks go hot. *Nothing. It had nothing to do with it.*

"I know I've been teasing you," he continued. "But truth is, I've just moved back to Charleston. Most of the people I hung out with here have moved on to new jobs. You're funny and smart and I thought maybe we could get to know each other a little better."

She frowned and stared at the road. *What*

a load of bologna. Especially after that kiss? Just want to get to know each other my giddy old auntie. From the periphery of her vision, she saw him lift his hands, palms up and shake his head. The international I-give-up sign.

"I'm sorry," she said, forcing the words out. "Yes. I like working in the emergency room very much. It's very challenging."

It took a moment, but he responded. "I'd probably pass out when I saw the blood."

"Blood doesn't bother me. Snot. Snot bothers me."

His laugh was beautiful. Rich and deep and real. "You and Josh, both."

"He needs to get over that. That child of Mickie's is the snottiest kid I've ever met. I don't know how she affords the amount of tissue she must go through."

"What a man will do for love," DeShawn said with a laugh.

"Wipe a baby's snotty nose apparently."

"I saw him have to do it once and he gagged."

"Dear Lord. Wait until the kid pukes on him. He's gonna die."

They both laughed and Tiana felt the tension ease. It wasn't like her to keep people at a distance and she didn't mean to be grouchy at him. But he was an itch that she so wanted to scratch and she had too many real grown-up problems to deal with. She didn't need a man, not even this one.

"So, what do you do as an engineer?"

"Right now, I'm doing the preliminary planning for a new highway interchange."

"Sounds… I got nothing. Not even a clue what that would involve," she said with a laugh.

"Measuring and taking pictures mostly."

"I'm sure it's way more than that."

"Math. It's mostly math and look, I can see your eyes glazing over already."

"Yeah. Me and math. Not really friends. I barely made it through algebra. Took one look at a calculus book and…nope. No way. No how."

"I love math. It's straightforward. Once you know the rules, it's easy. There's no waffling. No endless circle of discussion over meaning. Neat. Clean."

"I guess that's why they say there's something for everyone," she said as she turned into his apartment complex.

As she pulled into a parking space, DeShawn undid the seat belt and paused as he opened the door. He extended his hand. "Friends?"

She shook his hand with a smile. "Friends."

"Thanks for the ride."

She put the car in Reverse. "Bye, DeShawn."

As she drove away, she glanced at herself in the rearview mirror. There was a stupid, goofy smile on her face. She scowled at herself. "Don't you start thinking anything."

CHAPTER NINE

THE CROWD WAS still gathering inside the Circular Congregational Church for the Sunday Sound of Charleston concert when Lily tugged on her sleeve.

"Mommy? Is that the dog jump man?"

Tiana looked down at Lily. "Shh. Honey. Use your library voice."

Lily lowered her voice to a whisper. "The dog jump man."

Tiana frowned. "I don't know what you mean. What dog jump man?"

Lily pointed to the pew ahead of them and, sure enough, DeShawn scooted down to sit in front of her. "Tiana," he said with surprise in his voice and a wicked twinkle in his eye. "What a surprise."

She scowled at him. "Are you following me or something?"

Her mother leaned forward. "Bookstore man."

Lily shook her head. "Dog jump man."

DeShawn's smile widened. He held out a hand to her mother. "DeShawn Adams."

"Vivian Nelson. I'm Tiana's mother."

"A pleasure to meet you. You've raised a fine daughter."

Lily got to her knees on the pew and leaned forward with her hands on the back of his row. "I'm Lily!"

"Hi, Lily. I'm DeShawn."

"I know. I remember you. You're my mommy's kwantence not friend."

"Acquaintance, Lily," Tiana corrected.

"Wow. You remembered all of that? You're pretty smart," DeShawn said. "I remember you wanted to be a fish doctor."

"Now I want to be a cat doctor."

Tiana rolled her eyes and DeShawn laughed. "Cats are great pets."

"Do. Not. Do. That," Tiana ground out from behind clenched teeth.

"Kittens are even better pets," Lily announced.

"Okay, Lily," Vivian soothed. "Not now. DeShawn, have you been to any of these concerts before? It's our first."

"Yes, ma'am. This is my home church."

And that did it. Vivian side-eyed Tiana hard. Brushing off a churchgoing man? There'd be hell to pay later. "Your home church?" Vivian echoed. "Tiana is still looking for a home church."

He looked back at Tiana. "I'd be more than happy to escort her to services any Sunday of her choice."

"Can I come too? I like this church. It's round."

"Of course you get to come too, Lily."

"Mommy, can I sit with Mr. DeShawn?"

Tiana froze. The request was so out of the blue, she wasn't quite sure what to say. He must have seen it in her face because he shook his head.

"I'm not sitting here. I only came over to say hello. My friends are all the way over there so it'd be best if you stay with your mother."

He stood and gave a head tilt to Vivian. "A pleasure to meet you, Mrs. Nelson." He pointed at Lily. "Team Kitten!"

"Go away, DeShawn," Tiana said. He was not helping not one bit. She glared at him as he left. A hard finger pop on her shoulder grabbed her attention. "Ow. Mom, that hurt!"

"Educated. Churchgoing. Good-looking man and you're brushing him off like he's a nuisance?"

"I like Mr. DeShawn," Lily declared.

Tiana turned away from them, sliding down in the pew with her arms across her chest. "Concert's about to start. Y'all need to hush up now."

DESHAWN LINGERED AT the entrance after the concert. Waiting for Tiana and her family. He'd been surprised to see them there. Hesitant to approach her when her daughter was with her after how she felt at the Wildlife Expo. But her mother was another story. Mrs. Nelson, he had wanted to meet. What was it like to have had parents so strongly committed to your success?

At last, they appeared in the crowd. Lily was between them, holding each of their hands, swinging her arms and singing snatches of the gospel music they'd just heard. Tiana's mother smiled at the sight of him. Tiana? Not so much.

"Did you enjoy the concert?" he asked Mrs. Nelson.

"Yes! I didn't know quite what to expect, but it was wonderful. I've not heard some of those songs," she said, putting a hand on his arm.

"Those go back to pre–Civil War and the old slave spirituals. It's one thing I like about this church community. They don't pretend the past didn't happen. They elevate the lost voices."

He didn't miss the pointed look Vivian gave

Tiana. Nor the withering look Tiana shot at him. Maybe he was laying it on a little too thick.

"Thank you for the history lesson," Tiana said. "I'll see you tomorrow for the talk at the school."

She started to move away, but he walked with them. "I was going to offer to buy you all some dessert. Kaminsky's is just around the corner."

"Dessert!" Lily yelled. "Can we, Momma? Please, please, please?"

Tiana stopped. "It's a school night."

"No school tomorrow. Teacher's workday," Vivian added.

He suppressed a grin. "What's your favorite ice cream, Lily?"

"Strawberry. What's yours?"

"Mint chocolate chip. I don't know if they have strawberry ice cream, but I know they have a strawberry milkshake."

"I don't want ice cream," Tiana said. A little desperation sounded in her tone. She was losing this battle and she knew it.

"Well, something sweet would be nice. Tee, they have dessert martinis," Vivian said.

DeShawn smiled at Tiana. "Vote is three to one. Looks like you lose."

She looked at her mother. "Dessert martinis?"

"Mmm-hmm."

"Are we going?" he asked.

Lily slid her tiny hand into his and he felt a jolt of emotion he'd never felt before. Awed and humbled by her trust. "I am," she declared.

He smiled at her. "It's your mother's decision."

Tiana shook her head. "Fine. Whatever. Dessert it is."

"Yay!" Lily said.

"Yay!" he replied.

Lily stayed with him as they walked around the corner to the dessert shop. Tiana and Vivian walked behind him. Lily peppered him with questions. Where did he live? Where did he work? Did he like cats? Did he like unicorns? He answered all her questions, expecting Tiana to interrupt at any moment.

At the small shop, they lucked out with a booth. Sunday nights weren't prime tourist time. While Vivian nibbled on her pastry and Tiana sipped on her martini, he and Lily slurped down milkshakes, trying to outdo each other on straw-sucking sounds.

"So, DeShawn," Vivian asked. "What's this project you and Tiana are working on?"

He glanced over at Tiana. Her face was pure

stone, giving away nothing. "It's for a guy I know from my college job. He's a teacher at a rural school. We're going to try to mentor the kids there. Let them know college is a reality, even for them. If what Tiana has told me is true, you have some experience with this."

"Only with my own. Got all three of them through college."

"That's quite an accomplishment. I've been studying up on the Corridor of Shame. Seems like it's a problem all over the nation."

"It is. It's terrible. But we have to keep fighting for our kids."

"That's what I'm trying to do."

"That's not all you're trying to do," Tiana said. Acid dripping from each syllable.

He sat back. Had he overplayed this? "No," he said. Slowly. Deliberately. Holding her gaze. "It's not."

Her cheeks darkened and she sipped her martini with her eyes lowered. The kiss hung, unspoken, between them. She was attracted to him. She'd kissed him back. She had to know he was attracted to her. Wanted to get to know her.

Vivian looked from him to her. "Well. Thank you for the treat, DeShawn. It was a pleasure to meet you. Lily, come on. We need to get home."

Lily whined a bit but attainment of a to-go cup appeased her. Tiana remained stony. Vivian gave him a quick peck on the cheek with a whisper in his ear. "She's stubborn. Don't give up."

HE WAS WAITING on the sidewalk in front of his apartment. Tiana pulled into an empty space. She still wasn't quite finished being angry about the whole dessert thing. Nor was she sure she liked the way Lily had taken to him. But she was a hundred percent certain she was furious at DeShawn for being so damned perfect that her mother was probably planning the wedding already.

Frowning, she powered down the window as he approached the driver's side.

"We can take my car. I feel bad using yours every time."

She eyed his decidedly elderly Ford. "No offense, but no. Get in."

"I'll pay for gas then," he said as she powered the window back up. He climbed into the passenger seat and put on the seat belt. "It's a perfectly fine car. Just old. And paid for."

"I'm sure it is," Tiana said archly as she maneuvered out of the space. "We ready for today?"

"I think so," he said, rubbing his palms along his thighs. "Quick talk about our background. Then the fish paper chronicles."

She cut her eyes at him briefly before focusing on the road. "You sound nervous."

"You aren't?"

Her laugh was a harsh bark. "DeShawn, I survived nursing school. Nothing scares me anymore."

"I wish I had your confidence," he said.

"You had plenty of confidence last night," she said.

He was silent long enough for her to look over at him. "Yeah," he said. "I'm sorry about that. I should have cleared the ice cream thing with you."

Slightly mollified, she nodded. "Thank you. And don't go through my daughter ever again."

"I know. It was wrong. I didn't think it through. I really wanted to meet your mother."

"My mother? What on earth for?"

"The way you talked about her. How she supported you and fought for you to get through college. How she took care of Lily so you could do it. She's a good mother."

She gave him a long look. Couldn't tell if

it was more DeShawn charm or something real. "Didn't your grandmother do the same for you?"

"Yeah, but…" His voice trailed off as he turned his head to look out at the passing farmland. "Never mind. I am really nervous about today."

"You really are?"

"Yes," he said quietly. "I am. I still feel like I'm faking it. How am I going to stand up in front of those kids? Them looking to me for answers?"

"You aren't faking. These kids don't expect you to be perfect. They expect you to be real."

"Real," he said with a small laugh.

Tiana looked closely at him. He really was nervous. Strange to see him like this. She wanted to reach for his hand, fall into her role of caregiver. But she knew what touching him did to her. It led to all sorts of crazy feelings and longing. It was the smile that did her in. A weak, wavering smile in place of his cocky grin. She reached out and lightly touched the back of his hand. "You have a good heart, De-Shawn. The kids will see that."

He curled his fingers around hers and squeezed. "Thank you."

She pulled her hand free, trying to beat the warmth his touch kindled. A race she lost.

HIS NERVES INTENSIFIED as they checked in at the school office. He followed Tiana down the hall as he peeled the back of his ID label and pressed it to his shirt. The door to Henry's classroom was open and a wave of excited chatter rose when Tiana peeked in.

"Settle down, kids," Henry called out as he waved them in.

Tiana leaned against the front of the desk, her hands clasped while Henry introduced them to the class. DeShawn followed her example and looked around. There were maybe thirty young people crammed into the small space. The kids were looking back at them with grins and eyes shining with excitement. He suppressed a smile. He remembered that feeling. Anything that broke up the monotony of the day, anything new, was welcome.

There was a brief awkward moment after Henry finished the introduction. He and Tiana looked at each other. After all their planning, they'd never discussed who would take the lead. He grinned at her. "Ladies first."

But she didn't miss a beat. She turned to the kids and lifted her hands, palms up. "I just wanted to thank y'all for inviting me to speak to you today. I grew up about thirty miles inland from here and went to schools exactly like this one. Now I have a bachelor's degree in nursing and work as a nurse in an emergency department." She turned to him. "DeShawn?"

"I grew up just outside of Charlotte," he said. "Lived with my grandmother most of my life. Now I have a degree in engineering and work for the Army Corps of Engineers, which in spite of the name, is not a part of the army."

"Instead of us standing up here and telling you about our experiences," Tiana continued, "DeShawn and I got together and talked about things we wish we'd known before we got to high school and college. We're going to talk about each item and answer any questions you have." She motioned toward the chalkboard. "Your handwriting is much neater than mine, DeShawn. Why don't you write?"

At the chalkboard, he drew the number one and circled it. "First," he said. "The guidance counselor is your friend."

Tiana nodded. "I know at my old high school, there was one counselor for several schools so she was only there once a week. But when you get to high school, go talk to the counselor when you are a freshman. Don't wait until your senior year!"

Henry raised his hand from where he was sitting in the back of the class. "Can you explain what a guidance counselor can do for them? We don't have them until high school out here."

"Sure," DeShawn said. "The counselor is the person who will help you with picking out colleges, and applications not only for colleges but financial aid and scholarships also."

"And that's why you should start talking to them when you are a freshman," Tiana said. "So you have four years to plan. Planning is the key to succeeding."

DeShawn nodded, but inside he was grinning. He half expected her to suggest index cards. She glanced at him and he gave her some side-eye just to see if she'd get it and—yep—there was the scowl. Brief, and on half power, but there it was.

Several hands shot up. DeShawn pointed to the girl whose hand had gone up first. "Yes?"

"Do you have to know what you want to be before you start college?"

"That is an excellent question," he told her. "And the answer is no, you don't. You can take different classes and see what you are interested in."

Tiana pointed to a boy on the front row. "You had a question?"

"Where do you live when you are in college?"

The question took DeShawn by surprise. The knowing look Tiana shot him made him realize how big this project was. College was so foreign to most of them that they didn't know about dorms.

"There are dormitory rooms," Tiana answered. "Most people just call them dorms. And then there are sororities and fraternities, which are like girls' and boys' clubs that you might get invited to join. They usually have a big house and you stay in a room there. And a lot of people who have jobs while going to college rent an apartment with several other people."

"Where did you live?"

"Raise your hand, James," Henry said from the back.

James lifted his hand.

Tiana grinned and winked at the boy. Her smile about took DeShawn's breath away. Finally, a tiny chink in her armor. That's how she smiled with her family and friends, he just knew it.

"I lived in a dorm room for the first two years. Then when I got a job at the hospital, I rented an apartment with two other nursing students." She looked over at him.

"Dorm room all the way through," he said. "I had a job but I tried to put most of the money in savings."

A girl in the back waved her hand and Tiana pointed to her. "How did you find out you wanted to be a nurse?"

Recapping the marker, DeShawn put it down and moved to sit on the desk with Tiana. These kids wanted to talk, not for them to lecture them on what to do to prepare. That could come later.

"When I was six," Tiana said, "my grandmother gave me a doctor's satchel. Do you know what that is?"

The kids all shook their heads but one tentative hand crept up in the air. "Is it like a fat bag where the doctor puts his doctor things?"

"Yes. Exactly that!" Tiana said. "My grandmother found one at a yard sale. And it had an old stethoscope and the blood pressure cuff. Some bandage scissors. And a first aid book. I must have listened to every heartbeat and belly gurgle of everyone in town, including cats and dogs and a couple of my momma's chickens."

The kids all laughed at that and DeShawn felt himself smiling. He could picture a tiny, determined Tiana, stethoscope in one hand, chasing down fleeing chickens. It was as if another bit of armor had fallen away.

The smile dimmed a bit as the picture widened. Her family lovingly submitting to being doctored on. An entire community letting their heartbeats be listened to. A slight chill trying to raise goose bumps on his arms. She came from a place of love and support. They might as well have come from different planets.

"The idea of being a doctor was something that never occurred to me but by the next year, I knew I wanted to be a nurse." She turned to him and smiled. "How about you, DeShawn, did you always want to be an engineer?"

Her smile. Being this close to her. The warmth in her dark brown eyes. He could smell a trace of some perfume. A little tittering laughter from a corner of the room alerted his brain that he'd been staring at her a little too long.

"No," he said and cleared his throat. "I didn't. That was one of the things my high school counselor helped me figure out. She asked me a question—when I was a little kid, what was it that I liked to play or do more than anything else in the world. I told her, 'Build things with Legos.' She said, 'Engineering.' I said, 'What's that?' and she got me books to read."

Tiana shifted on the desk beside him, putting her hand down on the desktop, her fingers brushing against his. "And now he's building a road," she told the class.

She said it with such pride. His entire world shrank to the slight touch of her fingers. Did she feel that heat? How could she not? Another titter of laughter from the class snapped him back to the here and now.

"I'm planning where a road will go," he clarified. "Not actually building one."

Henry rose from the back. "We're running out of time," he announced as the questions from the kids finally slowed down, creating a chorus of boos. "Settle down."

Coming forward, he shook both their hands. "Thank you so much for coming out. Class, tell Ms. Nelson and Mr. Adams thank you."

DeShawn grinned at the group thank-you. "It was really fun," he said. "You guys are great. You'll be seeing us again."

As they stepped out into the hall, Henry put a hand on DeShawn's arm. "Your story gave me a great idea. We can talk about when later because if I leave them alone too long, it'll be chaos, but I'd like to do what your counselor did as a homework assignment. Then the kids can read out loud what they chose and we can brainstorm careers that follow that interest."

Tiana gave him a friendly bump and his skin came alive at the contact point. "It really is a great tool for getting them thinking. Good work."

He nodded. "We'll make it happen then."

As THEY WALKED back to her car, Tiana felt like her feet never touched the ground; she was completely amped up on the energy and hopefulness of the kids. DeShawn had a goofy smile on his face but she couldn't say anything about it because she knew she was wearing one too.

"That was amazing!" DeShawn exclaimed, holding a fist up.

She tapped his fist with hers. "It was. My heart is going like a million miles a minute."

As she cranked the engine and backed out of the parking space, she tried to put a word to what she was feeling. Happy, yes. But there was something else lingering there. More than happy, more than the high she was riding off the energy of the kids. She glanced over at DeShawn. He was staring out the passenger window, but his knee was bouncing in his own excitement.

"That was more than amazing," she said.

"I know. It was…fulfilling."

Fulfilling. That was the word she was searching for. "Yes," she said slowly. "I wasn't sure how the kids would respond but…"

"They were so hungry!" DeShawn interrupted.

"Exactly! They want to learn. To do better. And they get written off because they're poor."

DeShawn twisted in the seat to face her. "I was trying to figure out what I was feeling. My grandmother always believed in me. But I always thought on some level that was a given, your grandma has to be on your side. It wasn't until I was in high school and my guidance counselor showed me that she believed in me too that I began to start to believe in myself. I feel like that's what we did for the kids."

Tiana nodded. "We told them we believe."

DeShawn reached out and took her hand. "Now we have to show them we believe."

The rest of the ride was spent in alternate long moments of silence and bursts of conversation as they plotted out the next move. As the euphoria ebbed, it began to be replaced with a less exhilarating but no less exciting feeling of commitment. As she pulled into a parking space outside DeShawn's apartment, she put the car in Park.

"Come inside. I'll make you lunch. We can plan some more."

She turned a skeptical face in his direction. "What are you going to make? Bologna sammies and chips?"

He grinned. "On white bread with yellow mustard."

"Gross."

"Seriously. Do you have to go to work or get your daughter? I have some leftover lasagna I made last night. It's too much for one meal, perfect for two."

"You made lasagna?"

"Hand-shredded parmesan. Ricotta cheese, not cottage cheese. Sun-dried tomatoes."

"You can cook?"

He laughed and opened the door. "Come inside and see. Unless you're still into the whole running away from me thing."

She hesitated. She really wanted to keep the conversation going about their next visit. And the lasagna sounded amazing. The memory of last week's kiss rose in her mind and she felt her cheeks go hot.

"We can talk about that too," he said in a low voice.

"Don't need to talk about that," she snapped as she unhooked her seat belt and turned off the engine. "But this lasagna better be as advertised, Man Maid."

"I would never lie to you, Nurse Ratched."

He hadn't lied. The mere scent of the lasagna rewarming in the oven attested to that. Tiana sat at on the barstool at the kitchen island and watched as he moved around the small kitchen space. A glance around revealed a life in transition. Some very nice pieces of furniture side by side with college dorm make-dos.

"So what is next?" She asked.

He peeked into the oven and turned to her. "I really like the private Facebook group idea, but worry they might be too young for that."

"That's true. Didn't think of that. I got permission from the nursing school to do a tour of their teaching lab. It just can't be during a scheduled class, so I need to work that out."

"Yeah, I still need to talk to my boss about taking one or two kids out with me on the field. Show them how math works in the real world."

As he spoke, he reached into cabinets and

set plates and silverware on the island. "What can I get you to drink? I've got water or water."

"Water is fine."

He filled two glasses with ice and poured water from a pitcher. As he set the glass in front of her, she grinned. The ice maker had churned out the small pebbled ice chips. "Oh, fancy ice."

Pulling on oven mitts, he held his hands up. "Only the best for you, Nurse Ratched."

It made her laugh. She studied his back as he turned to pull the baking dish from the oven. Wide shoulders that tapered down to a slim waist. The dress shirt he wore was a dark silvery gray, neatly ironed and tucked into black pants. The sleeves were rolled up over nice-looking forearms. Her stomach rumbled.

"That smells amazing," she said as he slid a plate across to her.

"That's because it is amazing," he replied as he came around to sit beside her.

She took a bite and closed her eyes as the heavenly combination of cheese and tomato filled her mouth. Spicy Italian sausage. She might have moaned a bit. "It's good."

"You sound shocked. I am a man of many talents."

She shot him a scowl only to notice he was

looking at her mouth. Heat flared instanta-
neously. His gaze moved to her eyes and he
smiled a slow, sexy smile. "Eat your lunch,
Tiana."

She forked more lasagna into her mouth
and chewed before she said something stupid.
*What are you doing? Alone in his apartment
with him? Eat this and leave before you do
something.* Because this was bad. She could
feel him right there. As if the air between
them was vibrating. *Say something about the
kids. Anything. Get this back on track.* But her
brain ignored her command. Probably too busy
spewing out hormones.

"So," he said casually. "Next week, we'll
find out who is interested in doing a field trip
with us?"

Relief flooded her. "Sounds good," she replied. "And find out what their interests are
and maybe we can reach out to others for a
go-to-work day."

They bounced around the differing professions of people they knew while they finished
eating. Tiana lifted her empty plate and began
to stand. DeShawn took the plate from her, his
fingers brushing against hers.

"I've got it," he said. The warm sexy voice
was back. She needed to get the hell out of here.

"Thanks. That was great. Thank you. I should probably... I need to...do...some stuff," she stammered out as she got up and began gathering her coat and purse.

After putting the dishes in the sink, he crossed the small space to stand in front of her. "You're babbling, Tee."

"I'm not babbling."

His hand came up and he traced his fingers along the curve of her cheek. "I want to talk about that kiss."

"That was a mistake."

"I don't think it was."

"Fine. You don't have to."

He grinned that annoying grin at her. She scowled. Then he leaned in slowly and she should be stepping back but no, she was frozen to the spot, unable to move as his lips stopped millimeters from hers. She could feel his breath, warm against her skin. Her heart was pounding like a drum. *No. No. No. Do not do this.*

"Walk out that door if you think it was a mistake, Tee," he whispered hoarsely.

It was a mistake. But she so desperately wanted to make it again. Her entire body yearned toward him. She pressed her palms to his chest, intending to push him back. But the shudder that ran through his body at her touch and his sharp intake of breath undid whatever bit of resistance she had left. Her fingers gripped the fabric, pulling him to her and pressing her lips to his. His arms went around her, pulling her even closer as he deepened the kiss.

His hands traced hot lines of fire down her back as the kiss went on and on. Her own hands were busy, skimming up his chest to his shoulders and up to his cheeks. Finally, he cupped her jaw with both hands and pulled back. His gaze was hot on hers.

"I want you," he whispered.

"I can see that," she whispered back.

"Are you still leaving?"

Damn it. Her brain wouldn't work when he was this close. She rested her hands against his as he leaned in and kissed her again, his arms circling her and his knee wedging between her thighs. Her low moan was all the encouragement he needed to press closer. His lips moved from her lips across her cheek to her ear.

"Still leaving?"

No. She wasn't leaving. Not now. And he

knew it. She slipped her hands up under his shirt and traced across his skin. Hard lines of muscle quivered and jumped at her touch. Up on tiptoes, she caught his earlobe between her teeth for a tiny nip. "Only if you don't have protection, Man Maid."

"DON'T RUN AWAY NOW," DeShawn said as Tiana began to sit up. He tightened his arms around her. He wanted to stay here in this bed with her for the rest of his life.

"Not running," she said. "I need to check my phone."

Pushing the pillows up against the headboard, he sat up and watched her pad naked out of the room. The bed already felt cold. She scurried back into the room and dove under the covers, snuggling up close to him.

"Brrrr. Why do you keep it so freezing in here?"

He pulled her close and kissed her cheek. "So you'll do this."

She shook her head and did a quick scroll of messages on her phone.

"Anything urgent?"

She laughed. "Nothing urgent. But I don't have time for round two."

"Will there be a round two sometime soon?"

"This wasn't enough?"

He pulled her down. "This was not enough. This wasn't just sex. I don't want just this. I want you, Tee."

As he said the words, he realized how true they were. He was falling for her. Falling for this tough, smart-mouthed, strong-willed woman.

She reached up and pressed her palms against his chest. "My life is a package deal. You know this, right?"

That stopped the giddy feeling that was jumping around in his gut. "I didn't think about that. I'm sorry. Of course, we have to consider your daughter."

"You mean it? Now's the time to cut and run."

That hurt but he kept his mouth shut. Because she was right. There was a kid involved. He had to make sure he was in one hundred percent. Rolling over on his back, he stared up at the ceiling.

"DeShawn?"

"I have feelings for you. I really think we could make something here. I want this."

Her face appeared above him. That take-no-shit Nurse Ratched face. "But?"

"I want to be a part of your life. Of Lily's life. The only *but* is that I don't want to mess it up."

"It'll be complicated."

"I'm an engineer. I can do complicated."

"It'll be on a six-year-old's schedule, not ours. She's the boss."

"I'm patient."

"My heart can be broken but hers cannot," she said quietly, cutting through the banter.

That staggered him. Was he ready for such a commitment? He and Tee were adults. But once he let a child see him as part of her life? He drew in a breath. "Where's her father?"

He'd half expected the question to anger her but her expression didn't change. "We were young. Went away to different colleges. Lily stayed with my mother. He just drifted away. He tried to come around occasionally, but it was hurtful to Lily. She didn't understand why her daddy kept leaving her."

Reaching out, he brushed a curl away from her cheek. "And you'll not have that repeated. I get it."

"You see how big this is now?"

"I do. I'd never want hurt her, Tee."

"Still in? And you can say no and walk away and I won't think any less of you for it."

"I'm still in."

"Okay. I guess we'll figure it out as we go."

CHAPTER TEN

"How old is this pizza?"

Tiana had about two minutes for lunch. The nurses' break room was its usual horrific mess of half-full cups of coffee, half-eaten plates of food and a pot of sour, burnt coffee spitting and hissing on the burner. The box of pizza was in the middle of the table that never actually had people sitting at it to eat, which in Tiana's mind meant anything on it was up for grabs. The overhead paging system dinged and squawked. Controlled chaos. How could it be so busy on a Tuesday afternoon?

"I dunno," Kasey replied, flipping the lid open. "Congealed cheese." She pulled up a slice and banged it against the edge of the box. "Hard-as-a-rock crust. I'd say more than six hours, less than twenty-four."

"Sold," Tiana said, snatching the slice from Kasey's hand and tossing it on a paper plate into the microwave.

"So, what's up with this face of yours?" Kasey asked, pointing.

"What face? It's my I've-not-eaten-in-fourteen-hours face." Popping open the microwave, her stomach growled loudly as the scent of hot cheese hit her brain cells. "Microwave kills germs, right?"

"No. The I-haven't-eaten-in-fourteen-hours-but-I've-still-got-a-goofy-grin-on-my-face face. Something is going on. Tell me. I'm bored."

"We've been running like maniacs all day. How can you be bored?" Tiana took a huge bite of the pizza and immediately regretted it as molten lava hit the roof of her mouth. She swallowed quickly and fanned at her open mouth. "I have to put a catheter in that little old lady in bay 12 in five minutes if she hasn't peed yet. You got a point? Get to it."

Kasey shook her head, making her red ponytail dance. Crossing her arms, she looked over the top of her glasses. "My point is this—you got laid, didn't you? That's a remembering-some-really-good-sex smile."

One thing, she'd learned over her few months as an ER nurse: her scowl game was weak. These women were professional fierce face makers. She tried anyway. "Girl, you got too close to that meth head, inhaled too many fumes."

"Tell me. Tell me now. Is he cute? Does he work here? Is it that Mateo guy from radiology that's always flirting with you?"

"No."

"No he's not cute? No he doesn't work here? No it's not Mateo? Come on, Tee. Work with me here."

Devouring the rest of the pizza in three bites, she dusted her hands off. "Wanna go help me with that catheter? The woman's got a vocabulary of a demon-possessed sailor."

"Only if you help me get the meth head in the shower and delouse him."

"No deal."

"I'll help if we have a drink after work and you tell me about this mystery man."

"There is no mystery man."

Kasey raised her eyebrows and tilted her head back and laughed. And laughed. And laughed. Wiping her eyes, she let out a breath. "That's the worst lie I've been told since that girl told me rolling tobacco in the yellow pages and smoking it causes false amphetamine positives."

"Fine. Don't help."

"I'm coming. Meth Head can wait a minute. I want to hear about this man."

THREE HOURS LATER, Tiana was still feeling phantom lice creeping on her skin but the mimosa was helping. As was the stack of French toast she was demolishing. The Nurses' Lounge was the best thing about working downtown. A small, hole-in-the-wall dive that served breakfast and dinner and alcohol twenty-four hours a day. You had to be a nurse to become a member.

"This is the best place ever on the entire planet," she said around a mouthful. It was. She hated her three p.m. to three a.m. shifts because no matter how quiet she tried to be when she got home, she always woke her mother up.

"Seriously," Kasey said. She'd opted for the burger and beer route. "Tell me about this guy."

Tiana shrugged and took a sip of the mimosa. "You sort of know who."

Kasey's forehead wrinkled as she thought. "I do? Do I know him?"

"No. Not know. Saw."

"Saw?" She screwed up her face as she puzzled it out. "Oh. My. God. That guy! That hot, hot, hot man from the bird show? Chemistry man!"

"Yeah, him."

"You're grinning again!" Kasey exclaimed. "You just think about him and start grinning. Are you in luuurrrvveee?"

"I am not grinning." Except, she was.

"Sex must have been amazing."

"That it was."

Kasey lifted her beer and they clinked glasses. "To great sex. Now, tell me. Is it going to be more?"

Dropping her gaze to the plate, Tiana dragged the tines of her fork through the syrup. That was the million-dollar question. "I don't know."

"Do you want it to be?"

Did she? Yes. No. "It's complicated."

Kasey put her burger down and leaned forward. "Like he's married or something complicated?"

"No! God, no. I would never."

"Then what's complicated?"

"Lily."

"Ah. I see."

"I don't know, Kase. I really think there could be something with this guy. But I have to make every decision with her in mind. I'm not going to be bringing men into her life if they aren't sticking around."

"I understand that. But you can date, right? Until you know one way or another?"

Tiana forked another piece of toast into her mouth and chewed. *Yeah. We could date. But I'd have to lie to Lily.* Shaking her head, she put down the fork. "I don't know. I've never been in the position before. I've not dated anyone since Lily was born."

Sitting back in her chair, Kasey wiped burger grease from her fingers. "Is this about Lily or you, Tee?"

"What's that supposed to mean?"

"Exactly what I said. Is protecting Lily your way of avoiding relationships?"

She wanted to be mad. Except she couldn't. Kasey's brutal honesty and refusal to play emotional games was why they were friends. "You suck," she said petulantly.

Kasey laughed and took a sip of beer. "Not an answer."

"I don't even know anymore, Kase. I put everything on hold to get through nursing school. You know how tough it is. This is the first time in six years I'm not running at a hundred miles an hour. Let me catch my breath."

"Do you have doubts about him?"

Doubts? She shook her head slowly. "I don't think so. He seems to be a really nice guy."

"Then give it a try. Have some fun, Tee. You've earned it." Kasey's fingers closed around Tiana's. "Eventually you'll know if you can trust Lily with him."

"Thing is, if I bring a man around and let Lily love him, trust him, see him as a father figure, he's going to have to know that is a lifetime commitment."

"Lily doesn't have to go on your dates with you," Kasey said sarcastically. "This is what I'm talking about. You are pretending it's completely about Lily and it isn't. Do you even want to give him a chance?"

"Yes, I do. I'm just…"

"Scared?"

"Yeah, I made a stupid choice once and don't want to repeat it."

"You aren't that teenage girl anymore either. You are a grown-ass woman who knows what she wants. Start acting like it."

"Damn, you are bossy."

"And you aren't?"

Tiana stuck her tongue out at Kasey. Who returned the gesture. Taking a sip of the mimosa, she let out a sigh. Because she did want to try. DeShawn seemed like the total package. Smart, funny, educated, dedicated to building a career, compassionate with the kids they were working with. That he was smoking hot and amazing in bed were bonus points. But would that hold out over time or was she falling for a facade? That streak of smart-ass in him made her wonder.

"Give him a chance."

DeShawn slowed as he turned off East Bay Street onto Broad. A painted window sign caught his eye. Reyes Financial Management. Lena. He'd completely forgotten that she had made copies of all the information she and her Saint Toribio team gave out at the mission for him to use. Looping around the block, he found a parking spot on Meeting Street. He hesitated for a minute. Should he barge in on her like this? Call first? *Hell, man. You're here. Go see if she's got five minutes.*

He let out a low whistle as he approached the office. Nearly on the corner of East Bay and Broad. On the *south* side, no less. This was some expensive real estate. Maybe he should beg her to take over his miniscule savings. As a charity. The door was open and he leaned in.

"Hello. May I help you?"

The man's tone was cool as DeShawn approached the reception desk. "Yes. Hi. I don't have an appointment, but I was wondering if Lena, I mean Ms. Reyes, had a minute to talk?"

This earned him a slightly raised eyebrow and a lazy up-and-down look. No, he wasn't in a suit, but he wasn't a bum off the street. He hardened his gaze slightly. *Don't be pulling the South of Broad snob act on me.*

The receptionist lifted the phone. "A visitor for Ms. Reyes," he said. "An *unannounced* visitor." He motioned at the leather couch along the wall. "Have a seat."

"Thank you."

Sitting down, he realized he had some mud on the tops of his boots. He'd been out at the Maritime Center checking out a question about the Fort Sumter ferryboat's dock. Sliding his feet under the couch, he tried not to look as out of place as he felt. This office wasn't what he would have expected from Lena. Never. Lena's office would be sleek, modern and bright. This looked like a cross between a funeral home and some stodgy old law firm.

The door to the back opened and a beautiful blonde woman walked into the lobby. "Hello," she said as she crossed the room, holding out her hand. "I'm Chloe, Lena's assistant. How may we help you today?"

He stood and shook her hand. "I'm sorry. I

was driving by and remembered I needed to talk to Lena. Oh. I'm DeShawn Adams. She and I are working on a project for a school and she had some information about the work she'd done out at the mission."

Stop babbling, dude.

The blonde took her hand back. "Of course. She's mentioned it. I'll check with her."

He stood there for a moment, wondering if he was supposed to sit back down or stand here like a dork in the middle of the room. Before he could decide, Lena came through the door.

"DeShawn!" She gave him an unexpected hug. "Good to see you." She hooked her arm through his. "Come on back to my office."

As they went through the door, she glanced at the blonde. "Chloe," she said in a low voice. "Please go explain to your hire why we always ask for a name when people come in the door."

"It's no big deal," DeShawn said. He didn't want to get the guy in trouble. He followed her into her office, which, as he'd expected, was sleek and modern.

Lena shut the door and went to her desk. "Sit down. What can I help you with?"

"You said you had materials that you gave out at the mission?"

"Yes! I'd forgotten, sorry." She rummaged in

a drawer and pulled out an envelope with his name on it. "I put together a group. People with expertise in different areas. One is a librarian who knows all the ins and outs of getting free or cheap tutoring for SATs. Another is a financial aid counselor, so she talked about how to find and apply for scholarships. Their lectures are outlined and copies of all the handouts they give are on this flash drive. You may have to tailor them to meet the needs of the kids, but it's all yours to use."

He leaned forward. "Thank you. Tiana and I had been talking about presenting things that would have made the transition to college much easier."

"Sounds like the exact same thing. Our talks are aimed at high school kids, but I really think this will work for Henry's kids."

"I'm sure it will. Thanks again."

"No, thank you for thinking of it. I'm going up this weekend actually with the librarian I mentioned. We went on a massive book-buying spree. A lot of people donated money instead of books."

"Great. Do you need any help?"

"No. Matt's coming with us. He can do all the heavy lifting."

DeShawn grinned. "Sadie falls in love. Then Josh. Now you, Lena. You look very happy."

She smiled and hugged herself. "I am happy. You should try this love stuff. It's not bad."

"I'm working on it."

"Tiana?"

That took him aback. He tried to cover it by peeking in the envelope. "What makes you say that?"

"Oh, DeShawn. It's all over your face when you look at her when she's not looking."

He rolled his shoulders in a slow shrug, trying to make it seem like nothing even though some heat was stinging his cheeks.

"Maybe. Maybe not. We'll see."

"Just jump in!"

He laughed as he stood. "Who are you? The Lena I knew always had a plan and she stuck to it. Just jump in?"

She came around the desk to walk him to the door. "I learned how fun jumping can be. It was good to see you, DeShawn. You were always my favorite Crew guy."

"I'll bet you say that to all the Crew guys." He tucked the envelope with the flash drive in his pocket. Glanced around the room. "Can I ask you a question?"

"Of course."

"I have a little money in savings…"

"You want some help with it? No problem. I'm not taking new clients now, but my new partner, Moseley, is." Lena reached over her desk to pull a business card from the top drawer. "Give her a call and set up an appointment."

"Thank you. I'm trying to do this whole adult thing."

She laughed. "Being an adult is no fun. Feel free to stick your tongue out at Francis as you leave."

"Can I call him Frank instead?"

"Oh, yes. Wait. I want to listen at the door."

He stepped through the door and turned to wave. "Thanks again, Lena." As he walked to the front door, he lifted a hand. "Thanks, Frank!"

BEING BACK IN the Cleaning Crew office for Friday dinner was bittersweet. He'd had just enough time to get from Lena's office to home to change clothes and make it to the Crew office in enough time to keep Molly from nagging him about being late. It was good to be back with Sadie and Molly mothering him. DeShawn looked around the conference room and the people who had been a huge influence on him. Their guidance and friendship had taken him from a slightly overwhelmed college freshman to the man he was today.

"Feels weird, huh?" Malik said.

"It does. I only know a couple of the guys now."

"Aaron was here last month."

"How's he doing?"

"Great. Just started grad school. Something science-y."

"Science-y? And you're in doctor school?" DeShawn said with a laugh.

"Go play with your protractor, math nerd."

"Nice to see things never change," Sadie said as she leaned between them. "Be nice. You aren't setting a good example for the Baby Crew."

DeShawn snorted out another laugh. The new guys did all look about twelve years old. He caught Sadie's hand. "Can I talk to you later?"

She squeezed his hand. "You can talk to me anytime."

"What's up?" Malik asked as Sadie moved away. "You okay, brother?"

"Yeah. My mother called me. I'm not sure what I want to do about it."

Malik made a face. He knew the whole ugly

truth. "That's a hard decision. I'm here for you, DeShawn. Anything you need."

Molly leaned in to place a huge steaming platter of pot roast on the table. "What he needs, Malik, is to eat some food. Wasting away to nothing. And a kitten."

"I'm not taking a flea-ridden hair-and-poop machine."

"I want a kitten. What kind are they?" Malik asked.

Molly kissed his forehead. "You were always a man of fine taste and distinction, Malik."

DeShawn lifted his middle finger when Molly walked away. They both began laughing. DeShawn felt insanely happy and content as he dug into the melt-in-your-mouth roast. Good friends, possibility of a serious relationship with Tiana, good job. *Stay the course. Pay off those student loans. Look for a small house or condo to buy. Put down roots.* Once and for all, he needed to get this situation with his mother settled. He watched as Sadie circled the table, fussing over her guys. He'd been working here still when her half brother found her and she faced down her own mother, who had abandoned her to a childhood in foster homes. She'd never really talked about it with the guys but they all knew how hard it had been for her.

You have that strength, man?

He grabbed a dinner roll as the basket came around the table. The conversation seemed to dim around him. Did he have the strength? That he didn't know. Every time he tried to picture anything having to do with confronting his mom, the anger would begin to rise and he'd shut it down. Put it back in that box he kept in the darkest corner of his mind.

"Hello? Earth to DeShawn!"

He blinked and looked around. Malik looked at him with a frown. "You okay, man?"

"Yeah. Thinking."

"You aren't supposed to be thinking—you need to be eating," Sadie said. "You're so skinny Marcus Canard wouldn't hire you."

That made him laugh. Canard was the evil villain to Sadie's superheroine. "Is he still in business?"

"Barely," Sadie said with a delicate sniff, "but that's none of my concern." She raised her hand casually pointing to another Best of Charleston award on the wall.

That got Malik going. The party for the winners of the prestigious local award was always amazing, but for the Crew members who attended to collect the first award, it had been epic.

Malik waved at the newer guys. "You don't even know. That was a party like nothing we'd ever seen before! Complete freak show, in the best possible way. You had lawyers, doctors, artists, drag queens, bartenders, us and everything in between. It was at the aquarium." He point at DeShawn with a thumb. "This guy. We're not three steps inside and he's screaming like a little girl."

DeShawn laughed. "Dude. They were serving sushi in front of the fish tanks! The fish were horrified."

"Oh my God! Don't eat Bob!" they both yelled in unison.

And God, it felt good to laugh like this. To laugh over old memories with a good friend. His mother slipped from his mind again. He couldn't agonize over that all the time. He deserved to be happy.

The new Crew listened to Malik's stories with riveted awe while Sadie pretended to look humble. DeShawn shook his head. It felt so good, laughing here with his friends. For a moment, all his worries and doubts slipped away. He felt at home.

"THAT WAS JUST what I needed," DeShawn said as he settled on the couch next to Sadie in her living quarters above the office. "To be back with you guys. I saw Lena this afternoon."

"Really? Where?"

"I stopped by her office to touch base with her about that project I'm doing with Henry."

"Does she still have that snotty new guy receptionist who looks at you like you're a dog turd drug in on someone's shoe?"

"Yes! Francis! Thank you. I thought it was me."

"Nope. It was Francis. What did Lena tell you to do to him?"

"I called him Frank."

Sadie's eyes widened. "I wish I'd thought of that! I just sort of sat on his desk and asked him to print off my account balance. He's been pretty respectful since then."

"The power of zeroes."

Sadie turned on the couch to face him. "So, what did you need to talk to me about? Your mother still?"

Letting out a sigh, he nodded and wished they could go back to making fun of Francis. "Yeah. I need to decide what to do about her."

"Is she still calling you?"

"No. Her sponsor called me. Offered to act as an intermediary. I talked to Molly about it.

She said I should think about it too. I need to make some sort of decision."

"Do you want to do it? Meet with her?"

"No. I don't *want* to. But maybe…" He let the words trail off and leaned his head back against the couch cushion to stare up at the ceiling. He wanted all this to go away. That's what he wanted.

"Maybe you need to?"

The words were spoken softly. *Need. That's the problem.* Drawing in a slow breath, he sat forward, letting the air back out in a rush. "Do I? Do I need to?"

"Only you can say that, DeShawn."

"I want you to tell me."

"I can't do that. All I can say is that up until the very second I actually opened my mouth and spoke to my mother, I didn't want to do it. I wanted to turn around and walk away. I wanted to walk away and forget about it forever."

"That's about where I'm at right now."

He stood and paced around the room. The only thing different was the pictures of Sadie with Wyatt and Jules. She'd done it. She'd faced her past and moved on to create a life.

"I met this woman," he blurted out.

Sadie smiled and lifted her eyebrows. "I believe that is called changing the subject. It's a defense mechanism."

He smiled and sat back down. "Okay. But the two are related. Sort of. She's got a kid."

"Ah. A how-old kid?"

"Six."

"Do you know what a commitment that is?"

And Sadie would know. She was marrying a man with a nine year old. She was already undergoing the process of legally adopting Jules. "Yes. I do. It's why I need to make a decision about my mother."

"Okay. Let's break this down. What happens if you tell them no?"

"I don't meet with her. Simple. Next."

"No. It isn't simple. If it was that simple, you'd have already turned her down. Get rid of the smart-ass and get real now. Why haven't you already said no?"

"Because," he said, knowing it sounded petulant. He held up a hand and closed his eyes. "Let me think."

"Don't think. Feel. What did you feel when you heard the voice mail?"

"Anger. Fury. Hate. Pain."

His heart was pounding in his chest. He rubbed the back of his neck and unclenched his teeth.

"You're feeling that now, just talking about it," Sadie said quietly. "And if you don't meet with her…"

"It'll always be there. She'll always be out there. An unknown. She could spring up at any moment."

"More than that, she'll be in your mind forever." Sadie got up and went into the kitchen area. "Wine? One of Wyatt's beers?"

"No. Water?"

She returned and handed him a bottle of water. She sipped her wine. "And what if you meet with her?"

"Did it really help, Sadie? Did it really help to open that wound and bleed all over your mother?"

"I didn't think of it like that. I saw it as my opportunity to make her see me. *See* the pain and harm she did to me. Make her take responsibility for it. I made it her burden to carry, not mine."

He drained the bottle in several long swallows. "Damn," he muttered. Turning to face Sadie, he felt his shoulders slump. "I have to do it, don't I?"

She tilted her head and raised a shoulder in a small shrug. "You don't have to do anything."

"I don't know what I'd say."

Leaning forward, Sadie took his hand and squeezed. "The words will come. I promise. Do you want me to be with you?"

"I don't know. Maybe. Let me wrap my brain around actually doing it."

"Don't wait too long. It's like a splinter that's getting infected. It's gonna hurt like hell to dig it out, but you'll heal up cleaner once it's out."

"Awesome," he said with a groan.

"Now tell me about this woman you're falling in love with."

"I'm not. We just. Have this. Thing."

"DeShawn, don't even try that with me. A relationship with her is motivating you to face your mother. That means she is very important to you. I want details."

"She's a lot like you. Stubborn. Opinionated. Bossy."

Sadie nodded and took another sip of wine. "I approve already. You need your smart ass kept in line by a strong woman."

CHAPTER ELEVEN

A STRONG WOMAN. Sadie's words came back to him as he waited outside the restaurant. The air was still chilly but the sun was warm on his face. As February gave way to March, winter was on its way out. It felt odd, going on a date for lunch, but they were working around her schedule. Tiana's SUV turned into the parking lot and he felt his mood lift. He walked to where she parked and opened the door for her.

"Hey," she said almost shyly as she took his hand.

"Hey, yourself," he said, kissing her on the cheek. "Welcome to our first official date."

She smiled. "I thought lunch at your place was our first date."

"I said first *official* date."

"Okay, Engineer Man, you split that hair."

He hooked his arm around her waist and they began walking back to the restaurant. "Engineer. I've been promoted from maid at last!"

"This seems weird," Tiana said after the waitress left with their orders.

"Why?"

She shrugged. "I don't know. I've never really been on a date before."

"Never?" He leaned forward and put a hand over hers. He'd never seen her off-balance before.

Her cheeks darkened. "No. After Lily, I was focused on getting through school. I didn't date."

"Good to know. Now I just need to make this the best first date ever."

They stared at each other for a moment. DeShawn grinned. "Now I feel awkward."

Tiana picked her purse up from the chair beside her. "Luckily, I came prepared." She unzipped the purse and took out a small stack of index cards.

The sight of the white cards, bound with a rubber band, brought back a rush of memories and he began to laugh. Tiana smiled and undid the rubber band. "Oh, man," he said, wiping at his streaming eyes. "Okay, had a flashback there. Mickie sitting at her kitchen table desk last summer, six-inch stack of index cards, begging people to quiz her."

"Mickie is a brilliant woman," Tiana said

with a hint of her good old snark. She slapped a card down on the table between them.

He spun it around. "Tell me one unexpected thing about yourself," he read. "What? We each answer?"

"That's the idea."

"Where'd you come up with this?"

"My mother gave them to me."

"You told your mother we were going on a date?"

"Yes. It's not a secret, DeShawn, we're just keeping it amongst the grown-ups for now. Answer the question."

"No. Wait. Did you tell her anything else?"

Tiana rolled her eyes. "I didn't tell her about *that*. What's wrong with you? I told her we were going out today."

Now he felt his face go hot. Of course he hadn't thought she'd told her mother about sleeping with him. It was the ordinariness of it. She talked to her mother. Normal. He'd never told his mother one single detail about his life. In fact, he actively hid it from her. He looked back to the card. "I played the flute in my high school's marching band."

He laughed at Tiana's shocked face. He reached across the table and pushed up on her chin to close her open mouth.

"Flute?"

"My grandmother was determined that I would be in the band. She thought it would keep me out of trouble. So, she hit up every yard sale in a twenty-mile radius looking for any musical instrument she could afford. Ended up with a flute."

"Did it?"

"Did it what?"

"Keep you out of trouble?"

"Mostly. Your turn."

She scrunched up her face as she thought. "I tried out to be a cheerleader at USC."

DeShawn almost spewed the sip of water he'd just taken. "What?"

Tiana rolled her eyes and shook her head, making her curls bounce. "Temporary insanity. I was so excited to be there and wanted to have the complete college experience." She made air quotes on the word *complete*.

"And? How'd you do?"

"Not too bad but there's more to it than being loud. You have to jump around and sweat and that's not really my style."

"Tell me you joined a sorority too," DeShawn said with one of his trademark snarky grins.

"I did not. I may have been ignorant but I wasn't stupid. What about you?"

"No. All I did was study and work." He paused and the grin faded away to a more serious look. "There was something about the exclusivity of the sorority and fraternity life that bothered me."

"Yes," Tiana agreed. "I felt the same way about it."

"I thought, at first, being someone who didn't feel like I fit in, that being accepted into a fraternity would make me feel better."

"Wanted," Tiana echoed.

"But the idea of it. Being accepted while others were rejected? I couldn't do it."

The waitress returned with their food. Tiana unrolled her silverware and took a bite of the salad she'd ordered. She flipped the next card over. DeShawn put his hand over it. "No more cards. The other day, Tee. That meant something to me."

Her gaze met his and the flicker of uncertainty he saw there worried him. She swept the cards back into her purse. "It did to me also."

"But?"

"Like I told you. There is more to consider than what we want."

"I understand this. I'm completely on board with whatever you think is best."

Tiana looked down and pushed clumps of lettuce around in her salad. A cold feeling began to wash over him. She was having second thoughts. He waited her out. She put the fork down with a heavy sigh.

"It's just so complicated, DeShawn. My mother has essentially raised Lily since I went away to school. Now I'm trying to be her mother. And my mother is there and she won't go home and I'm trying to get things together so she will go home. I feel what you're feeling. I do. I don't want to tell you to walk away, but I'm juggling about ten things here."

"And I'm upsetting the balance?"

He tried to keep his tone even, friendly, but inside, he was in free fall.

"No."

"Yes." He took her hands in his. "Be honest, Tee. I can take it. I'm crashing in here, ruining everything."

"You're not ruining anything! It's just…"

"Complicated. I get it. Please, don't shut me down completely though."

"I promise I won't."

They each concentrated on their food for a minute. "So, your mom lives with you?"

Blowing out a breath that made the curls on her forehead sway, Tiana nodded. "Yes."

"What about your father?"

"He passed away a couple of years ago. I think she doesn't want to go home because she's lonely. Then I feel even worse about trying to make her leave. It's a hot mess."

He nodded and took a bite of his burger. "Your family sounds very close."

"Yeah. I was the last one to leave home. I have two older sisters who live in Florence. They are pretty awesome."

"Italy?"

Tiana snorted. "I wish. South Carolina." She tilted her head. "What about you? Brothers? Sisters?"

"Nope. An only child."

"Don't you have any other family?"

"Not since my grandmother passed. I mean, I have some aunts, uncles, cousins. But they aren't..." He trailed off as he searched for the right words. "Good for me."

Her forehead crinkled with a frown. "I'm sorry."

"No need to be sorry," he said, trying to be offhand about it. The conversation was getting depressing for a first date. "It is what it is. Finish up—I have a surprise for you."

"THERE'S NOTHING WRONG with your car," Tiana said as he pulled out of the parking lot. Looking around, she saw it was well maintained.

"I told you it was just old. You didn't believe me. Just wanted to drive around in your soccer mom van."

"I am not, nor will I ever be a soccer mom."

"You sound pretty sure of that."

"Lily is going to be an artist. And probably go to science camp. Didn't all the fish pictures give you a clue? Bet you get the oil changed exactly every three months on the dot, don't you, Engineer Man?"

"Yep. And rotate the tires every five thousand miles."

"What? Rotate the what?"

He grinned at her. "Don't tell me you don't."

"I didn't even know it was a thing. What's this surprise?"

"If I told you, it wouldn't be a surprise."

As he drove over the James Island Connector into downtown Charleston, she turned to look at him. "Tell me!"

"No."

"A clue?"

He laughed. "You're worse than a kid."

"A hint?"

"Clue and hint are the same thing."

"Pleeeaaaseee. Pretty please with sugar on top."

He reached over and caught her hand. "I'm going to have to remember this. Plan a surprise I want you to beg for."

Heat flooded through her. The thoughts that were running through her mind kept her distracted until he squeezed her hand. "That hushed you up."

His laugh was pure delicious promise. She sniffed. "More like you'll be the one begging."

"If that's what you want."

"Come on, tell me where we're going."

He turned on Meeting Street. "One hint. It's something I've wanted to do ever since I moved here but never did. So, it's a first for both of us. Your first date, my first time doing this."

She pulled her hand away from his. "Do? Does it involve exercise and sweat?"

"Nope. Involves sitting in a luxury van."

"What?"

Before she could figure that out, the mystery was solved as he turned into the parking lot for Gullah Gullah Tours. "Ta-da," he said.

"Really? This is so cool! I've been wanting to take Lily but I wanted to go on it first to make sure it would be age appropriate for her."

He lifted her hand and kissed the back of it. "Great minds. Come on, it should be fun."

And it was fun. They huddled together in the rear of the van, giggling and whispering snarky remarks. Then quietly held hands as the more painful truths of history were revealed. Finally, the pain transformed to pride as they reveled in the vibrant art and music culture that was born in the Gullah communities of the Southern Sea Islands along the Georgia and South Carolina coast.

When the tour was over, she stopped as De-Shawn held the car door open for her. Going up on tiptoe, she kissed him. "Thank you. That was an amazing tour. Perfect job on making our first date special."

He slipped his hands around her waist and pulled her to him. "You are welcome. You get to plan the next date, so you need to step up your game."

She smiled up at him. *Oh damn. You are falling for him.* Her heart was beating out of control, but as she wrapped her arms around his waist and pressed her cheek against his chest, she felt a calm wash over her. His strong arms around her. She felt his lips press against the top of her head. Forcing herself to step back, she met his gaze and nodded. "Challenge accepted."

He smiled and caught her chin between his fingers. The look in his eyes shifted from warm to hot. "What time is your curfew?"

"As much as I would like to make you beg, I need to get home. Saturday night is french fries and game night."

"French fries? As in that's what's for dinner?"

Tiana got in the car and looked up at him. "Yes. Why? Is that weird or something?"

"No. No. Not weird at all." He closed the door and walked around to the driver's side. "Okay, it's totally weird," he said as he got in the car. "Just french fries? No burger? No steak? No veggie?"

"Technically, potatoes are a veggie. I don't even know how this got started. But she is serious about her french fries."

"You eat french fries and play board games? What games?"

"Operation. The junior version of the Game of Life. Battleship. Lily is brutal at Battleship."

"All right then, let's get you back to your car. Do you have time to make out a little before you go?"

"If you ask nicely."

BACK HOME, HIS body still humming from the goodbye kiss Tiana had given him, DeShawn flopped on the couch. He stared at the ceiling. *What are you doing, man? She's got a family. Game night. What do you have?* "Nothing," he muttered. His phone vibrated on the table and he grabbed it.

Want to hit the gym? Need a spotter.

He dropped the phone on his chest. No, he didn't want to hit the gym. *Go to the gym. Stop wallowing.* He sat up, grabbing the phone as it fell. A couple hours with Malik would get his mind off this hamster wheel.

Sure. When?

Now?

Thirty minutes later, he was feeling marginally better as he and Malik took turns spotting each other on the free weights. At least the image of Tiana and Lily sitting at a kitchen table with a giant plate of french fries while Lily shouted *I sank your battleship!* was finally out of his mind.

"Dude," Malik said. "My old auntie can bench more than that."

"Your old auntie is stronger than me then."

Malik laughed and slid two more weights on the bar. "Come on. You can do 275."

"I know I can. Can you spot that much?"

"Jesus, man. If you can't, just say so, don't sit there whining."

DeShawn smiled at the trash talk. He positioned himself on the bench and grabbed the bar. It had been a while since he'd pushed himself. Since leaving the Crew, he worked out mostly just to maintain his weight, not to bulk up. The first two lifts were easy, but the third was a bit of a struggle.

"Pretty good," Malik said as DeShawn got up. "Now watch how it's really done."

After they'd made their way around the weight room, DeShawn was starting to feel the burn. It'd been a long time since he'd lifted at this pace. He wiped down the bench. "I'm done, dude."

"Me too. Want to get something to eat?"

"Naw. I'm tired. Just going home."

"Everything okay? You seem a little off."

"Yeah. I'm okay. Just stuff going on."

"Stuff with your mom?"

They walked to the locker room to get their

gym bags. Since he was going right home, De-
Shawn pulled off his shirt and wiped the sweat
off with it before putting on a dry shirt.

"Tiana," he said as he swung the locker door
shut.

"The woman from the dog jumping contest?"

"Yeah, we're sort of dating."

"You don't seem too happy about it."

"I am. She's amazing. But she's got this
whole family thing. Her kid. Her mother lives
with them. Sisters. All that."

"And? So?"

DeShawn slung the gym bag over his shoulder. "Nothing."

Malik caught him by the arm and pulled
him down to sit on the bench. "Obviously, it
is something, brother. Talk to me."

"What do I bring to the picture?"

Malik gave him a long look. A big brother
look. "You bring your own damn self to the
picture, fool."

"And my druggie parents out there somewhere. My greedy family who are still fighting over who got how much from selling
Momma G's land."

"Those people aren't in your life for a reason, DeShawn. You aren't like them. You de-

serve better. You've earned better. You're a damn engineer with a fancy degree to prove it. What do you bring to the picture? Stop looking at who you used to be and look at who are. Don't make me get Sadie on your ass. If you have feelings for this woman, don't blame your family when you're too afraid to pursue a relationship."

He stared down at the floor. Was he doing that? Using his family as an excuse? "It's complicated."

Malik stood. "Life is complicated. Get used to it. It never gets uncomplicated."

DeShawn laughed. "Damn if that isn't the gospel truth."

"The gospel of Malik. Chapter one, verse one—if life isn't complicated, you aren't doing it right."

Driving home, DeShawn realized he did feel better after the talk. Hearing that other people struggled with the complexities of being a grown-up helped. He'd been feeling like everyone had their shit together and he was the only one flailing around.

A memory came to him. From his first few weeks working at the Cleaning Crew—he'd made some stupid mistake and had to call Sadie for help. He'd been terrified, afraid she was going to fire him. But she'd only helped him fix it. Then as he apologized for the dozenth time, she'd looked him in the eye and said, "It's only a mistake if it can't be fixed. Fix your mistakes."

Pulling into his parking spot, he nodded. Time to fix some mistakes. The first one was putting off the decision about his mother for so long. He pulled his phone out of the gym bag and looked up the number before he could change his mind.

"Molly? Hey, it's DeShawn. Can I come over tomorrow? I want to talk about contacting my mother's sponsor... No. I do not want a kitten."

CHAPTER TWELVE

"ONE MORE GAME!" Lily begged. She was kneeling on the dining room chair, dragging the last of the french fries through the salt on the plate.

Viv walked over and took the plate away. "All that salt is bad for you."

Tiana raised her eyebrows. That. That right there was the problem. No matter how many talks she and her mother had, she never stopped. She just jumped right in and took over the parenting. Pushing back her chair, Tiana stood, trying to keep her thoughts off her face. "Come on, Lily, it's bath time."

After bath time and story time, Tiana pulled the door to Lily's room shut and walked to the kitchen. "I can get those dishes, Mom. Go relax."

Viv continued loading the dishwasher like she hadn't heard a word. Sighing, Tiana pulled a chair away from the dining table and sat down. She rehearsed her next words in her mind.

"I'll be off orientation next month," she said.

"That's good. Think you'll be ready?"

"Maybe. No. But I'm told that's normal. We've got a good crew there so I'll have a lot of people to help me. I wanted to talk to you about my schedule."

Viv finished in the kitchen and came to sit across from Tiana. "Is it going to get less crazy?"

"Yes. It should. Right now, I'm working Kasey's schedule because she's my preceptor. Her schedule is so crazy because her husband is a firefighter and they have to work around his twenty-four-hour shifts. But once I'm finished, I get my own schedule track."

"You get to say when you work?"

Making a face, she shrugged. "It means I get to say what I would like to work. But I may not get it exactly. But there's something else I want to talk to you about."

"You kicking me out?"

"No! I mean. Not like that. But see, Kasey and another woman from work, Jordan, they have this deal. They work opposite shifts so they can watch each other's girls. They both go to the same school as Lily and are about the same age."

"And you're going to make a third? Take care of how many kids?"

"Three, including Lily. Point is, Mom, I have care for her arranged. Twenty-four hours, seven days a week. Plus, the girls are as close as sisters. It's good for them also."

"What do you know about these women?"

Pressing her lips together against the words that wanted to fly out, Tiana took a deep breath. "I know they are good people. I know Lily is already best friends with Kasey's daughter. I know it gives both me and Lily a large safety net. It's time."

"Next month?"

"Yes. Mom, I will be forever grateful for all you've done for us. Really, I am. I'm not sending you away, but Lily and I need to do this on our own now."

"You want to do this on your own. There isn't any reason in the world I can't stay right here and help you raise my grandchild."

Except I don't want you to. If only she could say it that baldly. "Mom. We've talked about this. I'm Lily's mother."

"She knows that. I know that. We all know that." A touch of anger tinged her mother's words.

"You don't seem to really know that," Tiana replied, trying hard to keep her voice low. "You do, but it's your nature to mother people. So, you step right over me and mother Lily without even realizing that you're doing it."

"No, I don't. I told you I would defer to your decisions."

"Yet not an hour ago, you snatched that plate from her and told her salt was bad for her."

Viv pressed her lips together as her eyes narrowed. Tiana felt her stomach drop and she wanted to start babbling out apologies. "You're calling me out about a plate full of salt, young lady?"

Rubbing her face and shaking her head, Tiana fought to stay calm. "Mom. You need to go home. Who is looking after the house? The farm? You have a whole life back there. Friends. You could start watching kids again. Helping them like you helped me and all my friends."

"The house is fine. Rosa looks in on it every other day or so. And Mr. Jenkins's son is renting fields to grow soybeans."

"Mom."

"Just say it, Tee. You don't want me here anymore."

"That's your interpretation. Don't put words in my mouth."

"Don't be smart. I'm still your mother."

"I'm not being smart. You're taking this as

a rejection rather than the next step in the plan we've been working through since Lily was born. I finish school. I go to college. I get a job. Lily and I build a better life. You've sacrificed your own life for me for six years now. It's your turn to have a life for yourself. Do things with your friends."

Vivian looked a little less stormy. "I know. I didn't know it was going to be this hard."

"You aren't going away forever. There'll be holidays, birthdays, Granny summer camp."

"Next month?"

"Yes. But you don't have to leave right then. We can do a slow transition. Have Lily stay with Kasey one night a week, let her get used to it. We'll take it from there."

"That sounds like a sensible plan."

Tiana reached across the table and took her mother's hands. "I love you, Mom. You've been an amazing example for me. Lily and I are going to be fine because of the skills you've given me."

"Guess I'm going to have to figure out that FaceTime thing you kids are always talking about then."

"We'll get that all set up," Tiana said with a laugh. Her mother hated technology and still had her ten-year-old flip phone.

Vivian got up and Tiana stood to embrace her. "We're all going to be okay," she whispered.

"Of course we are. I'll come back and take a switch to you if you aren't."

"That's my momma."

"Are there more of them?" DeShawn asked as he stepped carefully into Molly's living room. There were kittens everywhere. Two of them were climbing his pant leg.

"A couple. The more the merrier," Molly said with a laugh. "The shelter knows I'm a sucker for a good sob story. This is rather out of control though. I'm up to fourteen kittens and two momma cats."

"How do you get anything done?"

"I don't. Come on in. Sit down. Let's talk."

As they settled on the couch, a kitten walked off the back of it onto DeShawn's shoulder and put its nose in his ear and purred. He pulled away and turned to look. It was the little gray kitten with the mint-green eyes. "You again," he said.

"Told you, you've been chosen."

"I am not getting a kitten."

"So you say. Now, tell me about your decision."

The change in topic left him feeling off-kilter. Because he hadn't really reached a decision. He wanted time. "I haven't made one yet. But I think I need to give an answer and not leave them hanging in the dark."

Molly nodded. "Do you want me to make the call?"

"No. I'll do it. I just need some…"

"Moral support?"

"Yeah."

"So tell me what you're going to say."

"Exactly what I said. I'm not ready to meet with her right now, but I haven't ruled it out completely. I'll call if I want to do it."

"When will that be?"

He spread his hands. "I don't know."

"But they'll need a time."

"They aren't getting one." He felt himself getting angry.

Molly smiled and patted his arm. "Sorry, I was trying to throw questions at you that the sponsor might. Wanted you to be prepared for some pushing. As a sponsor, she's going to be focusing on what is good for your mother, not necessarily what's good for you. You'll have to stand your ground and not let her make you feel guilty about your choice. It is your choice, DeShawn."

"Got it." He pulled out his phone and scrolled

through the phone log until he found the sponsor's number. "Funny if after all this agonizing, it goes to voice mail."

"Just say what you got to say."

Taking a deep breath against the nerves that wanted to creep in, he hit Redial. The phone rang twice.

"This is Gretchen."

"Hi. Gretchen. This is DeShawn. I'm Denise's son?"

"Yes. I know who you are. I'm glad you called back. Your mother is…"

"I'm sorry," he interrupted. "I called to let you know that I haven't decided if I want to do this or not. I didn't want to leave you hanging. I wanted to give you some sort of answer. But I don't think I'm ready."

There was a long pause. "Okay. I understand that. But here's the situation. Your mother is trying…"

"Ma'am. I'm sorry. My mother's situation is her situation. Not mine. I will let you know when, if ever, I am ready to meet with her. Thank you. Goodbye."

He ended the call with a trembling hand. The gray kitten climbed down from his shoulder to curl up on his chest. The rumbling purr was sort of soothing. He petted its tiny head with a finger and was rewarded with an even louder purr.

"You did very well," Molly said quietly.

"I feel like crap."

"Oh, the guilt. Yes. I'm well acquainted with the guilt. Addicts are experts at creating guilt."

"How do I deal with it?"

"First, you have to realize you have nothing to be guilty about. You did not create this problem. You did not make your mother an addict."

"I know that, but she *is* my mother. Shouldn't I try to help if she asks?"

"If she was asking you to come over and help her move heavy boxes up to the attic, yes, you should help. But she isn't. She's asking you to dredge up the most painful memories of your life. To mentally and emotionally go back in time and relive those with her. You have every right to say no to that."

"Sadie thinks I should do it. Have my say and move on."

"It doesn't matter what anyone thinks you should do. It only matters what you want to do."

"That's the problem, Molly. I don't want to do it, but I think Sadie is right. If I can face her and be able to say exactly what her behavior did to me, it will be like getting rid of something that's been festering in my mind all my life. But I'm afraid that if I let it all out, it won't leave and it'll be right there, in my face forever."

"For what it's worth, I don't think it will. When I cut my husband off, when I refused to participate in his constant cycle of sobriety and using, I felt that same guilt. What if my rejection made him worse? What if he went completely off the deep end and never got better? What if he died? It's hard to walk away. But you also have to know that you can't save that person. They have to save themselves. Destroying your own life isn't going to help them."

He looked down at the kitten, feeling even more confused. "I wish this whole thing would go away."

Molly stood and went to the kitchen, followed by about ten mewling kittens. "I'm going to make some lunch. Tell me about this woman you met."

"What? How'd you know about that?"

"Eric is a gossip."

After wrestling the kitten off his chest—seemed like for every tiny claw he pulled from the fabric of his shirt, the thing grew twenty more—he got up and joined Molly in the kitchen. "Eric doesn't know anything. She's an…acquaintance. We're doing a project together at an elementary school. She has a kid."

"Mmm-hmm," Molly murmured. "What do you think? A blustery day like today calls for grilled cheese and tomato soup, right?"

"Sounds perfect."

"Tell me more about this woman."

"She's a nurse. She's friends with Mickie—that's how I first met her. She has a six-year-old. I think that's all."

"Here, stir the soup while I make the sandwiches. You like her?"

"It's complicated."

"Not really. You either like her or you don't. Very simple."

"Yes. I like her. A lot. The complications are coming from her."

He stared down at the soup he was stirring. Molly stood beside him and dropped a giant blob of butter into the warming frying pan, tilting it this way and that to coat the bottom. His stomach rumbled.

"The child?"

"Yes. She's very careful about her. Doesn't want people wandering into and out of her life."

"Very good mother then." The sandwiches sizzled as she carefully placed them in the butter.

"It's one of the things I admire about her. She puts her daughter first and I respect that."

"That's because you're a very good man, DeShawn. You are both putting the child first."

A few minutes later, they sat at the kitchen table eating soup and sandwiches and detaching kittens from their legs.

"Feeling guilty?" Molly asked out of the blue.

The question startled him. "No, I'm not actually."

"See? This is how you know the guilt will go away. You go about your life. It'll creep up on you now and then, but you have to keep on living."

"I'm not so much worried about her recovery. I'm worried that by not addressing it, it's just out there. Waiting. Like a ticking bomb."

"Then detonate it. On your terms."

He took their dishes to the sink and rinsed them. "How's the dishwasher doing?"

"Perfect. Thank you. DeShawn, I don't like to tell people what to do…"

He cut her off with a real laugh. "Could have fooled me with that drill sergeant routine you pulled at the Crew."

"That's work. I mean in people's private lives. But I'm getting the impression that you want to do this but you're afraid. That's okay. If you need someone to go with you, I will. I'm sure Sadie would also. She took Lena and Josh with her when she met her own mother."

He put the dishes in the dishwasher and turned to lean against the counter. "You're right. I do want it done and over with. I just don't want to actually do it."

"Fine. But there are consequences either way. Once you decide facing the unknown is going to be better than living waiting for the other shoe to drop, let me know."

"True. I promise I will make a decision soon."

"Good. Your kitten will be ready for adoption pretty soon."

"I am not getting a kitten." He gave her a hug. "Thank you for listening to me whine."

"You weren't whining. Sometimes you need to talk things out."

As they walked to the door, DeShawn looked around at all the various kittens. "I might know someone who wants a kitten. Actually, I even mentioned you to them. Let me check."

"That would be lovely. I'll be keeping them until they are ten weeks old, but if they hit two pounds at eight weeks, they can be fixed and adopted."

"I'll let you know."

"I'm keeping that gray one for you."

"Goodbye, Molly."

"Call me if you need anything, okay?"

SUNDAY AFTERNOON, TIANA was regretting her talk with her mother. She had the entire weekend off, in fact didn't have to go back to work until Thursday afternoon. So her mother had gone home for a few days to check on things. And Lily was super mad that she couldn't go home with granny. Tiana was gaining new respect for her mother. Surely, she hadn't been half as stubborn as this child.

"It's not fair that I can't go to the farm." Lily plopped on the couch, arms crossed against her chest, and glared up at Tiana.

Taking a slow breath, Tiana put her arm around Lily's shoulders and tried to pull her closer. Lily twisted away. *It's okay. This is normal. Change. People leaving. Not easy.* "I understand you're upset that your Nana went back to the farm. It's okay to be upset. But you have school in the morning. And Nana will be back on Tuesday."

She was going to have to talk to her mother more in depth about this. They needed a more exact withdrawal plan if Lily was going to take it so hard. She was a sensitive little girl with a huge heart. *This is why you're right about De-Shawn. You can't let Lily get attached. Mom is coming back. A man doesn't have to.* "Well, it's still very unfair! I want to see my cat. You won't let him come here and you won't let me get another one and you're just mean."

"What cat? That old barn cat? Lily, honey. That cat would hate living here. He's used to being outside all the time and hunting mice. No mice here and he'd have to stay inside because he might get run over."

"Then why can't I get a kitten?"

Taking a deep breath, Tiana forced herself to stay calm. "I said you could have a fish. A goldfish or one of those pretty Siamese fighting fish."

"I don't want a fish! I can't snuggle and pet a fish. You're mean and unfair and I wish Granny was here because she'd let me have a kitten."

"That's enough. Go to your room. Ten minute cooldown time." Tiana went to the kitchen and grabbed the timer, twisting the dial to ten minutes and handing it to Lily. "Go on."

She ignored the slammed door and flopped down on the couch. Damn. Her mother had been right. This was going to be harder on Lily than she thought.

Her phone dinged out a text notification. She fished it off the coffee table with her feet, too exhausted to even sit up and reach for it. De-Shawn. Peachy.

When can we get together to talk about the take-one-of-the-kids-to-work stuff?

Now. She'd like to run away from her obstinate daughter right now. She could use a little DeShawn vacation. Ever since all that kissing the other day, her hormones were in a constant state of turmoil.

It would have to be on your lunch break. My mom is out of town until Thursday, so I have Lily.

A minute later, the phone dinged again.

I'll be doing field work on Tuesday so could swing a real lunch. Let you know time?

Too tired for anything else, she sent back a thumbs-up emoji.

Everything okay?

Dealing with a tantruming six-year-old. I'm mean.

There was a long pause before the phone dinged again.

My grandmother always said if a child didn't ever tell a parent they were mean, the parent wasn't doing their job right. Hang in there.

Unexpected tears stung at her eyes. He really was a great guy. And this solo parenting gig was harder than she thought. *No. She's just testing you because it's something new.* She heard the timer go off but Lily didn't come out. Sighing, Tiana got up. "Round two," she muttered under her breath.

In the room, Lily was sitting cross-legged in the middle of her bed, arms across her chest and a scowl on her face that left zero doubt whose child she was. What was that curse? *May you have a child that acts just like you?*

She sat down on the edge of the bed and rubbed a circle on Lily's back. "Lil, I know you're upset about Granny going home for a few days. It's a change and change isn't fun. It's okay to be sad but it's not okay to call people names."

"I didn't call you a name. I said you are mean. That's a description not a name."

Thankful Lily wasn't looking at her, Tiana struggled not to laugh out loud. "Okay. I'll make a deal with you."

Lily's scowl faded and she turned to look up at her. "Does this deal end up with me getting a kitten?"

"I'm not going to guarantee that. You have library day tomorrow, right?"

"Yes."

"Good. I want you to tell the librarian you need to research taking care of a kitten. All the stuff it needs, how often it has to go to the cat doctor, how much food it eats, how much those things cost. Got it?"

"Yes. And then what?"

"Then we'll look at it together and talk about it. When we have the facts."

Lily flopped back on the bed with a dramatic sigh. "I guess so."

Tiana leaned down to kiss her forehead. "I love you, Lily."

"I love you too, Mommy. Can we have french fry dinner again?"

"No. But we can play Battleship again."

AFTER GETTING LILY fed and bathed, after losing her Battleship twice in a fierce ocean altercation, Tiana tucked her into bed with a story and a kiss. She pulled the door closed and immediately went to the kitchen to pour a glass of wine. Curling up on the couch, she flipped on the television. Time for a little binge-watching. An hour into some really bad disaster movie that she couldn't tear herself away from, her phone dinged. Kasey.

How's it going?

She's trying to use it to get a kitten.

She got a laughing tears emoji back, and the only response to that was a middle finger GIF. A few minutes later it dinged again.

Want to try a sleepover sometime this week when you're available to come get her before we start with the real deal?

She thought about it. A sleepover would earn her some grown-up time with DeShawn. And that was very tempting. She sipped the wine and sighed.

No. I think she and I need this continuous chunk of time alone together. We can try it when my mother comes back.

Okie dokes. Let me know if you need anything.
See you Thursday!

She sent a thumbs-up and tossed the phone
on the couch beside her. So, no alone time
this week with DeShawn. Unless he could
take an extra long lunch break on Tuesday.
She grinned and stretched out on the couch.
That would be nice. She'd certainly have the
biggest smile in the school pickup line that
afternoon.

She was dozing off when the phone dinged
again. She grabbed it, thinking it was Kasey.
Nope. DeShawn. That woke her up.

You get everything settled?

Stalled. She has to do research on how much
work having a kitten will be.

My former coworker has fourteen foster kittens.
Want one of them?

No!

Want to meet at my place on Tuesday? I'll cook.
We can fool around.

Now she was really awake. Fool around. He was so adorkable. Yes, she was very interested in some fooling around.

Lasagna?

Whatever you wish. Sweet dreams.

You too.

Only if I dream of you.

Okay, Man Maid. You're backsliding.

There's my girl. Tuesday. Noon.

She sent a kissy face back. Turning the sound off on her phone, she checked the time. Nine. If she went to bed now, she'd be up at four in the morning. She got up for another half glass of wine, her absolute limit when alone with Lily, and cued up another disaster movie.

She tried to watch the movie, but she kept thinking she heard something. After checking on Lily a few times, she went into her room. Nothing in there. She peeked into her mother's room. This didn't feel right. She heard the sound again and fear flooded through her. Gathering her nerve, she crossed to the window and pulled back the curtain. It was a squirrel. Chewing on the window ledge. She rapped a knuckle on the glass and it took off. *What in the hell? Why's a squirrel out at night?*

Back in the living room, she turned the movie back on but couldn't concentrate. What if it was a rabid squirrel? Trying to chew its way into the house? She shook her head. "You've lost your mind," she muttered out loud. But that wasn't it. She felt a little afraid being here alone without her mother. She'd grown up sharing a bedroom with both of her sisters. She'd spent her college years either in a dorm or sharing an apartment with up to three other students. She'd rarely been by herself. Much less alone and one hundred percent responsible for a child.

She cut the TV off. *You've lost your mind, Tee. You miss your mommy.* Pathetic. She picked up the phone and scrolled through her contacts. Perfect.

Hey. Are you awake?

After a few minutes, she put the phone down. Obviously, Mickie was already in bed. So she'd just sit here acting like a fool in a haunted house. The phone lit up. She grabbed it up before the call went to voice mail.

"Hey. Sorry. I didn't mean for you to call me," she said.

"No problem. I'm up. Working on a research paper. I need the break. What's up?"

"Don't laugh."

"I can't promise that."

Scooching down on the cushions, Tiana put her legs up on the back of the couch.

"My mother went home for a few days and I'm alone with Lily and I think a rabid squirrel is trying to get in to kill us."

"You've lost your mind. You must have because the Tiana I know would have kicked that squirrel to the next county."

"Do squirrels even come out at night?"

"I don't have a clue. What's wrong? Are you scared?"

"I think so."

"Call-the-police scared or this-is-all-so-real-now-I'm-on-my-own scared?"

"Second. How'd you deal with it?"

She felt like a whiny brat even asking. Mickie had fled from her abusive ex and had been living on the run under an assumed name trying to keep her son safe. She'd lived with a fear Tiana couldn't wrap her brain around.

"I didn't. I was just scared all the time. But you learn to push it down. To do what you need to do."

"I'm sorry. I really shouldn't compare…"

"Don't be silly. Being a single mom is scary. But I really don't think the squirrel will kill you, even if it does get in. Maybe you should get a cat or something. That'll take care of any rodentlike creatures."

Tiana swung her legs down and sat up. "She got to you, didn't she?"

"She who? The squirrel? Tee, have you been drinking or something?"

"Lily. She's been on me about a kitten. Driving me insane."

There was a brief pause before Mickie snorted out a laugh. "You okay, really? I have five hundred more words to write on protocols for an evidence-based practice research project. My brain is about to dissolve into a pile of goo."

"I'm okay. Go back to work. Love you, friend."

"Love you too."

Tiana tossed the phone down. The entire world was in on this kitten conspiracy. To heck with being an artist or a vet. Lily was going to grow up to be the head of the CIA or something. Climbing to her feet, she double-checked the locks, peeked in on Lily and went to her own bed. *Maybe I should get a white noise machine. No. I'd want to hear an ax murderer breaking in.* Covering her face with her hands, she groaned. *You are a grown-ass woman. Stop acting like you're ten. No, you are not letting your mother stay because you're afraid of a squirrel.*

CHAPTER THIRTEEN

"THAT ISN'T LASAGNA," Tiana said as she lounged back on DeShawn's couch as he warmed up lunch. She looked down. The buttons on her shirt were quite catawampus. She rebuttoned them quickly. That would stir up some gossip in the school pick-up line. But then, everything was slightly off this afternoon. She'd expected a nice lunch. Some plans on the field trips with the kids. Food. Sex. Instead, DeShawn had pulled her into his arms the instant the front door shut and with one kiss, started a fire that would not wait.

"Even better. Jalapeño pimiento macaroni and cheese."

"Lordy. I'm going to be in a sex and carb coma."

"Just the way I like you. All the sass blissed right out."

She got up and crossed to the kitchen to loop her arms around him from behind and pressed her lips to the back of his neck. "Are you for real?" she whispered.

He turned in her arms and cupped her cheeks with his hands. "Real. Not perfect, but I'm real."

A dizzying sense of joy flooded through her. *You are falling for him.* The hot, crazy teenage emotion she'd felt for Lily's father, what she thought was love, was a pale imitation of what she was feeling right now. Along the heels of the realization came a nip of fear. She had been so wrong once and it had broken Lily's heart.

DeShawn kissed her chastely on the lips. "Come eat this food."

Sitting at the tiny dining table, Tiana pulled out a notebook as she spooned up the amazing mac and cheese. "This is so good. Tell me. Do you cook like this to impress me or is this your normal?"

He shrugged. "I don't cook like this every day but I can handle myself in the kitchen."

She opened the notebook. "And other places." She waited for him to stop laughing. "I got a list of all the days we can bring a group of kids to the practice lab. They are used to having school kids in and actually have a program where techs are on hand to show them how to use the equipment. I've forwarded all the information to Henry."

"Excellent. I've got two other engineers I work with interested in taking one of the kids around for the day. One is working on the environmental impact of building a restaurant dock on the Folly River. The other is supervising the dismantling and relocation of a historic building on the old navy base. And I'm doing the design planning for the new Cosgrove Avenue and I-26 interchange."

Tiana grinned up at him. This really was fun. She couldn't wait to have the kids in the learning lab, that had actual robot dummies programmed to simulate all sorts of medical emergencies. She was rewarded with a smile that burned her down to her toes. "Hold that thought." She looked at her watch. "I'm due in the school pickup line in an hour."

"My, how time flies when you're having fun."

"What else have you got? I don't know too many people here yet, so most of my contacts are hospital related."

"I've been in touch with a few of the former Crew members. One is in the Coast Guard and is willing to give a tour of the station downtown. I've got a K9 cop who's interested in taking a kid to a training session with the police dogs."

"Good, excellent," Tiana murmured as she added these to her list. She snapped her fingers. "My friend Kasey's husband is a firefighter. Maybe he can do a station and fire truck tour."

They bounced ideas off each other, each one sparking more until Tiana had quite the list to present to Henry. DeShawn stood and began to clear the table. "I think that's enough to get all this started. Send it off to Henry. He can match kids with career interests, then we can start setting dates."

"This is way more fun than I thought it was going to be," Tiana said as she tucked the notebook back into her oversize purse.

DeShawn came back and looped an arm around her waist. "Very true. I feel like...not a kid at Christmas, but like when you find that absolute perfect gift for someone and it's something they'd never guess in a million years and you are sitting there, waiting for them to open it."

"That's a perfect analogy."

"And I need to get back to work," he said,

He frowned as his phone rang. Fishing in his pocket, his frown deepened when he saw the number. That sponsor. He felt the heat of anger twist in his gut.

"DeShawn? You okay?" Tiana asked.

He left swiped the call into oblivion and tried to smile at her. "Yeah. Sure. It's nothing. Stupid telemarketers."

Her gaze lingered on him for a moment before she lifted her purse to her shoulder. "Okay. I should get to the school pickup line or I'll be there for an hour."

He walked her to her car. "Hey," he said, pulling her close. "I'm glad we got to spend some time together. Are you still in for pursuing this?"

"I'm in."

He kissed her again. A kiss that made being last in the pickup line seem like no big deal. He stepped back. "You're going to make me lose my job, Tee."

"Go measure something, Engineer Man," she said with a laugh as she climbed in her car. Driving away, she kept glancing at him in the rearview. He was watching her. *This is so much more than sex*. The thought zoomed through her mind, leaving her shaky and unsure. She so wanted to pursue this. But Lily. But her mother. But her job. Shaking her head, she hit the turn signal and pulled out of the apartment complex. She'd tackled bigger problems. They could figure this out.

SATURDAY MORNING, AS Tiana left work, she stopped by the Starbucks in the cafeteria and bought the largest, strongest coffee available. The timing of this outing was horrible, but there was nothing to be done about it. Except try not to drive off the road into a ditch somewhere.

In her car, she punched the address into the GPS and downed half the coffee. "You are so going to regret drinking this," she said out loud. It might keep her eyes open for now, but the caffeine was still going to be jittering in her blood later when she tried to take a nap. She dropped the car in gear and made her way out of the parking garage.

Luckily, the morning rush hour traffic was going in the opposite direction so it was a quick drive to the K9 training center in North Charleston. Glancing at the dashboard clock, she saw it was just a little after eight in the morning. The demonstration was starting at nine. *Perfect. I'll just rest my eyes for a bit.* She finished off the now lukewarm coffee and pushed the seat back. *So tired.* There had been no full moon, but the shift had been extraordinarily psych patient heavy. And dealing with psych patients took a lot of work. It was mentally exhausting. And usually quite frustrating because you ended up spending hours on the phone trying to find placement. Then there were the ones who just walked out and you worried about them being okay. And...*damn it, Tee. Shut it down. Stop going over everything.*

A sharp rap on the car window jolted her out of sleep. She wiped at her eyes, disoriented and woozy headed. The rap came again and she looked over to see a police officer standing by her car. She powered down the window.

"Yes, sir?"

"Checking to make sure you're okay, ma'am."

"Yes. Thank you. I'm part of the group of schoolchildren who are coming to see the training demonstration today."

He looked down at her uniform and badge. "Night shift nurse?"

"Yes, sir."

"My wife's a nurse. I understand. Your group should be here in about ten minutes or so. Did you want to come inside? We've got coffee."

"That would be wonderful, thanks."

She shut down the engine and climbed out to follow the officer into the building. After getting coffee and a biscuit he insisted she have, she sat in the small lobby area to wait. She let her head fall back on the sofa cushion and closed her eyes.

"Hey, sexy lady."

She raised her middle finger at the sound of DeShawn's voice without opening her eyes. The cushion shifted as he sat beside her.

"Don't tell anyone, but those scrubs are kinda hot."

She opened her eyes to his grin. "Oog. That's so weird."

"And you like it. Did you work last night?"

"Yep. Seven p.m. to seven a.m."

He frowned. "Are you going to be okay? To drive home?"

She shrugged. "I've had coffee. We'll see."

He took her hand. "Seriously, Tee. You don't have to be here for this. Henry and I can handle it. Go home. Get some sleep."

She stretched and let out a jaw-popping yawn. "No. I want to be here. It's the first activity we're doing. Plus, I really want to see the dogs."

He looked at her doubtfully but whatever argument he was about to launch into was interrupted by the sound of a bus pulling up outside. "That must be them. Lena rented the bus."

"Really? Is she super rich or something?"

"I believe the correct answer is 'filthy rich' but Lena's good people. She grew up just as poor as us. Made every penny on her own."

He got up and walked across the room to the door. "Yep. That's them. You ready?"

She tilted her head as she watched him. The black leather jacket fit him perfectly. As did those jeans. *Yum.* He turned and caught her staring. "I'm ready. Just pinch me if I start falling asleep standing up."

Following him outside, she saw that the bus was really one of those passenger vans. Henry was standing by the door, ticking names off a list as the children got out. There were ten of them. This was good. In today's world, these kids needed positive interactions with the police.

"Hi, guys," DeShawn said as he approached the group. "Ready to have some fun?"

They all yelled, *"Yes!"*

The officer who'd tapped on her window came to stand beside her. "Good morning, everyone. I'm Sergeant Harris. If everyone is here, we can get started. Follow me."

They followed him around the building to the back. There was a large area of grass. But there were also small buildings and a car.

Three police officers and their dogs, two German shepherds and one bloodhound were already on the field. The kids all squealed at the sight of them.

"You'll have a chance to meet the dogs later," Sergeant Harris said. "These are working dogs, not pets." He led them over to a small set of bleachers where they could sit down. They put the kids on the bottom row. Tiana climbed up to sit behind them, thankful she wouldn't have to stand the entire time. DeShawn sat beside her.

Once they were settled, the officers with the dogs came forward. "Now," Sgt. Harris said, "when most people think about police dogs, they think about them chasing down and biting the bad guys. And while they can do that, we prefer they don't. Most of the time, they find things for us."

One boy raised his hand. "Because they can smell so good, right?"

"That's exactly right. They are taught to find drugs or bombs or people. First up, we're going to show you some of the obedience training. The dogs and their handlers train almost constantly."

For the next fifteen minutes, Tiana watched, spellbound, as the officers put the dogs through a variety of commands. From the basics of sit and stay to jumping through the glassless windows of the buildings. A simple one word command had the dogs either barking, growling, or being completely silent.

"Question?" Sgt. Harris asked, pointing to the bleachers.

"Why are the commands in another language?" DeShawn asked. "It sounds like German, but it isn't."

"Good catch. These dogs were trained in Europe. They learned their commands in Dutch so it's easier to teach the police officers Dutch phrases than to reteach the dogs English."

Next up was the find demonstration. The officer with the bloodhound stepped forward. "Last night, I hid a doll somewhere on the property. Groot's going to find it for us."

Several of the kids giggled. "Why is his name Groot?" one of them asked.

The officer looked down at the dog and spoke a phrase. The dog lifted his nose and let out something between a bark and bay. *Guroorooroo.* Tiana collapsed against DeShawn as she laughed at the sound. He was laughing just as hard.

"I should get one of those," he said. "What a goofball."

"Your neighbors would love that."

"Ready?" The officer took a small cloth from his pocket and held it out to Groot, who eagerly sniffed at it, his tail swishing in the air. "*Vind!* Find."

Groot trotted to the center of the field and lifted his nose in the air. He turned in a circle, then bounded off toward the old car. He circled the car once, then sat down at the passenger seat door and let out one short bark. The officer trotted to the car and opened the door. Groot jumped in the car and emerged with the doll.

As the demonstration went on, Tiana found herself leaning more and more on DeShawn. Fighting to keep her eyes open, smothering yawns. All the coffee in the world wasn't going to help at this point.

"Do you need a pinch?" DeShawn whispered in her ear.

"Mmm. Is this almost over yet?"

"I think so."

Thankfully, it was. The kids were called over to pet the dogs and ask questions. Getting up and moving helped. As long as she was moving, she was okay.

"All right, kids," Henry said. "Tell the officers thank you for taking the time to show you how police dogs work."

"Thank you!" they all chanted.

"And Ms. Nelson and Mr. Adams for arranging the visit."

Another round of "Thank you."

"You are welcome!" Tiana said as they walked back to the van. "This was an exciting start and I'm glad so many of you were able to come out today."

After making sure everyone was accounted for and in the van, Tiana walked back to her car. "Hold up there, Nurse Ratched. I'm not comfortable letting you drive home."

She frowned at him. "I'm fine. As long as I'm doing something. I've been awake way longer than this before."

"Studies have proven that sleepy driving is as bad as drunk driving," he said, pulling her into his arms. He touched his forehead to hers and looked down into her eyes. "I don't want anything to happen to you."

"Nothing is going to happen to me."

"For Lily's sake then. Tee, you were swaying on that bench. You could barely keep your eyes open. If you get in an accident on the way home, I'll never forgive myself."

She let her shoulders slump. She was awfully tired. And he'd thrown the perfect guilt bomb—Lily. "Let me see if it's okay to leave my car here."

He handed her his car keys. "Go get in, I'll ask."

Five minutes later, they were pulling out of the parking lot. "Where to?" he asked.

She gave him the name of her apartment complex and leaned against the door. It was just her eyes. Her eyes were so tired. She just needed to shut them for a minute.

"Hey."

She came awake at the touch on her leg. The car was idling just inside the entrance to her complex. "Damn. I fell asleep."

"About a minute after we left. Which apartment is yours?"

"Keep going. Third on the right past the pool."

As he pulled to a stop in front of her building, she turned to him. "Thank you for doing this."

"Not a problem. Let me know when you're ready and I'll take you to get your car."

"It's okay. My mother is coming back from the farm today. She can take me. I don't have to work tonight."

His eyebrows raised in surprise. "Who's watching Lily?"

Leaning forward, she kissed him on the cheek. "She's at a friend's house. I'll get plenty of sleep. But it's cute that you worry about me."

"Of course," he said, shaking his head. "Of course she's with someone."

Tiana rolled her eyes. "Of course she is."

He caught her hand and pulled her back for another kiss. "Think we can sneak a date in sometime this week?"

"Definitely. Now, go away. I need some a nap."

CHAPTER FOURTEEN

SUNDAY AFTERNOON, DESHAWN and Malik hit their backs hard in the gym. Started with classic wide-grip chin-ups to get everything loosened up, then moved through set after set of rows—barbell, dumbbell, and cable—before going upside down on the decline bench for some pull-overs that left DeShawn's lats feeling scorched. FedEx Fred strolled in, still in his uniform, en route to the locker room with his gym bag over his shoulder, and DeShawn gave him a fist bump as they passed. Then, Malik waved him over and handed him a curl bar. Their backs already toast, it was time to hit the biceps. Pull day, Malik called it. DeShawn thought of a few other words he could use to describe it!

He was still feeling it after his shower, gingerly slipping his shirt on in the locker room and feeling that good hurt way down deep in his muscles that meant he'd done what he came to the gym to do.

He was happily groaning and buttoning his shirt when his phone meep-meeped a message notification at him. He reached into his locker, slid his finger across the screen and tapped his code in to unlock it. The message was from Tiana.

I quit! I absolutely quit! Who is this friend with the ten billion kittens?

DeShawn laughed out loud as he read it. That scored him a couple of annoyed glances from a couple of guys who apparently came to the gym just to watch ESPN on the wall-mounted TV in the far corner of the locker room. Whatever. But Dan-Dan the Sun Salutation Man gave him a nod and a knowing grin from three lockers over. Good old Dan—how long had he been coming to the gym? Years. Always wearing shades of purple and blue and always the exact same routine: twenty minutes of yoga, twenty minutes on the stair-climber, twenty minutes of free weights. Never saw Dan without a bright, blissed-out smile on his face. DeShawn returned Dan's nod and smile, then looked back to his phone.

Was Tiana finally ready to pick from Molly's

latest litter? Well. Seemed like her daughter was just as stubborn as Tiana could be.

"What's up?" Malik asked as he returned from the shower room. He had his towel wrapped around his waist and the flip-flops he wore as shower shoes made wet schlup-schlup sounds as he made his way to his locker. He dropped his shoes on the floor, plucked his shirt off the back hook in the locker and began dressing.

"Looks like I'm going kitten shopping instead of grocery shopping," DeShawn said.

Malik nodded. "Molly still has all those cats?"

"Even more now. It's out of control. Have you been to her house? You can't get inside the door without two or three of them climbing up you."

"You're getting one?"

Sitting down, DeShawn grabbed his shoelaces and tied them. He shook his head no and stood. "Nope. Tiana wants one for her daughter."

"You guys a thing now?"

He shrugged, stuffed his workout clothes in the gym bag and grabbed his phone. He quickly swiped a message in reply to Tiana. His brow knit, perplexed, when autocorrect tried to change *look* to *Luke*. Seriously? He repaired the text, then hit Send.

Want to look today? I can call her. Let you know time.

Her reply was immediate. Thank you!

"I gotta run," he said to Malik as he shouldered his bag. "Need to set up a kitten deal."

Malik laughed. "Go make your woman happy."

His woman. The word burned hot in his mind. He wished. He hoped. In the car, he called Molly. No texts for her. That kind of thing was pure *Star Trek* as far as she was concerned, she'd once told him. And he was quite sure she was picturing a young William Shatner in the Captain's chair as she said it, definitely not Chris Pine. He chuckled, bit his bottom lip and waited as the phone rang.

"Hey, I may have an interested party for a kitten," he said when she answered.

"Lovely," Molly said. "Did you want to come by this afternoon? I have, I think, six of them over two pounds so they are eligible for adoption."

"Hold on a second, let me check."

Two?

Tiana's text came back immediately.

Perfect. Meet you at your apartment.

"Okay, Molly. We'll be around a little after two."

He hung up with a smile. Still had time to get the grocery shopping done before meeting Tiana. This was shaping up to be a good day.

HE'D JUST FINISHED putting the groceries away when there was a knock at the door. He opened it to a thoroughly irritated-looking Tiana. He said hello to her and then looked down. Lily. "Hi, Lily," he said, smiling at her and then back up at Tiana.

"Hi, Mr. DeShawn! I'm getting a kitten!"

"So I hear." He grinned at Tiana. "What happened?"

"She wore me down. Plus, that librarian at her school is obviously a crazy cat lady. All the research I had Lily do into the responsibilities and cost of owning a cat came back with nothing but all the benefits of pet ownership. Then my mother started in and I've got way too many real battles to fight without fighting over a dang cat."

He managed not to laugh, but couldn't help smiling. She looked and sounded so much the Tiana he'd first met last summer. Full of sass and salt.

"I sank her battleship," Lily said, crossing her arms against her chest and looking smug.

He couldn't stop the laughter this time.

"Don't laugh at me," Tiana snapped, but a smile was playing at the edges of her lips. "I made my mother swear she would be responsible for teaching Lily how to clean the litter box. Filthy, smelly things."

"I'll do everything, Mommy. Even pick up the poopoo."

"There's always toilet training," he said. He wanted to touch her. Put an arm around her. Something. You leave the little box up on the seat for a while and they learn to…"

She waved it off, then said, "I'm going to look into that. Trust me."

Grabbing his coat, he shrugged it on. "Come on. Molly's expecting us. You have six total kittens to choose from, out of the fourteen."

"Good God! Fourteen? Is she crazy?"

"No. A softhearted foster mom. Apparently, this winter was mild enough to spark an early kitten population explosion and the shelter was overrun. What kind of kitten do you want, Lily?"

"A fluffy one."

"Fluffy," he repeated slowly and cut his eyes at Tiana. "Extra furry. What color?"

Lily pushed her lips out and tilted her head to the side as she considered. "I like orange cats. But I like striped cats too."

"What about a fluffy orange striped one?"

"Do they have one?"

"I don't know," he said, grinning at the excitement in her eyes. "I guess we'll find out."

"A normal cat is enough. Don't need extra cat hair all over everything," Tiana said as they walked the sidewalk to his car.

"That's what lint rollers were invented for."

"I'm not lint rolling my entire apartment."

"DeShawn!"

He froze at the voice. Angry, that edge in it. It froze him in place, just for a second. There was a rush of cold pin-pricking in his gut as he finally turned around. A woman—hard, haggard—stood in the center of the sidewalk behind them. Her eyes were locked on him.

No.

She looked older. Older than she should

be. She advanced on him like she wanted his throat.

He put a hand out to move Lily behind him.

"What in the hell do you mean you aren't going to even talk to me?" The woman said this as she approached, her voice dangerously clipped. She was on him before he could register the words in his head. "Your own mother? I'm trying here, DeShawn! Trying. And you turn your damn back on me like you've done all your life."

"How…how did you find me?" He stood there, not moving, not knowing what move to make, until something slipped into his peripheral vision. Lily was peeking around him to see what was going on. He reached out and gently pushed the child back.

Something hit his chest and fluttered to the ground. He looked down, confused. Paper?

"You trying to show off to your family with fucking Christmas cards," the woman said. The woman. His mother.

He felt Tiana's hand close around his arm, but he shook her off and stepped toward his mother. "You need to go home. This is not the time. Not the place."

Denise lifted her hands, palms to the sky. "When, then? You sitting up here in this fancy apartment with your fancy college degree and fancy job. You always thought you were so much better than any of us. Well, guess what, you aren't." She spat the words at him, inches from his face. "You aren't anything but an ungrateful brat who won't even help his own mother."

He couldn't think. It was that feeling. That same feeling. Being small. Being scared. That voice. So angry. Angry at what? He never knew. Never knew what she was so angry about, all the time. And always at him. His fault, all that anger, just for being there, for breathing? He went blank, silent, expressionless.

His mother turned her lip up like she'd won.

When the words broke through, they came out in a rush.

"What in the hell are you even talking about?" he said. "You're a goddamned drug addict. That's it! That's all! You've never been a mother to me. Don't you say you're a mother. I've been nothing to you except a way to blackmail your way to drug money. Money for drugs! Momma G! Remember her? Remember *your* mother? Do you? Don't you even know what you did to her? How much pain you put in her? In me? Damn! If you'd come here and said sorry—it wouldn't matter. But you didn't. You came here to lay all of this on me. Don't you dare come here and try to lay any of this on me."

His voice was too loud, he realized, as little snaps of awareness began to pull him back to himself, to where he was and what he was doing. His muscles were tight and locked, his hands clenched into fists. Looking at her infuriated him. Having her throw blame in his face was too much.

She held her hands palm upward, before on him. She looked like she was about to cry. "That was the past," she said. "I'm trying, DeShawn. I'm trying. I thought you, my only son, would want to help me." Then, her hands dropped and her mouth twisted into a scowl again and she jabbed a finger at his face over and over as she spoke. "But that's you. Selfish through and through. Your grandmother spoiled you. You don't care about anyone but yourself."

"Selfish? Me? How about you? How about you loving your drugs more than you ever loved me? That's selfish. You never did one damn thing for me my entire life. You left me wallowing in shit and filth until Momma G took me away. I don't owe you a damned thing."

"You owe me your life! I didn't do drugs one single time until after you were born!"

"You want credit for that? You aren't supposed to do drugs at all when you have a kid. You seriously want cookies for not poisoning me in the womb? Not poisoning your baby isn't an extra credit point. It's a basic part of being a mother."

"I want credit for what I'm doing now."

"No! I told you no. I told you I want nothing to do with you. Go away. Go away. I don't care. Do you get that? I don't give a damn if you stay clean or die. Go away! I. Do. Not. Care." Denise looked past him to Tiana and Lily. "Who's this? You got a woman and a kid now?"

Those words went straight to his gut. *Tiana. Lily.* Watching this. Hearing this. He stepped forward. Feet apart, chest to chest with Denise, looking down at her, his hands still clenched in fists.

"Go. Away," he said quietly. "Now."

His voice was quiet, but Denise recognized the look of pure fury in his eyes. He'd taken a deliberately threatening stance with her. She took a step back.

"Go," he repeated.

Denise shuffled a few feet down the sidewalk and lifted her hand to point at him. "Oh,

I'm gonna go for now, Mr. Big Man. But this isn't over. I'm gonna have my say."

With a withering glare, she turned and hurried to a car parked at the end of the sidewalk. He watched her go. The rage swirled in him. He needed to get away from here. He needed to do…something. "DeShawn," Tiana said quietly from behind him.

Shame crumpled his anger. Lily. And Tiana. With her perfect family. Parents who loved her. Parents who did right by her. Now she knew the truth about him. He'd exposed Lily to this poison.

"You go too, Tiana," he said without turning around. He didn't want to see the look in her eyes. Or Lily's.

"No. What's going on here?"

It was just an instant. One second of weakness. He spun around and brought his fist down on the hood of his car. "Go."

Tiana's flinching back doused the rage with ice-cold shame. But it was what she needed to do. Go.

Turning away before she could say anything more, he walked back to his apartment. He had to get away.

Slamming the apartment door behind him, he paced through the small space, rage and hatred boiling through him. It was all he could do to not put a fist through the wall. What the hell just happened? They were going to look at kittens. Damn fuzzy kittens. He sank down on the couch and put his hands to his head.

He should have taken care of this. He should have known better. After everything he'd been through, his mother was still ruining his life.

"MOMMY, WHAT HAPPENED? Why was that lady yelling?"

She scooped Lily up into her arms to settle her in the booster seat. "I don't know, Lily."

"Why won't Mr. DeShawn take us to see the kittens?"

Tiana didn't know what to do or what exactly had happened but she knew he was in pain. She'd seen her share of raw emotional outbursts in the emergency room, but the pain she'd heard behind DeShawn's angry words had stunned her. She would have never guessed he carried that much pain within him.

It was the flash of violence that scared her.

She had to get Lily away from here, talk to her about what she'd just seen. *Give him time to calm down.* She climbed in the driver's seat and locked the doors. The woman had gone, but everything seemed poisoned with the words that had been spoken. She rested her head on the steering wheel as she cranked the engine. What in the hell had just happened?

"THAT WAS QUICK," Vivian said as they came through the door.

"We didn't go," Tiana said. She helped Lily out of her jacket and took her hand. "I want to talk to you, Lils."

"What happened?" Vivian asked.

"A lady was there and she was yelling at Mr. DeShawn and he was yelling at her and saying bad words," Lily answered.

Vivian looked at Tiana. She met her mother's gaze and shook her head. *Damn it. All your fault. Exposing Lily to this.* "Come sit down with me, Lily."

She got settled on the couch but had no idea what to say. "I'm sorry you saw that," she began. Now that the shock was wearing off, anger was beginning to creep in. Anger at DeShawn. But mostly at herself. "It's scary to see grown-ups yelling like that." She looked up at her mother. She was floundering here. She had no idea how to explain this.

Vivian sat on the coffee table facing them. "Were you frightened, Lily?"

"No. Well. Maybe a little when she first starting yelling."

"Yeah, yelling isn't good."

Tiana took Lily's hand. "People are different. When you and I are disagreeing, we don't yell. We try to talk about it. But some people yell. I don't like it but that's just the way some people express their feelings."

Lily thought about that for a moment then nodded. "I don't like it either. But can I still have a kitten?"

Tiana laughed. "Yes. But not today, okay? Mommy needs to get this straightened out first."

Vivian stood up and held a hand out to Lily. "Come on, we'll make some cookies. Go wash your hands first though."

As Lily dashed off to the bathroom, Vivian sat back down and took Tiana's hands in hers. "What happened?"

Tiana told her quickly, in a low whisper, as guilt twisted in her gut. All her fault. Vivian shook her head as she listened.

"Look at me, Tiana," Vivian said. She met her mother's gaze. "Don't be beating yourself up about this. Put fault where it belongs. Is DeShawn okay?"

"I don't know. He wouldn't talk to me.

Just told me to leave. I had her with me so I couldn't stay."

"It'll be all right. She doesn't seem too affected by it."

"I hope not."

"Try to talk to DeShawn. See if he's okay."

Tiana pulled her hands away from her mother's. "I don't know, Mom. When he hit the car... It frightened me."

"I understand, Tiana. But talk to him, at least. That doesn't seem like DeShawn."

"No, mother. It doesn't. But it still happened. And Lily doesn't need to be around that."

AN HOUR LATER, Lily was happily eating cookies as fast as she baked them. Tiana hadn't gotten over the trauma of the scene quite as easily. She reached for her purse. "I've got a few errands to run. Do you need anything?"

"Not that I can think of," Vivian said.

"My kitten," Lily mumbled under her breath.

It made Tiana smile. If she felt okay enough to be sassy, she was going to be fine. "It's still a yes, Lily. Just not today."

In the car, she got her phone out of the purse and dialed Kasey's number.

"Is everything all right?" Kasey picked up. "You never call."

"No. I mean, I'm okay. I… Something happened. Can I come over? I need to talk."

"I've got about ten guys here watching some Sportsball thing. Are you in West Ashley? Meet me in Barnes & Noble for some Starbucks?"

Ten minutes later, Tiana was in line, ordering tea. *Tea was supposed to calm nerves, right?* She had enough adrenaline rushing through her, she didn't need a caffeine boost. Finding a table as far away from other people as she could, she sat down and waited. Her hands shook on the table and she clenched them into fists.

Kasey skidded into the area about five minutes later, hair in a messy ponytail, no makeup, in jeans and a faded T-shirt that said Nasty Woman. "What's wrong?" she asked as she sat across from Tiana and took her hands.

Tears stung at Tiana's eyes. "Did you just throw on shoes and run out of the house?"

"Didn't even brush my teeth. What's wrong?"

"I don't know." She told Kasey everything.

"Yikes. Tiana. That sounds like a scene straight outta the ER. Poor Lily. What are you going to do?"

She felt her shoulders slump. "I don't know. That's why you are here."

"Is Lily okay?"

"She seems to be. We talked about it when we got home. She was more concerned about still being able to get a kitten."

"That's good. Don't make a huge deal about it. She probably didn't understand what was happening. Are you okay?"

"I don't know what I am. It tore me up to see all that pain he was carrying around. I think the worst is that it scared me. To see the anger behind that pain. I understand it, but it was so completely out of character for DeShawn. And now I'm having doubts. Is that there all the time? Have I just never seen it until now? How can I trust him around Lily? Am I making another mistake?"

Kasey chewed on her bottom lip as she stared at Tiana. "Okay. That's a lot. Let's break it down. First. You were falling in love with him?"

The past tense of the question stabbed at her. Was it still true? "Yes."

"I think you should talk to him."

"But. Lily. I have to think about who I let around her."

"Stop using her as an excuse."

"Excuse me?" A real anger rose in her.

"Unbunch your panties, Tee. You know I'm

not going to sugarcoat anything. That's why you called me. I meant don't use Lily as an excuse to walk away from him without even trying. Talk to him. Find out what exactly is going on."

Only slightly mollified, Tiana stalled by sipping at the now tepid tea. "I don't think he's going to talk to me about it. I tried. He told me to go away."

"One minute after it happened. And you had Lily. Ever cross your mind that he didn't want to talk to you because he didn't want Lily to hear any more? This is the way I see it. You got a man who came from a pretty shitty home life yet still managed to graduate from college, start a good career and—when not being ambushed by his estranged drug addict mother—is a generally all-round nice guy. Don't throw all that away because of one moment."

"Sometimes a moment is all you need to see into a person's true nature."

"You don't believe that. If you believed that, you would have washed your hands of him already. You wouldn't be sitting here talking to me."

Clapping her hands over her face, Tiana groaned. Kasey was right. She was struggling against her first impulse to run away, to burn down all her feelings for DeShawn.

"Relationships aren't all hot sex and calorie-free cupcakes, girlfriend. Sometimes it's raw and messy."

"I didn't get any calorie-free cupcakes."

"Not denying the hot sex, I see."

Slinging her purse strap over her shoulder, Tiana sat up straight. *Get some spine, woman.* "I'm going over there right now. Make sure he is okay and if he wants to talk."

"Maybe give him some time," Kasey suggested.

"No. I think it has to be now. If I let it wait, it'll just be easier to talk myself out of it."

As they walked out of the store, Kasey gave her a tight hug. "I hope it works out. Call me later. Promise?"

"I promise."

She went to her car with a pounding heart. *What are you going to say?* Her brain had no answer for that question. What if she couldn't look at him the same way? What if this was all over? She took in a deep breath.

CHAPTER FIFTEEN

THE KNOCK AT the door was so tentative, he knew it was Tiana. Shame burned through him. Lily. She'd seen it all. Heard all the terrible things he'd said. And the dent his fist had left in his car? Tiana had certainly seen that. Tiana, whose best friend Mickie had nearly been beaten to death by her ex-boyfriend. She wasn't going to let that go lightly. His phone buzzed.

Please open the door.

He rolled off the couch and, crossing the space in a few long strides, cracked open the door. "Just go home, Tiana."

She put a hand on the door and pushed. "Are you okay?"

He turned away and returned to the couch. He knew she followed him inside but couldn't look at her. She'd come to tell him goodbye. He could feel it. And as much as he didn't want to hear it, it was the only decision she could make.

"No. I am not okay," he said, throwing himself down on the couch. "Go home."

She came and sat on the table in front of the couch and took his hand. "DeShawn. Talk to me. What happened? What was that all about?"

"That was my lovely mother. Sorry I forgot to introduce you."

"Don't be like this," she said with a bit of heat in her voice. "Talk to me."

"Go home, Tee. You don't deserve this. Lily doesn't deserve this."

"I don't even know what you mean by *this*."

He sat up and she walked over so she could sit next to him. "My life," he said. "The reality of it. That's my mother. My father is even worse. My whole family is one giant ball of either codependent dysfunction or actively involved in substance abuse."

"But you aren't."

"Just because I don't abuse doesn't mean I escaped harm. Doesn't mean the damage isn't there. You saw that." He looked at her. She didn't look away.

"I saw you get surprised and emotionally attacked out of the blue," she said.

"And you saw what happens. Rage. Violence. Honestly, are you willing to expose Lily to me? Knowing that anger is inside me? Don't even answer that. Just go away. Go."

It hurt to say it to her. More than he could imagine. He could feel her gaze on him. He could feel the pain in it. Still, he couldn't meet her eyes. If she couldn't end it, then he had to. For her own good. For Lily's own good.

"You don't mean that." Hearing her words, spoken so softly and shakily, ripped at his heart. "Look me in the eye and say that."

It was the hardest thing he'd ever done but he did it. Turning his head, he looked into her shocked brown eyes. "Go home, Tiana. It's over."

As she stood and walked out the door, he fought against the urge to call her back, to run to her, to tell her this wasn't really what he wanted. But it was the right thing to do. So he let her go.

"What's wrong?" Viv asked as Tiana walked through the door.

Glancing at Lily, who was reading a book in the living room, Tiana shook her head. "Nothing."

She continued straight to her bedroom and shut the door. Sinking down on the bed, she thought she should be crying or something. But there was nothing. Nothing but an awful empty, hollow feeling. Stiff and brittle. As if she might break into pieces. *You love him. Great. Now you're sure.* She looked up as her mother opened the door.

"Close it," she said, hearing the tears wavering in her voice. She didn't need Lily to see her crying over a man.

"What's happened?" Viv asked, sitting beside her and taking her hand.

"My heart is broken."

With those words, the tears came. She leaned into her mother's embrace and cried. It had all been so sudden. One moment, laughing and teasing. Going to look at damned kittens. The next…it had ended. Her mother asked no questions, for which she was grateful. She didn't want to talk. All she needed were her mother's strong arms around her, the comforting sound of her voice in her ear.

"Momma? What's wrong? Are you hurt?"

Lily's worried voice shut the tears off like a faucet. Wiping at her face, she held her arms out and tried to smile. "I'm okay, love. Just a little sad." Gathering Lily on her lap, she kissed her on both cheeks.

"Why are you sad though? Is it because I want a kitten?"

"No, baby girl. It isn't that at all. Mommy had a friend who she can't be friends with anymore and it made her sad."

"Was your friend mean to you? That happened to me and Claire. This girl wanted to be our friend but then she said mean things to Kara so we couldn't be friends with her anymore. Because Claire and I don't like mean people."

That got a real smile. "I'm proud of you for sticking up for other people and not liking mean people."

Viv stood up and took Lily's hand. "Come on, little miss. Read me a story while I finish folding laundry. We'll let your mother alone for a nice long bubble bath."

"Thanks, Mom."

She had been planning on crashing for a nap; she felt exhausted. But a scalding hot bath with the new sugar cookie–scented bubble bath she'd gotten at the mall sounded really good also.

Her thoughts kept returning to DeShawn as she sat on the edge of the tub, one hand spinning circles in the water to churn up more bubbles. *Believe people when they tell you who they are.* She knew this to be true. But she also knew people in pain sometimes said the worst they believed of themselves, not the truth of themselves. Sighing, she turned off the water as soon as it began to run cool.

Easing into the almost scalding water, she felt her muscles relax. One of the many reasons she was paying the scandalous rent for this apartment was this full-size garden tub. It took the entire water heater to fill but she could sink down to her neck and still stretch her legs out straight. Tilting her head back with another sigh, she closed her eyes. *Maybe. No. No maybes. It's over. He said so. Deal with it and move on.*

She kept the ugly crying at bay, but let her tears run down her face until the bathwater cooled and she was forced to climb out.

Problem with being a grown-up was all the relaxing benefits of a bubble bath were ruined because you had to clean out the tub after. *Here's where a maid would come in handy.* Meeting her eyes in the bathroom mirror, she straightened her shoulders and took a deep breath. *No wallowing. No crying. Not around Lily.*

THE INCENSE IN the foyer burned his nose as DeShawn passed the altar with the statue of

Buddha. Offerings of food were on the small table in front of the statue. He continued on into the restaurant, feeling an odd sense of relief as if passing by the altar had let him leave the world outside. He hadn't felt normal since sending Tiana away the day before. Wandering around in a state of numbness punctuated by moments of anger or regret. He blinked as he glanced around the dim space. The hostess approached him just as he spotted Sadie sitting in a booth in the rear of the quiet room.

He slid into the booth. Taste of Thai had been one of his favorite takeout places when he was a crew member. Good food. Lots of it. Good prices. While other restaurants were full of loud chatter and the clanking of silverware on plates, it was always quiet here. Even when all the tables were occupied, there was an unspoken rule that voices were lowered.

He'd called Sadie in a moment of weakness and told her whole ugly mess with his mother and Tiana. This earned him an order to be at the restaurant by six p.m.

"You okay?" she asked as he sat down.

He shrugged and flipped open the menu. She let him get away with that. That she hadn't gone all mother bear on him meant he was about to get some serious Sadie talking-to soon, though.

After they'd given their orders, he looked at her. "I don't know how I am."

"You loved this woman."

"I still do. But I can't see any way back."

"Maybe not right now. Tell me what happened."

As he began to describe the incident, she listened for a little while then covered his hand with hers. "I don't need the play-by-play, De-Shawn. How do you *feel*?"

"I feel like crap. I can't put it out of my mind anymore. Before, I could push it all away and function. Now it just keeps popping up."

"What do you mean by *it*?"

"The anger. The sheer anger. It's just there. I can't make it go away."

"Well, you have a right to be angry. What she did was very wrong. You know that, right? The things she said aren't true. That was an addict talking. You did nothing wrong."

He pushed the lemon in his water down to the bottom of the glass, pinning it there with the straw. "Intellectually I know. Emotionally I feel worse than I ever did as a kid."

They sat in silence until their food arrived. Taking a sip of his absolute favorite, the coconut chicken soup, he let out a sigh. The sweet creamy coconut milk laced with level-three spice was a perfect one-two punch on the tongue. Matched the constant boxing match going on in his mind. "You feel bad about the things you said. That's because you, unlike your mother, are capable of empathy," Sadie She reached out, put her hand on top of his and said his name. "DeShawn." Then, she took her hand back and put it to work forking pad thai into her mouth. "Sorry," she said. "This stuff is really good, and I'm hungry."

He smiled and nodded. He picked his spoon up, then placed it back down. He became quiet. Then he said, "I have to do something." He looked toward the windows as if that something would be waiting for him right there in the parking lot. It wasn't. He looked back to Sadie. "I have to do something. I can't walk around feeling like this. I want my life back. The life where I was happy."

It was the truth. If he could rewind time, make it never happen. If he could still be with Tiana, moving slowly forward. Still falling in love. It was as if his mother had taken all the joy out of his life. No. That was a cop-out.

His mother triggered him, yeah, okay, but his actions, his words, what he did—that's

what had taken all the joy out of his life. You
can't control what other people do. But you,
yourself, what you do? Maybe. Maybe you had
a shot at that.

*Yeah, well, rewind the tape and remember
that then instead of now.* Damn! This empty
feeling, this numbness. This was not the way
to be. This was no way to be.

Sadie swallowed and pointed her fork at
him. "You need to call her sponsor. See if she
knows about this. Then you need to meet with
your mother under controlled circumstances.
I'll go with you. Don't even try to argue with
me. You're doing it. I'm coming with you. The
end."

"What happened to all that 'it's your choice'
stuff you were peddling last time?"

"You were okay then. You weren't being actively harmed by waiting. Now you're bleeding
all over the place and won't even let anyone
help you put a Band-Aid on it. So, I'm pulling
my boss status and insisting."

"You're not the boss of me anymore."

"Ha! Bullshit I'm not. Call the sponsor.
Right now."

"Not here. Let me eat my dinner."

She brightened as if that was the most sensible thing he'd said yet. "Okay, yes. Eat. But we will have this arranged before I leave you."

He ate his soup, trying to feel angry at her. But he couldn't. She was right. Sadie was always right. *That's why you called her, dude. You knew she'd make you do the right thing.* He had fallen right into his mother's manipulation. She'd tried to make him feel bad. To make him think his refusal to talk to her was his failing instead of his choice. He had to make it clear that he wasn't going to play the game anymore. He had to fully let go of his parents. Dropping his spoon into the soup with a splash, he sighed.

"It's scary hard," Sadie said knowingly. "I understand."

"I feel like I'm killing something."

"You are. It's called hope. There was a part of me that, no matter what, hoped that my mother would wake up and be sorry for what she did. That she'd take responsibility and apologize and really change and then everything would be sunshine and riding unicorns over rainbows. But when you grow up, you know that isn't going to happen. And you have to let that dream go or you're going to stay right where you are."

A wry smile turned up the corners of his

mouth. "I'd ask how you got so smart, but I know."

"I will always be here for you, DeShawn."

He nodded and spooned up more soup to wash down the lump that had risen in his throat. They ate in silence for a while. When he'd finished, he pushed the bowl to the side and picked up his phone.

"Is this DeShawn?" Gretchen asked when she answered.

He lowered his head and his voice and tried to hide his surprise. "Yes, it is."

"I am so sorry about what happened. Denise told me about it after she got home. She almost used over it, she felt so bad."

"I really don't care about her feelings on the matter. But I think we need to sit down and finish this. You, me, my mother and my friend Sadie."

Sadie reached out and took his hand, giving it a squeeze. He felt her strength flow into him.

"That's a good idea. Can we do it this week? I don't want too much time to go by before we address it."

"Fine. Prepare my mother. I'm going to be saying goodbye to her. Forever. Make sure she understands this is her only chance to do that amends thing she needs for her sobriety.

I'll give her the opportunity for that. But only once. Then we're done."

"Fair enough. I understand."

He ended the call feeling more relieved than he'd expected to feel. He squeezed Sadie's hand. "That was easier than I thought."

"Because you are taking your power back. She threw you for a loop and made you doubt yourself. But you know who you are. You know what you want. You know what you are capable of doing. You've got this."

His heart filled with her words. "Thanks, boss."

"I'm not your boss. I'm your cool, always right big sister."

"Certainly pain in the butt enough to be a sister."

She grabbed the check. "Let's go over to the mall and I'll let you buy me a cupcake."

"Deal."

CHAPTER SIXTEEN

KASEY CAUGHT TIANA by the arm and swung her into an empty treatment room. "You okay?"

"Yes. Bay 8 is out for an MRI. I'm waiting on orders for the sore throat lady. I'm getting ready to go discharge the stitches in bay 10. Waiting on blood work to come back on altered-mental-status granny. Sheesh, why can't the whole no-patients thing be every Tuesday?"

"Not with your assignment, Tee. With *you*. I know you've got this stuff down," Kasey said with a hand flourish toward the chaos of the emergency department.

"Oh. Yeah. I'm fine. Tired."

Tired. Try exhausted. She couldn't sleep. Between pretending everything was okay in front of Lily and her mother and Kasey deciding she needed to start having her own full assignments before coming off orientation in a couple of weeks, she was simply worn out. Every time she closed her eyes, she saw the pain in DeShawn's eyes when he told her to go away.

"Have you tried to talk to him again?"

Shaking her head, she swallowed down the tears. "No. It's best if I just accept that it's over and move on."

Kasey looked at the clock. "Shift is over in an hour. Come have dinner with me at the Nurses' Lounge."

"I can't stay late. I have to take Lily to school in the morning."

"Just do what I do. Put a coat on over your pajamas and go back to bed when you get home," Kasey said. "Amateur."

"Fine. But you aren't going to get me drunk and weepy and spilling my guts all over the place."

"Promise. We'll play a nice game of rate the boy nurses."

Tiana's work pager buzzed to life in her pocket. "Duty calls."

AN HOUR OR SO later, they were ensconced at a table at the Nurse's Lounge. It was just after eleven at night so the place was packed. "I can't believe we actually got out on time," Kasey said and she looked over the menu.

"Seriously. That means tomorrow is going

to be a horror show, doesn't it? Nothing ever ends nice and neat in the ER."

"Probably. I want a burrito."

Tiana slapped the menu down. "And a margarita."

"Hell yes, my friend."

While waiting for their food, they talked about the shift. Tiana had done the entire patient load while Kasey stood back, available for guidance or assistance. "Overall, you did great. Everything that needed to be done, you did. Your charting was sickeningly perfect. You'll get over that pretty soon. Very good for your first solo day."

"Good to hear. I felt like I was running around like a squirrel in the middle of the road."

"That's just work flow stuff. Nothing to do for that but practice. Want to come off orientation early? I think you're ready."

"Absolutely not. I'm taking every second I can get. I'm not ready to swim in the deep end yet."

"You are. Every nurse feels like that. We've talked. It's going to be a full year before you stop feeling like a complete fake. Two years before the feeling of sheer terror leaves you. Just keep swimming."

Their burritos and margaritas arrived and they dove in. On twelve-hour shifts, nurses were supposed to have a thirty-minute lunch and two fifteen-minute breaks. ignored he reality was that getting two minutes throw some food in your mouth was considered a good day. And then there were the shifts when if you managed to find thirty seconds between alarms, you invested that thirty seconds in dipping into the bathroom to empty your bladder.

"Are you ready to talk about DeShawn yet?"

"Don't ruin my margarita experience, Kase."

"You were falling in love with him."

I was in love with him. Am *in love with him.* She swallowed hard on the chunk of burrito stuck in her throat. "That's neither here nor there. He told me to go away. He told me to leave him alone. I'm not sure that he's not right. That I shouldn't go away. There's a lot there I don't know about."

"Doesn't mean you have to. I think you should try to talk to him again."

"It's not going to make any difference. He's completely shut me out."

"How do you know? Have you tried to talk to him? Text? Phone call? Knocked on his door?"

Dragging a tortilla chip through the salsa,

Tiana shook her head. "No. What good would it do? Have him tell me to go away again? Make a fool of myself? No thank you."

"I think you may get a different reaction now that a few days have passed. He was upset and angry. Probably more than a little embarrassed. You really ready to throw it all away? The way you talked about him, I thought he was going to be the one."

"Me too. But look how wrong I was. I'm a fast learner—I don't need to be taught the same lesson twice."

Kasey finished off her drink with several long swallows and brought the glass down hard on the table. "You throwing clichés at me? Some things are worth fighting for. How's that?"

"Don't beat a dead horse."

"When you reach the end of the rope, tie a knot and hang on."

"Don't keep doing the same thing expecting different results."

"The dogs bark, but the caravan passes by."

"That doesn't even make sense," Tiana said with a laugh.

"I blame the margarita. Come on. Do you want it to be over?"

Finishing her own drink, Tiana shook her

head. "No. But to use another cliché, the ball is in his court."

"I'm sorry, friend."

"Me too. But I've got other things to deal with right now."

"Your mother still won't leave?"

"She goes home when I've got a long stretch off. I think we need to arrange for a practice sleepover for Lily and Claire while she's here. So she can see that Lily likes it. That it really is good for her to have that sibling-like experience. That I have a good circle of support."

"Then we'll set it up. We'll get Jordan in on it too and have all three girls together. We can do it at your house. Your mom can meet us all and see how the girls get along. It'll be fine."

"I know. I think it's that Lily is her last baby. She's spent her life caring for her own kids and every kid back home. I'm down to begging one of my sisters to get pregnant."

"Any chance that's going to happen?"

"I think Shanelle and her husband are trying. They just don't want to say it because Mom would be up there offering advice and cooking get-pregnant food or something."

"That's a thing? Get-pregnant food?"

"My mom thinks so. She also thinks there is a have-a-boy diet and a have-a-girl diet."

"Does it work?"

Tiana arched her eyebrows. "Planning something?"

"No. Maybe. Don't you want more kids? We thought we just wanted one. But now we're talking. A little boy would be nice."

Picking up the napkin, Tiana wiped her hands. "I would love more. Always wanted at least three. Someday."

Kasey reached out and took her hand. "Yep. Someday."

"Someday is going to have to wait. It's almost one a.m. and I need to get up at six."

CHAPTER SEVENTEEN

FRIDAY MORNING, TIANA waited nervously on the sidewalk. Why she was so nervous, she didn't know. The simulation lab workers were going to lead the tour. *Maybe because you don't have DeShawn here with you.* She shook her head. *Stop thinking about him.* Henry was driving up with four of the kids from his class who expressed an interest in medicine. She needed to be on her game, not moping around over a man.

Pacing, she pulled her coat tighter and frowned at the man sitting on the low wall of the parking garage smoking a cigarette. Flicking her eyes to the No Smoking sign just above where he was standing, she shook her head and reversed direction.

She heard her name and looked back to see Henry herding the kids up the sidewalk. One look at their faces made her grin. They were looking around in awe of the tall medical building surrounding them, the hustle and bustle of people coming and going.

"Hey, guys! Glad you made it," she said as they caught up to her. "Y'all ready to have some fun?" A chorus of yeses rang out and she laughed. "Come on then."

First stop was at the registration desk, where they signed in. They all got name tags, slipped between the plastic sheets of a badge. The badges were just flimsy, cheap, throwaway things, but the kids puffed up with pride when they pinned them on.

A tall blonde woman came down the hall to meet them. "Hi, everyone. I'm Susan. I'm going to be showing you around the lab today."

As they followed her down the hall, one of the girls slipped her hand into Tiana's. "There isn't going to be real blood, is there?"

"No, honey. There won't be."

One of the boys turned. "How can you be a doctor if you're afraid of blood, Diane?"

"No down talking," Henry said firmly.

"It's okay. I was afraid of blood when I started nursing school," Tiana said. She leaned down to whisper in Diane's ear. "And vomit."

The girl giggled. "Ew. Me too."

"All right," Susan announced as they reached the lab. "We're going to take a tour of the whole lab. I'll talk a little about each of the mannequins and what we can do with them. After that, if you are interested in any particular one, we can help you do actual procedures."

The lab really was an amazing place. You could draw blood. Learn to intubate. Even deliver a baby, but she supposed that would be a bit much for the kids. She trailed along behind the group, remembering her first days in a similar lab while in nursing school. She'd been so afraid. Every test, every skill check-off day, every clinical day was another chance at failure.

Looking around now, she sighed. Why had she been so afraid of failure? She knew she was smart enough. She knew she was determined enough. Diane fell back and took her hand again. She smiled down at her and it clicked. *Lily.* The fear had been for Lily's future, not hers. Because deep down, she'd known she could do it. Just like deep down, she knew that… *No. Stop it. Doesn't matter what's deep down. He's gone.*

She cleared her throat. "Are you having fun?"

"Yes. Do you think I can really be a nurse when I grow up?"

"I think if you want to be a nurse, you will be a nurse. Come on, let's catch up with the others."

As they walked toward the little crowd, Diane pointed at one of the mannequins. "That's for having a baby, right?"

"Yes, it is."

"I saw a baby be born. My sister."

Tiana stopped walking. "You did? How'd that happen?"

"My daddy had the car. My mom was at the neighbor's trying to borrow theirs when she just laid down on the floor and said it was coming."

"That must have been scary." Tiana put her hand on the girl's shoulder.

"It was, but it was also kind of neat. I was on the phone with the 911 people and they told me what to do. I dried the baby off and put her on my mom's chest and kept her warm until the ambulance got there."

"Wow. You're a hero! A superhero!"

Diane blushed. "Maybe. But later, I heard my momma talking to our neighbor and they said this happens a lot. We are so far away from the hospital. They said last year, a woman had her baby on the side of the road."

A frown crossed Tiana's face. "That's horrible. There isn't any place closer women can have their babies?"

"No, ma'am. We're pretty much equal distance from Hilton Head and Hardeeville. That's it. When you came to school that first time and talked about being a nurse, I thought…"

She looked down at her shoes and her fingers played with the hem of her shirt. Tiana put both her hands on Diane's shoulders and turned the girl to face her. "You thought what? You can tell me."

"Well, I thought that when my baby sister was born, it was a special kind of nurse who was there, not a doctor. And maybe, what if I could be that kind of nurse and I could help?"

"That's an amazing idea," Tiana said. Diane looked up at her with a smile. "You're right. That is what is called a nurse-midwife and they can deliver babies. I think you'd make an excellent one."

"You do?"

"Yes. Most kids your age would have been too scared to help your sister like you did. But someone needed help and you did it. That's what nurses do. It's who we are."

She stood and took Diane's hand. "Come on, we're going to miss all the fun stuff."

As they caught up with the group, she stayed

with Diane. Giving her a little more in-depth
description of the simulations they were being
shown, she began to really enjoy it. They got
to learn how to feel for a vein and draw blood.
They got to practice giving saline shots to or-
anges. They tried to do chest compressions.
Tiana and the tour leader, Susan, did a round
so they could see how it really looked, which
was not the stuff they'd seen on television.

"Have you done that in real life, Ms. Tiana?"
Diane asked.

"Unfortunately, yes."

"And they were okay?"

Tiana looked up at Susan and over to Henry.
He gave a little shrug. Putting her hand on Diane's shoulder, she shook her head. "Not all the
time. Sometimes, no matter how much you try,
some people die."

She hated that she'd asked the question but
couldn't lie to her. She only hoped it didn't
scare her away from her dream. Diane frowned
and looked around. She looked up at Tiana.
"That's why all this is here, right? So we get
smarter and better and less people die, right?"

"Exactly!"

They wrapped up the tour with a question-
and-answer session. Susan touched Tiana on

the arm as they left the room. "If you have a minute, I'd like to talk to you."

"Of course. Just let me walk them to the door and say goodbye."

Susan was waiting when she got back. "Have you ever considered teaching?"

Tiana felt her mouth drop open. "Teaching? No. I'm a nurse."

"No, I mean becoming a nurse educator. You were amazing with that girl. I was watching you. I think you'd be an excellent nursing instructor."

Tiana laughed. "Sorry. Really. I'm too fresh out of nursing school for me to think I'm half as smart as the women who taught me."

Susan smiled. "Maybe not now. But keep it in mind. The hospital has scholarships for employees. Tuition reimbursements. Online classes."

"Tempting. I will keep it in mind. I love the floor, but can't imagine me running around the ER at fifty or sixty."

They shook hands. "Thanks for bringing the kids out. They were really fun."

"Yeah, they're a great group."

As she left and began the hike to her assigned parking spot, she thought about what Susan had said. She loved that Diane had confided in her. She loved the look in her eyes when she told her a little bit more about the procedures. But teach full-time? Encouraging a twelve-year-old was one thing. Running herd over a group of stressed-out, high-strung nursing students? Nope.

She got all the way home before she realized she hadn't thought about…*him. Until now, dork.* Sitting in the parking lot, she pulled out her phone. No new messages. She pulled up the log. She still had all his texts. She should delete them. Was this the twenty-first century's version of old love letters stuffed in a shoe box, undeleted texts? Shaking her head, she hit the Back button to close it down but accidentally opened a new text box. Composing and deleting about five texts, she hit the Back button again and threw the phone into her purse with a frustrated growl.

"Come on, woman," she said out loud. "Pull yourself together. Why are you sitting out here trying to text a man who doesn't want you around when you could be inside taking this damned bra off?"

"I'M NOT SURE I want to do this here," DeShawn said as he looked around the conference room at the Cleaning Crew office on Saturday morning. It was empty. Quiet. Too many good memories here.

"I thought it would be a good, private spot," Sadie said. "And don't underestimate the home turf advantage."

He shrugged. "Well," he said. "I'm not sure I want the memories of all the good times here tainted."

Sadie frowned. "Shit," she said, then tapped her lips with her fingertips. "Damn it, I'm not supposed to swear so much anymore. Jules. It's a bad example. Anyway, that's a fair point. Want me to call Gretchen? Arrange for another place?"

He pointed a thumb toward the front entrance. "I think it's too late. I just heard a car pull up."

Sadie stood. "Come on."

"Where?"

"We'll do it in my office. It's big enough. Go back there. Grab a couple of chairs from the reception room on your way. I'll bring them back to you." She pursed her lips and whistled. Jack, her shaggy black-and-white dog, came padding in from the kitchen. "Go with De-Shawn, Jack."

It still didn't feel quite right, but as he grabbed the chairs and got settled in Sadie's office, it felt better than the conference room. That room was full of memories of laughter, pranks and too many Friday night dinners to count.

Jack came over and rested his head on De-Shawn's thigh. "Stick with me, okay, buddy? I'm not sure I can do this," DeShawn murmured as he scratched the dog behind the ears. Jack looked up at him and let out a tiny little whine. He took that as an agreement. He went cold at the sound of voices in the hall. Sadie. Gretchen. And not speaking, but surely there, his mother.

He shifted in the chair and reached down to put his hand on Jack's neck. The dog lifted his head but stayed beside him, pressed against his thigh.

The door opened. Sadie stood in the doorway. "You ready?"

"Yeah, let's get it over with," he said quietly.

Gretchen, the sponsor, turned out to be a slightly overweight older woman who looked like she could be related to Molly. Her warm smile made him feel a fraction better. He dropped his gaze to the floor as Denise came in.

"Okay," Gretchen said in a calming voice. "I know this is awkward, so let's just acknowledge that and start from there."

Sadie pulled her chair from behind the desk and sat beside DeShawn. Gretchen and Denise sat facing them. Jack leaned in closer and DeShawn's fingers tightened in the thick fur. Gretchen cleared her throat.

"I'm sorry for what I did last time I saw you, DeShawn," Denise said. "It was wrong and unhelpful."

Snorting out an angry laugh, DeShawn shook his head. "Wrong and unhelpful. That's all you have to say?"

"No. Actually, I have a lot to say."

Her tone was hot and Gretchen put a hand on her thigh. "Deep breath. Focus on why you are here. To complete your next step."

Denise looked down and fiddled with the hem of her shirt. DeShawn looked her over almost clinically. How could she be his mother? He had not one positive feeling or memory of her. Sadie was right. It was time to let the hope for a magical fix die.

"I wanted to apologize and admit to the wrongs I did to you," Denise said. She began slowly. She kept her eyes on her knees while her fingers worked the fabric of her shirt. "I was worse than a bad mother—I was no mother at all. I didn't care for you properly. I hurt you with my behavior."

She paused and peeked up at him. He kept his face neutral. No anger. No sympathy. But his heart was pounding so hard, he was sure Sadie could hear it. He could actually feel his palms go slick with sweat. He slid his fingertips through it as he watched his mother say what she had to say.

Sadie was silent but shifted a little in her chair so her shoulder was just touching his.

"Everything you ever said about me is true," Denise said. "I didn't care about anyone or anything except getting my next fix. If it hadn't been for your grandmother, you probably would have died when you were a baby. And, yes, I was horrible to her. I used the threat of harming you to blackmail her into giving me drug money when I had reached rock bottom. I'm ashamed of these things. I'm sorry."

Silence fell. *That's it? That's all she has to say about it?* The anger rose but he struggled to keep it from showing. He wasn't fooling Jack though, who put his head back on DeShawn's thigh with another small whine. He felt cold. Frozen. When he blinked, he could hear it. He realized he wasn't breathing. He forced himself to draw in in a slow, steady breath and hold it deep down in his belly. When he let it go, it was measured, under control.

"DeShawn?" Gretchen asked. "Anything you'd like to say?"

Sadie shifted so that her shoulder was more firmly in contact with his. What she was trying to convey, he didn't know. "Yes," he said. "I do have a question." His voice sounded so composed. Strange, that. It was the exact opposite of how he felt inside. "What the hell was that?"

"What?" both Gretchen and Denise asked in unison.

"All that washed-over bullshit you just served up to me like a sandwich." Anger grew as the words began to pour out, getting hotter and hotter as he spoke. "You almost killed me. I was septic from the open sores from diaper rash. I was six months old and I was in the hospital, almost dead. Momma G had made *funeral arrangements*. Don't you get that? The doctors don't know how I survived. And you say 'I didn't care for you properly'?"

"I said you would have died without your grandmother, yes," she said. "I know how bad I was."

"What about the time you pulled me out of bed when I was…when I was ten and told

Momma G you were taking me to the meth house to sell me to men? You remember that? Because I spent two nights in that house in sheer terror because I knew what you meant. You… And then you… You pass it off as being at 'rock bottom'? That's the most self-serving line I have ever heard."

Sadie leaned in. "DeShawn," she said softly.

Gretchen raised a hand and spoke. "No, Ms. Martin," she said. "DeShawn is right. Denise needs to hear this. She needs to face the full impact her behavior had on DeShawn. She needs this spotlight turned on her rationalizations. She has to acknowledge this. She has to accept that she did those things as a result of her drug use."

"How am I supposed to even believe you?" He continued. "Last week you were out of control. Calling me selfish. Calling me all sorts of things. Implying that I was a bad person for bettering myself. You're just jealous. All I've ever seen you do is try to drag people down. So you can justify yourself to yourself. It didn't work with me. That's what bothers you. I got out. I got away. You hate that."

"Because that's what I wanted for myself," Denise whispered.

DeShawn leaned forward, placing his forearms on his knees. He caught his mother's gaze. Holding it, he shook his head. "That is your problem. I have nothing to do with that. Nothing. Fix your own problems. I hope you do. I wouldn't wish your life on anyone. But it's your life. You did all this to yourself."

"I know that. I really do."

"Fine. I forgive you. But I really do not want to see or hear from you again. I am grateful you were strong enough to stay off drugs while you were pregnant and not completely screw up my brain. That's all. Do you agree to this?"

"I want to try to be a mother to you."

"It's way too late for that. Way too late. Go. Be sober. Be happy. But stay away from me. I will get law enforcement involved if you even try. Understand?"

He didn't wait for her answer, but rose and quietly left the room. He heard footsteps following behind him. Sadie. He walked faster.

"DeShawn. Stop it."

He stopped in the kitchen and let Sadie catch up with him. She pulled him into a hug. "Are you okay?" she whispered in his ear.

"Was I horrible?"

"No. You told it like it was. You laid out your terms and expectations. You did well. Like you said. This is her mess to clean up. You gave her the courtesy of listening. You don't owe her anything else."

He let out a long breath and nodded. "I need to go."

"Are you okay?"

"I need to take all this in. Saying those things stirred up a lot of stuff. I need to sift through it. Find a way to leave it behind for good."

"Call me. Anytime. Day or night. I mean it."

"I will." He gave her a fierce hug. "You were right."

She smiled at him. "If you guys would just realize that I am always right, we'd save a lot of time."

The smile he gave her felt real. He kissed her quickly on the cheek and slipped out the back door. He had to get home.

HE SAT IN his car, in the parking lot of his apartment, aware that he had no memory of the drive home. Cutting off the engine, he stepped out. The sun was bright in his eyes and the air was decidedly warmer. Seemed wrong. Seemed like it should be the dead of night. *Sunshine is the best disinfectant.* He heard Momma G's voice in his mind as clearly as if she was standing beside him. She'd say that every time he'd complain about having to hang towels and bedding out on the clothesline that ran through her dirt-and-weed backyard.

Was that it? He'd cracked open that old wound and let the sunshine in? He looked around with a sense of pride. He'd created this life. With only his grandmother, who'd not finished high school, pushing him on. Nothing nor no one was going to take any of his pride in reaching this stage of life away from him.

Inside, he paced around, unable to sit still. Finished up the breakfast dishes. Put on a load of laundry. Neatened up the living room. Dusted. Contemplated the vacuum. Finally, he sat on the couch and kicked off his shoes. Swinging he feet up on the coffee table, he let his head fall back. He'd expected to walk away full of rage and poison. But he hadn't. He felt… he couldn't put a finger on it. Not relieved. Not happy. It was quieter than that.

Maybe you're just numb. In shock. Or denial. Maybe any minute now, it's all going to come back. He waited. Nothing happened. He kept going through the entire conversation over and over again. How he started out with that burst of anger over her lame admission to wrongs and apology. But Gretchen's words had encouraged him to continue to speak as he was. Raw. Unfiltered. She said Denise needed to hear the ugly truth. It had made him feel validated.

It wasn't until he'd said he would use law enforcement to make her leave him alone that he realized he had fully accepted he would never have the family he wanted. He was on his own and he was okay with that.

The washing machine signaled the end of the cycle and he got up to put the load in the dryer. Halfway to the laundry room, he stopped. *Peace.* That's what he was feeling. He was at peace. With the past. For the first time since she'd reached out to him, that free-floating dread was gone. For the first time since she had ambushed him on the sidewalk, the anger was gone.

It felt pretty good. He loaded the dryer and returned to the living room. The past was settled. What about the future? He sank down on the sofa and picked up his phone. Pulled up Tiana's number. He stared at the Call button for a long time before swiping left and putting the phone down. *No, man. That's done. Just because you got your mother situation settled doesn't change what she saw. Doesn't change a thing.*

He grabbed the phone and texted Malik to

cancel their lifting session at the gym. After this morning, he felt justified in vegging out for the rest of the day. He found a stupid movie and was nodding off before the opening credits finished.

HE WOKE UP to a pounding on his door. Fumbling for the remote, he switched off the television and stood up. "Who is it?" he growled. For a brief moment, a fear flared that it was his mother and he'd have to make good on his promise to call the police.

"Sadie. Open the door, you idiot."

He flung the door open. "What's wrong?"

"What's wrong? I've sent you about twenty texts and called four times and I get nothing! I was afraid you were over here…"

"I fell asleep. I had the sound off on my phone. Jeez. What'd you think I was doing?"

"I don't know. I'm glad you're here. Hey—" She took off, exploring the apartment. "This place is nice. Granite countertops. Gas cooktop. I'm dying of jealousy here. I like Wyatt's house. But the kitchen is unchanged since the '60s."

"I'm fine, Sadie. Today actually helped a lot. I'm at peace with it all now."

She went down the hall and poked her head

in the bathroom. "A full-size garden tub! That's it. When we get married, we're buying a new house."

She came back to the living room and took his hand. "Come sit down." She pulled him to the couch and pushed him down before sitting beside him. "Yes, you're very at peace now. But it's a process. You might not feel that way tomorrow. It took me a couple of months before my feelings about the confrontation with my mother settled down. I want you to know that it's normal and okay. My offer still stands. I'm always here."

"I really am okay. Formally cutting off my ties with my family was the right thing to do. I can't be around them. Not the ones using or the ones who turn a blind eye to the drug use. I've got to build my own life."

"Well, you're off to a good start. Have you spoken to Tiana?"

He shook his head. "That's over. And like I told you. She has a great family. The last thing she needs is me and my crazy-ass family. She didn't see me at my best that day. She's never going to let me be around her daughter now that they saw me screaming at my own mother and punching out my car."

"Is there nothing to be done? Does she not understand where that came from?"

"It doesn't matter. It's over."

"You loved her."

"I did."

"Did she love you?"

"We hadn't gotten to the words yet, but I think so."

"Then maybe give it another try?"

He shook his head again. "Family is the most important thing to her. I have nothing to offer her. I have no family."

Sadie's eyebrows came together in a scowl. "That's a crock. You're Crew. You have a family. Me. Josh. Wyatt. Jules. Mickie. Molly. Malik. Eric. We aren't your family?"

"Yeah, but you know what I mean."

"You're full of shit. Family of choice is the strongest bond there is. Blood family is happenstance. You get born into one. Maybe it's a good one. Maybe it's not. But the family you chose because they love you, they believe in you, they support you? That's a bond that will never break." She stood up and pointed a finger at him. "You better remember that."

He felt completely chastised. He'd taken the love she and the Crew had given him and treated it like nothing. "Wait," he said, scrambling to his feet to catch her at the door. "I'm sorry. You're right."

She smacked him on the arm. "I thought we settled this issue. I am always right. Always."

He wrapped his arms around her. "Of course you are. I don't know why I ever doubt you. Except that dude you're marrying."

She pushed him back. "What are you saying about Wyatt?"

"He's kind of that suburban dad type, don't you think? White bread. Like at forty, he's going to give it all up and blimp out like the Pillsbury Doughboy? Go full dad bod?"

"You are uninvited to my wedding. Take all that back."

He laughed. "I take it all back. Wyatt is a good guy. I love how happy he's made you."

She pointed at him. "Wyatt and I had some serious hurdles to get over before we could be together. Maybe you should think about whether you and Tiana can get over your hurdles."

"Yeah, yeah. I hear you." He spoke the words lightly enough, but they had hit him hard.

"What do you have to lose?"

"Sadie. Enough. I can't fix every aspect of my life in one day. Let me get through this first."

"Fair enough. But promise me you won't rule it out."

He held up his right hand. "I promise."

After she left, he went to the kitchen and began rummaging around. He'd skipped lunch but wasn't really hungry. In the freezer, he found a Tupperware dish with lasagna in it. That reminded him of Tiana. "Give it up," he muttered as he popped the lid and tossed it in the microwave. *Damn it, Sadie.*

Because the peace was gone. It had been the situation with his mother buzzing his head like a mosquito. Now all he could see was Tiana's face. Nowhere in this apartment was safe from memories of her. He'd pushed her away. Told her to go. What was he going to do now? Go crawling back? Beg for forgiveness like his mother had begged him? He shook his head. Tiana would send him packing. And he'd deserve it.

Putting the reheated lasagna on a plate—he wasn't a savage—he sat at the dining room table. While waiting for it to cool, he noticed the dog fur on his pants leg. Jack was a good dog. He'd seemed to sense the need for support. Maybe he should get a dog. Or a cat. Cats didn't need to be walked. Cats didn't care if you were gone all day as long as you left enough food out. Maybe if he had a pet, he wouldn't feel so alone here.

"What you need to do," he said out loud. "Is to stop wallowing around. Eat your food. Go outside and do something."

Like get a suit for Sadie's wedding. He had jackets and pants, but no real suit. A black suit. The invitations had been specific on the dress code. Black suits with red or white shirts and/or ties. Black or red dresses for women. He had no idea why. After eating, he rinsed the dishes and put them in the dishwasher. Maybe he should head out to the mall. See what Dillard's had in the way of suits.

He gave the lasagna another test. It had cooled just enough for him to dare stabbing the tines of the fork down into the layers, spinning a string of cheese around until it broke away. It was so good, almost decadent in its saucy, cheesy deliciousness and it made him happy in the moment.

After eating, he rinsed the dishes and put them in the dishwasher. Maybe he should head out to the mall. If he was lucky, maybe he could find a nice Ralph Lauren or Hart Schaffner Marx at Dillard's. Weren't they running one of their famous 30 percent off deals right now? That'd kick the happiness of the moment up another notch. And if not, well, he was doing okay.

Doing okay other than all the *what if*, that was.

What if. It kept running through his mind. What if he told her everything?

Too much. *Let's just go get that suit,* he decided.

"HMM. I'M THINKING more like a 42R."

DeShawn looked up. He'd found a nice section of suits in the men's department at Dillard's—and hey, hey, they were having a sale after all, how great was that?—and was browsing through the selection when she walked up. She had her thumb on her jaw, index finger pressed to her lips, appraising him. "What's that?" DeShawn asked.

"Definitely 42R," she said, decisively. She extended an arm to her left. "Which means maybe over here."

"Oh," he said. The section he was in was marked 40. So close! "Okay, we can try that."

She lifted a fine looking specimen off of the rack. It was black, but not just a flat black, it had a little something else threaded through it, giving it a touch of texture. The words *warp* and *weft* ran through DeShawn's mind, but he left them there. It was a really nice suit. He accepted the jacket from the salesperson and shrugged it on. It fit him perfectly.

"Mm-hmm," she said. "Told you so."

He looked at himself in the triple mirrors and…yeah. This suited him, this look. He could see himself wearing this. He added a black shirt and red tie to the mix. Looking at his reflection in the mirrors, he thought, *Not bad. Not bad at all,* and told her, "I'll take it."

Perfect," she said, handing him the matching pants. "Let's get these right and we'll have you ready to go."

He slipped the pants on in the changing room, pulled the unfinished ends up over his shoes, and walked back out.

"I'm Tammy, by the way," she said, between the pins she held in her lips as she rolled up the bottoms of his pants legs and measured them out. "How do you like them hemmed?"

DeShawn watched a worried expression cross his own reflection. "You know, I've mostly been a jeans and T-shirt kind of guy… until now. What do you recommend?"

"Nothing wrong with a classic half break," she said and adjusted one cuff as an example.

He took a look at the bottom of the pants in

the mirror. "Good choice, I like that," he said. "Make it so."

She had the pins in on both sides within a few seconds. A few minor adjustments to the jacket later, they were at the register and he was the proud owner of a great looking new suit. Well, at least of an alterations ticket that promised the suit to him within a few days. He was good with that. He was happy with the relief it gave him to have made the decision to get it done and do it.

But as soon as he was back in his car, it started again. *What if?*

"Okay, dude," he said out loud, looking at himself in the rearview mirror. "Are you going to do this? Or just torture yourself with it?"

CHAPTER EIGHTEEN

"So WHERE ARE all these girls going to sleep?" Viv asked in a skeptical tone.

"In my bed. I'll sleep on the couch. It's going to be fine, Mom."

Kasey and Jordan were coming over for dinner with their daughters. Then the girls were having a sleepover here. So they could get used to her place. So her mother could meet everyone and stop acting like she was letting random strangers take care of her baby.

They'd chosen this night, Sunday, because the girls wouldn't have been in school all day, but having school the next morning would give Tiana practice getting all three of them there.

She turned back to the meatballs she was rolling. Spaghetti with meatballs and garlic bread. Seemed like a kid-friendly kind of meal. "I don't know. You sure you can take care of two extra girls? Get them all up and to school on time?"

Clenching her teeth, she drew in a slow

breath. Then threw a fake smile at her mother. "I guess we'll find out tomorrow." She turned the heat on under the pot and began chopping sweet onions.

"Okay. But you better not add too many onions to that sauce. Little girls can be picky eaters you know."

"Okay, Mom."

"You got a backup meal in case one of them won't eat this?"

"Yes, Mom."

"I like s'getti!" Lily said. "Can I help?"

"Thank you, Lily. In a minute, I'll need to stir the sauce once I get it going, okay?"

She resisted sticking her tongue out at her mother. Barely. She was nervous enough without a professional childcare expert standing around judging her every move.

Half an hour later, her nerves were forgotten when Kasey and Jordan showed up with their girls. Ear-shattering noise erupted as Lily, Claire and Shay ran off to play in her room.

"Lordy, it sounds worse in here," Tiana said as she hugged Kasey.

"Girl. You should hear it when they are in my den with the ten-foot ceilings. Echoes for days," Kasey said.

"Y'all. This is my mother, Vivian Nelson.

Mom, this is Kasey, the brilliant and wonderful preceptor you've heard so much about. And this is Jordan, the brave nurse who threw herself between me and an arrogant medical student and saved my career."

"Pleasure to meet you both," Viv said. Her tone was a bit icy.

"Ugh. Medical students. They're the worst," Jordan said.

"Nope. The worst would be the baby docs," Kasey replied.

They both groaned. "Baby docs?" Tiana asked.

"First of July. The brand-new baby doctors start their residencies. It's our job to not let them kill anyone while not puncturing their egos."

Kasey stepped forward. "Let's not talk shop around your mother. I'm sure it's very boring for her." She turned to Vivian. "I just wanted to tell you what an amazing job you did with Tiana. She is so smart and such an amazing nurse already. Compassionate. No-nonsense when she has to be."

The ice thawed a bit. "Well, thank you. She was a project."

Tiana waved a hand toward the living room. "Go sit down. Dinner is almost ready."

DINNER WAS A huge success with all three girls asking for seconds. Tiana tried not to smirk as she and her mother cleared the table.

"I saw that," Viv murmured.

"Saw what?"

"That look. Don't get a big head just yet."

"Hey!" Kasey said as she plopped down on a barstool at the counter that separated the kitchen from the living room. "I've got a great idea. Jordan and I should take your mom out for a drink and a movie. Let you do this solo."

"My mother doesn't drink."

"Oh, I'd have a glass of wine," Viv said.

Panic began to nibble at her guts. Tiana turned to Kasey. "Well, if you think that would be best."

"Sounds like a plan!" Jordan said. She scrolled through her phone. "I've been wanting to see this movie and my husband refuses to go with me because he says it's a chick flick. And it's playing at the Citadel Mall, so we'll be just down the road."

She handed her phone to Mom, who put her reading glasses on to see. "Oh, yes. I've heard wonderful things about this movie."

"Awesome! Hey, Claire, Shay, come here."

All three girls came reluctantly out of Lily's bedroom. "We're going to take Ms. Vivian out to a movie," Kasey said. "Ms. Tiana will get you ready for bed and I will see you after school tomorrow. Okay?"

"Okay. Can we go back and play now?"

The two women hugged and kissed their daughters while Viv got her coat. Tiana could not believe this. They were all going? All of them? Leave her alone with three kids?

"You think they'll be okay?" Viv asked Jordan.

"Yeah. They've been spending nights at each other's houses since they were babies. This is normal for them. They love it. Makes them feel like they have a sister. Now with Lily, they'll each have two sisters."

"Okay then." Viv shrugged on her coat and kissed Tiana on the cheek. "Have fun now, you hear?"

And they left. Just like that. Out the door. *Since when does my mother drink wine?* She closed her open mouth and returned to the kitchen. *This was nothing. Easy. You made it through nursing school. You can handle gunshot victims without breaking a sweat. Three little girls? Piece of cake. Get the bubble bath going, toss all three of them in the tub. Pajamas. Story time. Lights-out.*

She made a face as she thought of Mom,

Kasey and Jordan in the movie theater. *All three of them are going to be staring at their phones, waiting for me to call for help. That ain't going to happen.* She finished rinsing the dishes and loading the dishwasher listening to the happy chatter of the girls. This really was good for Lily. To have friends.

She went down the hall to peek in on them. They were playing some sort of very involved game with Lily's stuffed animals.

"You guys doing okay? Need anything?"

"We're playing, Momma."

"Okay. You play."

Back on the couch she flicked on the TV, decided on something child appropriate to watch and kicked back. An hour to bath time. When that was done, it'd be bedtime. She was worrying for nothing.

Until bath time came. Oh, the girls were all in for a group bubble bath in the giant garden tub. What she had underestimated was how much water three giddy, splashing girls could displace. Her bathroom looked like a pipe had burst. She gave up on towels and threw a blanket on the floor. Then there was the accidental flinging of soap into the eyes. She was surprised none of the neighbors called the police because it sounded like people were being murdered in here.

She carried the towels and blanket to the laundry closet—right next to the bathroom, so she could keep an eye on the girls—and tossed them in the washer. *At least the bathroom floor doesn't need to be mopped anytime soon.* Glancing at the clock, she shook her head. She had to have those girls into their pajamas and in bed, preferably asleep before her mother, Kasey and Jordan returned. She had about forty-five minutes. Anything less would be failure.

Returning to the bathroom she clapped her hands. "Show me your fingers!" They all held their fingers up. "Look at all those wrinkly fingertips. You're waterlogged. Come on, everyone out." She handed them clean towels as she helped them out.

Then came Pajamagate. Shay wanted to wear Lily's Hello Kitty pajamas but Lily wanted to wear them. Then Claire wanted to wear Shay's Minnie Mouse pajamas if Shay got to wear the Hello Kitty ones. She was about to send them all to bed in their underwear when she remembered her own Hello Kitty T-shirt. That was perfect. Until both Shay *and* Lily wanted to wear it.

After settling that dispute, she felt as if she was qualified for a diplomatic position anywhere in the world. But finally, at long last, she got them settled. All three of them in her bed.

She heard the key in the lock as she was coming down the hall and sprinted to throw herself on the couch. Feet up, remote in hand. *Look bored.*

Her mother peeked in and she waved. Put a finger to her lips as Kasey and Jordan followed her inside.

"How'd it go?" Kasey asked.

"Fine. Not a problem."

Jordan snorted out a quiet laugh. "Liar."

"Okay. Everyone is alive and asleep. How that came to be will be between just me and God."

"Only answer that counts," Kasey said. "Okay. Call us if anyone freaks out about being in a different house. Vivian, it was so nice to meet you. We're going to have to go out drinking again. Tee, your mother is wicked funny."

Looking between the three women, Tiana shook her head. "I'm too tired for this. Screaming girls. Drinking mommas. I can't even. Y'all go home."

After they left, Viv came and sat beside her. "Your friends are very nice."

"Thank you. I kind of like them."

"You were right, Tiana."

She sat up. "Wait. Hold on. Where's my phone? Can I get this on video?"

"Oh, hush up with yourself. I can admit it. You were right. Lily's got two great friends there. And you've got a good support system with their mothers."

Tiana scooted over and put her arms around her mother. "Thank you, Momma. This is all going to work out."

"You've done very well. I'm proud of you. I'm sorry I've been sniping at you."

"I understand. You love Lily. It's hard to let go. I get it."

"But it's time that I let you take over."

"Getting there. Like I said, we can take it slow."

"You're the boss now. You tell me."

"I'll tell you this. This boss is exhausted."

"I can take a hint. Good night, Tee."

"Night, Momma."

She snuggled back under the blanket she'd thrown on the back of the couch. A warm sense of pride glowed in her chest. She'd done it. Convinced her mother that it was safe to go home. She turned off the TV and squirmed around until she was comfortable. She *was* exhausted. But her eyes stayed open and she stared at the ceiling. She'd left the hallway light on in case one of the girls got up and was confused in an unfamiliar house. She had everything she wanted now.

Except DeShawn.

TUESDAY AFTER MEETING with his mother, he was pretty much settled. Sadie had been right. The feeling of peace he'd felt the afternoon after hadn't lasted. It came in waves: the doubt, the anger, the guilt. But it didn't stay. And he always felt in the end that he'd done the right thing.

Good thing because he had Henry bringing two students to spend the day with him. He was looking forward to it and a bit worried. How to make engineering exciting to a couple of twelve-year-olds? He'd gone out to the project site early that morning and was just finishing up entering the data when Henry arrived.

"Come on in," he said as he waved them into his little cubbyhole.

"DeShawn, this is Darius and Abigail. They are both honors math students. We're looking into STEM programs for them," Henry said.

"Great. Okay. I thought I'd take you around to a couple of the different projects our office is working on. Give you an idea of how varied engineering jobs can be. Sound good?"

They started at his project. The interstate exchange. As they stood on the road the current overpass lead to, DeShawn explained about the new railway that was going in and how this interchange would need to be moved.

"So, my job is to figure out where to put the new road. The safest place for it. The place that will minimize the number of houses and businesses that will have to be relocated or torn down."

"What happens to the people who live in the houses?" Abigail asked.

"Their houses are bought and they are helped to move somewhere else."

"Oh, okay."

He tried to paint a happy picture of it, but the truth was, relocation was the part he hated most about his job. The elderly people who lived along the proposed route would come out and ask him, "It isn't coming through here is it?" And the only answer he could give was that he was looking for the best way to keep as many people in their homes as possible.

"For right now, my job is mostly doing measurements and mapping out buildings in the area. Once that is done, I'll start drawing up proposed routes for the new road."

"Do you build the road too?" Darius asked.

"Nope. Once a design has been approved, it's turned over to the Department of Transportation to build."

As they got back in the car, DeShawn turned and looked at them. "I think you'll like this next one. They're moving an old building brick by brick and putting it back together in a new place."

It was a short drive to the old navy base where the moving of the Sea Chapel was well underway. "It's an historical building, so no one wanted to just tear it down. But it was also pretty unstable, so to move it in one piece might have caused it to collapse. So the engineers on this project had to figure out how to take it down without it collapsing."

"Like that game Jenga?" Darius asked.

"Exactly," DeShawn answered. He looked over and saw Alex, the lead engineer. Waved him over. "Hey, man, how's it going?"

"Good. Almost done. The more we take down, the slower we have to go."

"This is Henry Gardner and two of his honors math students, Darius and Abigail. I'm giving them a look into a day in the life of an engineer. Anything you can show them?"

"Sure. Perfect timing. We're doing tests on a load-bearing wall right now, trying to decide the best way to start dismantling it. Come on, kids."

DeShawn leaned against the side of the car as Alex led the kids into the construction site. He stopped at the entrance and got them each a hard hat. Abigail turned and grinned at Henry when the hat was set on her head.

"Oh, that made this whole trip worthwhile," Henry said.

"Right? Hold up. Let me check on something," DeShawn said. He pulled his phone out of his pocket and scrolled through his contacts. Hit Dial. After a moment, Sharon picked up. "Hey, Sharon, it's DeShawn. Are you still out at the Folly dock site…? Yeah? Cool. I'm showing a couple of STEM students around and one of them is a girl and… Yeah… Yeah… Perfect. See you in about an hour?"

An hour later, they were pulling up to a site along the Folly River. A restaurant was wanting to expand its dock and Sharon was doing the environmental impact study. As they got out of the car, she spotted them and walked over.

"Sharon," DeShawn said. "This is Abigail

and Darius. They are the students I'm showing around. Do you have time to tell them a little about what you're doing out here and why?"

Both the kids stared up at Sharon. She put her hands on her hips and grinned down at them. "Yes. I'm a real black girl engineer. We exist." She motioned at the dock. "Come on. I'm sure DeShawn has been boring you with measurements and such. I'll show you some real fun stuff engineers get to do."

Henry smacked DeShawn on the arm. "That's perfect. Just what Abigail needed to see."

"I was going to bring them here first, but Sharon is going to hang on to them for a while."

"That's fine. I'm going to wander down there and listen in. Learn something I can use in class."

DeShawn waved him on. "Of course. I've got my laptop. I can get some work done."

Almost an hour later, they came back to the car, babbling excitedly. "This was the best field trip I've ever been on," Darius said.

He looked at the two of them. Their eyes were bright, they were laughing and, most of all, they'd glimpsed a world that they now knew was in their reach. "I'm glad," he said. "Now, I'm starving. Who wants lunch?"

AFTER HE'D GOTTEN Henry and the kids back on the road home, he finished up his day with a sense of accomplishment he'd not felt in a while. Not since…working with Tiana on this project. He tossed some leftovers in the oven and went to change. He wanted to talk to her. He wanted to call her and tell her all about today. About Abigail's face when she saw a black woman engineer. She would be ecstatic. The good feelings from the day drained away.

Forgoing the plate this time, he sat on the couch and ate the food straight out of the plastic container. *This just sucks. Finally got my life together and I lost the best part of it.* Then it came back. The what-if. He'd sent her away. She hadn't wanted to go. He'd seen that in her eyes. What if he called her? *What if she tells you to get lost?*

DESHAWN ROLLED OUT of bed Saturday morning and grabbed his phone. Nine. *Nine on a Saturday morning isn't too early, is it?* Maybe. He shuffled to the kitchen to start a pot of coffee and went to shower while it was brewing. After he'd dressed and had a cup, he pulled up his contact list.

He'd made a mistake. Now he had to see if

he could fix it. If not, he could move on. But he couldn't just give up on Tiana.

"Hey, Molly. It's DeShawn. It's not too early is it?"

"Of course not. I'm an old lady. I get up at the crack of dawn whether I want to or not. What do you need? A kitten?"

He laughed. "Actually. Yes. I need a couple of kittens. Three or four kittens."

"Have you lost your mind?"

"No. Yes. Maybe."

"Come on over. Have you had breakfast?"

"I had coffee."

She tsk-tsked him. "I'll make you French toast. And we'll talk about why you've gone insane."

Twenty minutes later, she was letting him in. Her house smelled like cinnamon and butter and all sorts of good things. The kittens were splayed out on the couch, chairs, the rug, everywhere. A sea of tiny furry islands.

"Nice to see you," Molly said as she headed back to the kitchen. "Don't close the door on anyone and don't let any of them out. These creatures are becoming troublesome."

"Troublesome?" He followed her to the kitchen after carefully shutting the door.

"Have you ever had fourteen six-to-nine-week-old kittens in one place? It's constant chaos."

He sat at her kitchen table with a grin. "I think you like constant chaos, Molly. Why else would you put up with all of us Crew guys?"

She flapped a hand at him. "Y'all were easy compared to these little terrorists." She crossed the room to put a plate of French toast in front of him. "Butter, syrup. It's maple but I might have some blueberry syrup somewhere."

"This is perfect. Thank you."

After she brought her own plate to the table, she gave him her stern grandmother glare. "What do you need four kittens for?"

"Maybe three. There's this woman I know…"

"The woman you were supposed to bring over to look at kittens and never showed up and never called and I had to find out from Sadie what happened?"

He felt his face go hot. He had forgotten to call Molly. "I'm sorry. Yes."

"I understand. So, you're going to take some kittens for her to see?"

"Yes."

"Why not bring her here? She can see all of them."

"Well, it might be more than just that."

"Are you using my kittens as a lure to try to win her heart back?"

"Sadie talks way too much."

Molly got up to pour some coffee. "How do you like it?"

"Black is fine. Has Sadie been sharing my business with the whole Crew?"

"No. Just me. Are you going to talk to her? Tiana? Is that her name?"

"Yes. She'll probably take a kitten and kick me to the curb, but…"

Molly smiled and reached over to pat his hand. "It'll work out, DeShawn. You're a good man. If she's a good woman, she'll see that."

"I'm going to need your fluffiest, most-likely-to-make-a-little-girl's-heart-melt kittens."

Molly sopped a piece of toast through the syrup on her plate and popped it in her mouth. She nodded as she chewed and swallowed. "How old?"

"Six."

Nodding again, Molly ate more toast. He tried to eat more, but his stomach was in knots. His heart was racing. What exactly was he doing? Did he really think this was going to work? "Eat!"

"I'm trying. I'm nervous."

"Okay," Molly said, getting to her feet. "I'm going to assume you don't have a carrier."

"A what?"

Molly made the sign of the cross. "Dear Jesus, protect my innocent kittens."

"I will keep them alive. I promise."

Molly got a cat carrier from a back room and returned to the living room. "A six-year-old girl. We'll need a very easygoing kitten who likes to be picked up and cuddled. Something fluffy and cute."

"How do we tell?"

"Pick one up."

"Who, me?"

"Yes. They know me."

DeShawn looked around the room. "That orange one looks fluffy." He crossed to the chair and picked it up. The kitten stretched and turned into butter in his hand. He had to catch it with his other hand and cradled it against his chest.

"That's a contender," Molly said, taking the kitten from him and putting it in the carrier. "Oh, wait. I think this guy will be a good choice."

She picked up a kitten from the couch. It was solid white except for its tail, which was a fluffy gray plume. It lifted its head and yawned. DeShawn noticed a gray patch over each eye. "He's certainly unusually marked."

Molly flipped the kitten over. "Yep. It's a him." She put him in the carrier. "One more."

He picked up a little striped cat who arched back and bit his thumb. "That's a no."

"There's your friend Smokey," Molly said.

He turned to see her holding up the gray cat with the bright green eyes. He reached out and the kitten meowed. "Give him to me." The kitten snuggled up against his throat and purred. "Is he like this with everyone or just me?"

"I'd imagine everyone. You aren't exactly the cat-cuddling type."

"Gee, thanks. Okay put him in."

"You'll bring them back to me today? They need to eat. I'll give you some food. And a disposable litter box."

Thirty minutes later, he was pulling out of the driveway with Molly still shouting advice at him. He was doubting his plan at this point. Taking care of kittens for the day seemed more work than taking care of a real human child.

Once he was back in his apartment and the kittens had been set free, he realized the flaw in his plan. He had no idea if Tiana was working or sleeping or what. He might be taking the kittens right on back to Molly, which he suspected she might be relieved about if it happened. He sat on the couch while the kittens hesitantly left the comfort of the carrier and began venturing out into the new environment. The little gray one found him, climbed up the couch and up on his shoulder.

"What do you think, little guy? Is this going to work out?"

He pulled up Tiana's contact information again and stared at it. This definitely wasn't the time for a text. He had to call. His heart rate amped up a bit. *What if she just hangs up? Refuses to even listen to me?* He gathered his courage. Hit the Call button.

CHAPTER NINETEEN

TIANA PICKED UP her phone. It was actually ringing. This could not be good news. The only phone calls she got were from Lily's school or the hospital wanting her to work extra. She'd had a shift until three last night, so that wasn't going to happen. The phone kept ringing.

She froze. *DeShawn.* She stared at the phone until it stopped ringing. Sitting up, she wiped a hand across her eyes. Was she seeing things? Pinched herself. Was she dreaming? The phone buzzed in her hand. New voice message. It slipped through her fingers and fell on the bedspread. Why was he calling her? What could he have to say? Hope, that nasty, evil, lying bitch, soared in her heart. *Stop it.*

She scooped up the phone and burrowed back down into the blankets. Last thing she needed was her mother to realize she was awake. She needed time to think. Did she even want to hear what he had to say?

"Is Mommy going with us?" Lily asked loudly at her bedroom door.

"No, honey, she worked late last night. She's sleeping. She'll be awake by the time we get home from the grocery store."

Perfect. Grocery day. That could take a couple of hours. Once the front door had closed and she heard the lock turn, she waited for ten minutes in case they'd forgotten anything. But she was alone. Alone with a message from DeShawn. She sat back up and hit the voice mail button.

"Hey. It's me. I'm sorry about the other day. I have some kittens if you're still interested for Lily. I'd like to talk to you. Call me. Or text."

Frowning, she plopped against the pillows and let the phone fall on the bed. *Kittens? He has kittens?* "What the hell does that even mean?" she asked the empty room.

He wants to talk. Suddenly, she was back to the pain and heartache of him telling her to go away. The fear of that scene. She knew he'd been surprised by his mother. But the way he got aggressive with her? Going into that dominant posturing? The dent his fist left in the car? *What could he say about that? Do you want to hear it?* She didn't know what to do. Throwing the covers back, she climbed out of the bed. In the kitchen, she found a pot of coffee ready to go on the percolator, compliments of her mother. She pushed the on button and went to plop down on the couch.

"Do you want to hear him out?" she asked out loud. Hope said yes. Fear said no. *Do you want to walk away from him without giving him a chance?* The answer to that was no.

She brought up her phone log and hit return call before she could think about it too much. "Hey," she said when he answered.

"Hey. Thank you."

"For?"

"Calling back. I didn't know what your schedule was today. Can we talk?"

"You have kittens?"

"Yes. Three. Handpicked to be good pets for a little girl."

Okay, that melted her heart a little bit. "Is everything okay?"

His voice dropped. "A lot has happened, Tee. I need to talk to you. Please."

"Give me an hour."

An hour later, she was showered and dressed and sitting in her car outside his apartment, her insides a quivering mess of hope and practicality. She hadn't realized how much she missed him until this moment. But who had she been missing? The man she'd come to know? Or was there another DeShawn in there? Angry? Violent? Gathering her courage, she pulled the key from the ignition and got out of the car.

He opened his front door before she knocked and pulled her inside. "Careful. Molly will kill me if anything happens to them."

She looked around. There were three kittens snuggled sleepily together on his couch. Turning her gaze back to him, she reached out and took his hand. "Are you okay? That thing with your mother. That was terrible. I've been worried about you."

He tried for a smile. "Always thinking about other people, Tee. Yes. I'm okay."

She kept hold of his hand. She wanted to pull him into her arms but didn't quite dare. He'd sent her away once before. She wasn't sure she should be here at all.

He let her hand go and ran a hand over his hair. "Can we talk?"

"That's what I'm here for."

He moved the pile of kittens to the armchair and waved his arm at the couch. Crossing the room, she sat down and turned to face him as he sat. "Tell me."

"You saw what happened. The background. My parents were...are drug addicts. Heroin.

Meth. Doesn't matter. I was very neglected as a baby. My grandmother took me in. Raised me."

"I know all this. What changed?"

"My mother called me. Weeks ago. Said she was clean and sober. Wanted to meet with me. Do some amends things. And I stalled her. I didn't know if I wanted to do it or not."

"Those were all the 'telemarketer' you kept getting?"

"Yes. I should have told you about this. I was embarrassed. I wanted it to just go away."

"Why?"

"Because I don't want her to be in my life. I've broken away from all that dysfunction. I've created this new life. But I'm not a monster. If it would help her to stay clean, I was willing. But I didn't want her to think it was an invitation back into my life. There was too much damage."

Her heart hurt at these words. That a mother could so alienate a child. What must he have gone through? She reached out and took his hand.

"I was communicating through her sponsor. I told them not yet. That I needed time. That I would get back to them when I made a decision."

"And," she whispered, "your mother took it as a rejection. The addict showed up."

"Exactly," he said. "It was a complete ambush. I reacted poorly. I'm sorry you saw that. That was the hurt child in me screaming at her."

She nodded. She could see this. He'd clawed his way out of a situation that had been worse than hers, she realized now. Walked away. Thought he was free and clear and then was blindsided. She knew enough about the behaviors of addicts and the cycle of codependency to understand why he'd reacted the way he did.

But.

"I understand all this," she said quietly. "Except the violence. The way you went after her. The car."

He lowered his head. "I know. I'm sorry. But she noticed Lily and I just…don't know. It was extremely wrong, but I wanted to get her away from Lily as fast as possible."

Tiana let go of his hand. She replayed the scene in her mind. He was right. His mother had just said "You got a woman and a kid" when DeShawn got aggressive.

"I know this sounds like self-serving crap that men say because I've heard it in my own family too many times, but I'm not a violent person. I'd never hurt you or Lily. And I'd understand if you told me you don't believe me."

"What's changed? Between then and now, DeShawn? What's changed? Why am I here?"

He looked to the pile of sleeping kittens. "I met with her again."

"You what?"

She was stunned. After that horrible scene? He'd reached out to her? Met with her?

"Yes. I arranged it through her sponsor. I wanted to say what I needed to say and make it a clean break. She and I had our say. She's not coming back. I hope she does well and lives out a happy, drug-free life, but she can't be a part of mine."

"Is that what you want?"

He turned his gaze to her and the sorrow she saw there nearly broke her heart. "It's what I need. Whether she means it or not, she's poison to me. She accused me of being selfish." He paused there, looked down, shook his head side to side. When he brought his head back up, his hands were pressed together as if in prayer, thumbs under his chin, index fingers against his lips. "Yeah," he said, nodding, dropping his hands down to his thighs. "Okay. Maybe. But, you know what? I'm trying. I'm trying to build something better. A good life. And I refuse to be taken down to an addict's level."

"DeShawn," she whispered. Her lips were pressed tight, eyes shut. She patted her cheeks twice with the tops of her fingertips as words raced through her mind. Fast words, wrong words, words she was lining out and revising as soon as they formed. Finally, she whisked all words away, reached over to him and pulled him into her arms.

"I love you, Tiana," he whispered in her ear. "I want to be a part of your life. I don't know how to fix this."

Tears stung at her eyes. She hugged him tighter. "I don't either."

"Do you love me?"

She hesitated. She did. But Lily. She pulled back and put her hands against his cheeks and looked into his eyes. "I do. I do love you."

"But?"

"There shouldn't be a *but*. I understand everything you've told me."

"The nurse in you understands," he said, his smile measured and his eyes unwavering, watching her reaction calmly and carefully. "The mother in you isn't sure."

She sat back. Held up a hand. "Give me a minute. I have to think."

She watched the kittens as they stretched and climbed over each other in constant motion. Paws padding the air, thin slivers of claw popping out and retracting. Rolling over, showing their bellies, nuzzling into one another, neck to neck. Seeking comfort, seeking warmth.

Kasey had told her to not use Lily as an excuse to cut and run. She had a second chance here. But the *love* word had been spoken. And she did love this man. She loved that he was sitting there. Quiet. Letting her figure this out. He never pressured her. He instinctively put Lily first also. Until this thing with his mother, she'd thought him perfect. But now, his outburst had been spurred by his seeing a threat to Lily. She wasn't sure how she felt about it.

"I need to tell you something," she said.

"Tell me."

She turned to him. "I'd known Lily's father all my life. Small town. You know everyone. He was a good kid. Tried to do right. Hoped for a football scholarship because that was what he loved. But he was a small-town kid, playing in a small-town league. He never could accept the fact that he wasn't good enough for college level."

He took her hand and it felt so good. She

closed her fingers around his. "Sounds like the athletic equivalent to our academic shock."

"But we coped. We adapted. We worked harder."

"He didn't?"

"No. He dropped out of Lily's life when she was three. Remember? We had this conversation. She was old enough to know her daddy didn't come around anymore. It hurt her, De-Shawn."

"And you can't risk it again. I understand. I'm not asking for full acceptance here, Tee. I just wanted to tell you everything. So you can decide. I love you. I want us to continue. But it's your decision."

She shook her head. "No. You're not getting it."

"Getting what?"

"I'm not that same girl anymore. I know what it's like to have to turn your back on someone you once loved so you can be the person you want to be. I know the strength and courage it takes to do that."

He looked down at his hands. "It's not a choice I wanted to make."

"But you made a choice. You chose a life free of substance abuse. You chose yourself. You chose to hope."

She leaned forward and kissed him. His hands—lightly at first, fingertips just brushing—moved from her shoulders down the length of her arms as he returned the kiss. Their hands met at the bottom, locking tight. Hot and desperate and hopeful. He turned his head, pressing his cheek against hers. "Thank you," he said.

"For what?"

"Understanding. I love you, Tiana. I want to be a part of your life. You. Lily. Your mother. All of you. I love you."

She sat back and looked at him. Looked at the kittens. "Pack them up."

"What?"

"Come on. Pack them up. You're coming to my house. Let Lily pick out a kitten."

"Are you sure?"

"One hundred percent. But I'm leaving you in charge of the whole toilet-training thing." She stared straight ahead just for a beat, then shook her head, smiling.

AS HE FOLLOWED Tiana up the stairs to her apartment, carrier full of mewing kittens dangling from his hand, DeShawn felt more nervous now that he had when he'd made the phone call that morning. He couldn't mess this up.

"Hey, Mom? Lily?" Tiana called out as she opened the door. "I have a surprise."

She turned to wave him through the door. Heart thumping, he stepped over the threshold. Lily popped up from the large comfortable-looking couch. "Mr. DeShawn!"

Vivian came down the hallway. She gave him a long, appraising look then tilted her head to toward the carrier in his hand. "What do you have there?"

Lily let out a squeal. "Kittens! You brought me kittens!"

Laughing, he crossed to the living room and set the carrier down on the rug. "Just one, Lily," Tiana said as she joined him. "He brought a couple for you to choose from."

Lily threw her arms around Tiana's waist and squeezed. "Thank you, Mommy!"

"Okay," DeShawn said as he sat down on the floor. He motioned at Lily to come sit with him. "Let's see what we have here."

"I'll get some supper started," Viv said. "De-Shawn, will you be staying for supper?"

He looked over at Tiana. "Will I?"

Her smile warmed him to his core. "Of course you will."

He returned the smile and felt something deep down within him relax. It was going to be okay. "All right, Miss Lily. These three kittens were handpicked by a friend of mine to be the best kittens for you."

"Yay!" she said, clapping her hands. Her smile was like Christmas morning and he found himself grinning with her.

"First, we have this little orange kitten. I remembered you wanted a fluffy, striped orange one." He took the biggest of the kittens out. "She is going to be a little fluffy when she grows up."

He set the kitten down in Lily's waiting hands. She handled it carefully. "She's so pretty. Don't you think she's pretty, Momma?"

Tiana sat on the edge of the couch. "Very pretty, Lils."

"Next, we have this little boy kitten. My friend says he is very lazy and snuggly and just wants to be petted."

"He's got a gray tail and spots!" Lily exclaimed as she put down the orange kitten and took the white one from him.

"Very unusual-looking cat, isn't he?" De-Shawn agreed as he took out the last kitten. The little gray one with the mint-green eyes. "Now this guy. He's also a cuddly cat. Loves to sit on you and purr."

"Oh, look at those gorgeous eyes," Tiana said. "Let me hold him, Lily."

Lily carried the kitten to the couch. "How am I going to pick, Mommy?"

"Play with them for a little while. One will pick you," DeShawn said. "That's what my friend believes."

He moved to the couch to sit beside Tiana while Lily crawled around on the floor with the kittens. Viv brought them two glasses of sweet tea. "Thank you, Mrs. Nelson," he said.

She held on to the glass for a beat as she handed it to him and he looked up into her eyes. "You are welcome, DeShawn."

A lump rose in his throat. The emphasis she'd put on the words. He was welcome here. Tiana smiled and touched his hand.

A giggly squeal rose from the floor. The gray kitten was standing on Lily's back, sniffing at her ear. "The purring is tickling me," she said, reaching back to pick the kitten up. "You are a purr bug." The kitten sat calmly in her palms and he could hear the purring from where he sat on the couch.

"I think he picked you," Tiana said.

Lily titled her head. "Did you? Do you want to live here?"

The kitten squeaked out a meow and they

all laughed. "I think that's a yes," DeShawn said. Secretly pleased that she'd chosen the little gray.

"Okay then," Tiana said. "We've got a kitten."

Lily looked solemnly up at her mother. "Thank you very much. I will take good care of him."

Tiana stood. "I know you will, Lily. Hey, Mom? About when will supper be ready? DeShawn has to return the other kittens and I'll need to run out and get some supplies."

Viv waved a hand. "About an hour. I want to see you both back on time."

Draping his arm on Tiana's shoulders as they walked down the stairs to the parking lot, he gave her a squeeze. "That went well."

"Of course it did. My mother is good people."

He stopped at the bottom of the stairs and took her hand. "We're going to do this?"

"We are. No way you're backing out now."

Pulling her into his arms, he kissed her. "I'm not going anywhere."

A rather loud mewing rose from the two kittens in the carrier. Tiana stepped back. "Get those kittens out of the cold. I'll see you in a bit."

"Wait," he said. "Do you have a black or red dress?"

"What?"

"I've met your family. I'd like you to meet mine. My real family. My family of choice."

CHAPTER TWENTY

April 1

MEET HIS FAMILY. The words came back to her as they walked down King Street, past the hot new restaurants, the marquee lights of the American Theater, and crowds of people out on the town. They'd parked in the garage because, come on, you had better odds of winning at roulette in Vegas than of scoring a parking meter in this part of Charleston.

When DeShawn finally said, "Here we go," and pointed, she drew a breath.

"Whoa," she said. "That's a lot of really old stuccoed brick."

He laughed. "Yeah," he said with a smile, squeezing her hand. "Yeah, I guess it is."

The rest was arches and pediments and the kind of fine architectural detailing that just wasn't made anymore. It couldn't be made like that these days, she thought. Too expen-

sive, even if you could find artisans with the
right skills.

This was old Charleston, moneyed Charleston, the kind of building on King Street that
maybe predated the Civil War, the kind of
building that got the tourists lined up snapping pictures for Facebook and Instagram. Just
standing in front of it made you feel like you
were long away in the distant past. Hm. Yeah,
but, the past meant different things for everyone, didn't it? Still. This was something, this
building, no two ways about that.

A small wedding, he'd said. Tiana looked
up at the building again. This was a high-dollar small wedding. Who were these people,
again? She smoothed down the sides of the red
dress she'd found, suddenly hoping it wasn't
too plain. She felt odd wearing red to a wedding, but she certainly wasn't going to wear
a black dress. Realizing she was nervous, she
looked over at DeShawn.

He smiled and took her hand. "Mickie will
be here."

They stopped at the door and he kissed her
on the cheek. "You really are so beautiful,
Tiana."

She curled her fingers around his tie, pulled
it straight and then smoothed it against him.

As she slowly slid her hands away, she looked at his eyes directly and said, "You clean up pretty well yourself, Man Maid."

"Come on, let's go see if this wedding actually happens."

"Yeah? You have doubts?"

"Hey, it's April first. The theme is Fools For Love. We'll see."

They were greeted by two good-looking guys in black and red. "Uh-oh, the Cleaning Crew royalty is in the house," the first guy said, clapping a hand on DeShawn's arm.

"Ha!" DeShawn said, exchanging a first bump with him.

"Oh. My. Gosh," Tiana said once they were inside. "You weren't kidding!" The room, with its ancient pine flooring and exposed hand-made brick was a veritable carnival. Red, white and black tablecloths. Masquerade masks. The centerpieces at each table were jester's hats complete with jingling bells at the tips of the curls. On the other side of the room, chairs were set out in rows. Everyone in the room was dressed in black, white or red, grouped in small clusters, chatting and catching up.

In the far corner, she could see staff already setting out food. There were several dozen people walking about, greeting one another, laughing and embracing. It wasn't a huge wedding by any means, but one thing she saw immediately: the people who were here really cared about one another.

"Tiana!"

She looked over the small crowd to see Mickie rise up from her chair and wave at them. They made their way to the seats. The two women embraced and DeShawn leaned over to kiss Mickie on the cheek.

"Where's Josh, my fine Miss Mickie?"

"He's giving Sadie away. They should be starting soon. Isn't this the best theme ever?"

Tiana nodded. "It's so fun."

"Lena's mother is quietly freaking out. She's convinced they're going to yell 'April fool' at any moment."

That's when the first notes from the organ signaled to everyone that it was time to take their seats.

The minister came in to stand before the crowd. There were two columns at the front of the room with a backdrop of a medieval castle stretched on the wall.

A hush came over the room as the groom and the best man entered.

"That's Wyatt," Mickie whispered to Tiana. "Isn't he gorgeous?"

He was wearing a black suit with a black-and-red diamond-print tie. Tiana nodded. "Easy on the eyes, for sure."

Again the music spoke to the crowd and everyone turned to look to the back of the room. Coming down the aisle was a beautiful young girl of about nine or ten. The red velvet princess dress perfectly set off her raven-black hair and olive complexion. In her hands, she carried a black-and-white basket with red ribbons tied to the handle. In the basket were the reddest rose petals Tiana had ever seen. The little girl threw them to the floor with such an imperial grace one could think her a real princess.

She reached the front and the groom leaned down to kiss her on the cheek before she moved to her spot. Next down the aisle was the maid of honor. Recognizing Lena from the school project, Tiana leaned close to DeShawn. "Is she related to the flower girl?"

He shook his head and turned to whisper back. "Long story. Later."

As Lena approached the front, there came a wolf whistle from the crowd. Everyone laughed and when she scowled into the audience, several people laughed even harder. "What?" Tiana whispered.

"Lena and Matt," DeShawn said, pointing

to a man near the front. "First man to ever irritate Lena on purpose and live to tell about it."

The music swelled as the "Wedding March" began and the crowd turned with a collective intake of breath. Rose to their feet. After a moment, Josh appeared with the bride. The usual oohs and ahhs rose from the crowd at the sight of the bride. Sadie. DeShawn's former boss. She'd heard about her. A strong, independent, fiery woman. DeShawn hadn't told her how beautiful she was. Her long black curls were the perfect veil for the simple yet elegant gown she wore.

She heard Mickie sniffling beside her and took her hand. She didn't even know the woman and she felt the tears stinging. Some about a wedding. The love and hope in the air. Brought out the romantic in everyone.

Josh escorted Sadie to the front of the room. As she turned to face Wyatt, he lifted his hands and gave her a puzzled look. Placing her hands on her dress, Sadie lifted it enough to show the red-and-black diamond-print stockings she wore.

THE CEREMONY WAS BRIEF, informal. The vows they exchanged were simple words about love and about respecting one another as equal partners in their life together. It told a story of connection and communication, of learning to trust, of learning to try. When Tiana felt the teardrops well in eyes, she didn't even try to conceal it, because everyone—the entire group assembled there—seemed to be wiping at tears, dabbling at tears, letting the tears run freely.

Because this was all of their stories, shared, combined. This was an extended family that had found one another through chance and experience and luck and effort and never, ever giving up.

It was beautiful.

When it finished, everyone moved to the other side of the room, so the reception began immediately. The staff had seemingly swept a perfect reception hall into being while no one was looking.

As Tiana walked hand-in-hand with De-Shawn, a handsome young man with a tray to his shoulder offered both of them puff pastries stuffed with shrimp, crab and sheer deliciousness.

Over on the side of the room where the ceremony had taken place, an elegant young woman in black took just a few formal photographs of the bride and groom. It gave the wedding guests a few minutes to get settled.

There was already a line at the book where guests could write notes and wishes to the newlyweds. The table with the wedding gifts was piled high.

The buffet was nothing short of spectacular. Tiana smiled as she imagined how Lily would have reacted to it: eyes wide, her mouth a wide O of appreciation. She hoped she was having tons of fun on her special Granny-Lily night. She deserved that happiness. Really, they all did.

The buffet was replete with roasted chickens, perfect crisp skins glistening. Mini Thai beef salads portioned out into little dishes, the beef seared and the vinaigrette ginger-lime. Oven-roasted Brussels sprouts, each with a perfect char. Potatoes with garlic, butter and chives. There were mounds of seafood resting in ice, wedges of lemon all around.

And the cake. The cake looked like a showstopper. Elegant lines, many-tiered and true to the theme. The jester motif was so subtly but perfectly there alongside the berries, blossoms and greenery. That cake was made by an artist. As Tiana waited in the line to greet the newly married couple, DeShawn tapped her shoulder and motioned toward Josh and Mickie. The two of them were glowing. Looking at them made her smile. Mickie especially deserved happiness, after all she'd been through, and look, she'd found it at last.

Then it was Tiana's turn to tap and motion. "Oh, that's why he's alive," she said to De-Shawn.

"Who?"

"That guy over there with Lena," she said, nodding. "He could irritate me all day long."

DeShawn laughed and put his arm around her waist. "That's my job now."

"And you're so good at it too."

Then there was Sadie. "DeShawn!"

He hugged the radiant bride, lifting her off her feet. "Congratulations, Sadie. I never thought I'd see this day."

"I know! Can you believe it?"

Sadie turned to Tiana. "You must be that amazing, stubborn, strong woman DeShawn was telling me about."

"I'd better be," she replied with a smile and threw DeShawn some side-eye. "I'm Tiana," she said, turning back to Sadie. "Congratulations. I love this theme. It's so much fun."

Sadie laughed. "Thank you."

"Sadie," DeShawn said. "I brought Tiana so she could meet my real family."

Wyatt, who'd wandered over to join them, let out a laugh. He pulled DeShawn in for an embrace. "All of us at once?" he said. "The entire gang of insanity? You're a braver man than I."

"Oh, hush up," Sadie replied. She held out her arms and embraced Tiana. "Welcome to the Crew, Tiana. We might be a little crazy but we never, ever give up on each other."

As they moved away to find a table, Tiana took DeShawn's hand in hers. "I think I like your family."

He looked around, nodded. "You know, I like them too," he said. Then, he leaned close to kiss her cheek. His lips were warm, brushing against her tenderly as he said, "They're going to love you and Lily as much as I do."

* * * * *

Get 2 Free Books,

Plus 2 Free Gifts—

just for trying the Reader Service!

YES! Please send me 2 FREE Harlequin Presents® novels and my 2 FREE gifts (gifts are worth about $10 retail). After receiving them, if I don't wish to receive any more books, I can return the shipping statement marked "cancel." If I don't cancel, I will receive 6 brand-new novels every month and be billed just $4.55 each for the regular-print edition or $5.55 each for the larger-print edition in the U.S., or $5.49 each for the regular-print edition or $5.99 each for the larger-print edition in Canada. That's a saving of at least 11% off the cover price! It's quite a bargain! Shipping and handling is just 50¢ per book in the U.S. and 75¢ per book in Canada.* I understand that accepting the 2 free books and gifts places me under no obligation to buy anything. I can always return a shipment and cancel at any time. The free books and gifts are mine to keep no matter what I decide.

Please check one: ☐ Harlequin Presents® Regular-Print   ☐ Harlequin Presents® Larger-Print
                      (106/306 HDN GLWL)   (176/376 HDN GLWL)

Name	(PLEASE PRINT)	
Address		Apt. #
City	State/Prov.	Zip/Postal Code

Signature (if under 18, a parent or guardian must sign)

Mail to the **Reader Service:**
IN U.S.A.: P.O. Box 1341, Buffalo, NY 14240-8531
IN CANADA: P.O. Box 603, Fort Erie, Ontario L2A 5X3

Want to try two free books from another series?
Call 1-800-873-8635 or visit www.ReaderService.com.

* Terms and prices subject to change without notice. Prices do not include applicable taxes. Sales tax applicable in N.Y. Canadian residents will be charged applicable taxes. Offer not valid in Quebec. This offer is limited to one order per household. Books received may not be as shown. Not valid for current subscribers to Harlequin Presents books. All orders subject to approval. Credit or debit balances in a customer's account(s) may be offset by any other outstanding balance owed by or to the customer. Please allow 4 to 6 weeks for delivery. Offer available while quantities last.

Your Privacy—The Reader Service is committed to protecting your privacy. Our Privacy Policy is available online at www.ReaderService.com or upon request from the Reader Service.

We make a portion of our mailing list available to reputable third parties that offer products we believe may interest you. If you prefer that we not exchange your name with third parties, or if you wish to clarify or modify your communication preferences, please visit us at www.ReaderService.com/consumerschoice or write to us at Reader Service Preference Service, P.O. Box 9062, Buffalo, NY 14240-9062. Include your complete name and address.

HP17R2

Get 2 Free Books,
Plus 2 Free Gifts—
just for trying the Reader Service!

HOMETOWN HEARTS ♥

YES! Please send me **The Hometown Hearts Collection** in Larger Print. This collection begins with 3 FREE books and 2 FREE gifts in the first shipment. Along with my 3 free books, I'll also get the next 4 books from the Hometown Hearts Collection, in LARGER PRINT, which I may either return and owe nothing, or keep for the low price of $4.99 U.S./ $5.89 CDN each plus $2.99 for shipping and handling per shipment*. If I decide to continue, about once a month for 8 months I will get 6 or 7 more books, but will only need to pay for 4. That means 2 or 3 books in every shipment will be FREE! If I decide to keep the entire collection, I'll have paid for only 32 books because 19 books are FREE! I understand that accepting the 3 free books and gifts places me under no obligation to buy anything. I can always return a shipment and cancel at any time. My free books and gifts are mine to keep no matter what I decide.

262 HCN 3432 462 HCN 3432

Name	(PLEASE PRINT)	
Address		Apt. #
City	State/Prov.	Zip/Postal Code

Signature (if under 18, a parent or guardian must sign)

Mail to the **Reader Service**:

IN U.S.A.: P.O. Box 1867, Buffalo, NY. 14240-1867
IN CANADA: P.O. Box 609, Fort Erie, Ontario L2A 5X3